Dear Reader,

P9-CQT-171

Home, family, community and love. These are the values we cherish most in our lives—the ideals that ground us, comfort us, move us. They certainly provide the perfect inspiration around which to build a romance collection that will touch the heart.

And so we are thrilled to have the opportunity to introduce you to the Harlequin Heartwarming collection. Each of these special stories is a wholesome, heartfelt romance imbued with the traditional values so important to you. They are books you can share proudly with friends and family. And the authors featured in this collection are some of the most talented storytellers writing today, including favorites such as Laura Abbot, Roz Denny Fox, Jillian Hart and Irene Hannon. We've selected these stories especially for you based on their overriding qualities of emotion and tenderness, and they center around your favorite themes—children, weddings, second chances, the reunion of families, the quest to find a true home and, of course, sweet romance.

So curl up in your favorite chair, relax and prepare for a heartwarming reading experience!

Sincerely,

The Editors

LAURA ABBOT

Growing up in Kansas City, Missouri, Laura Abbot was deeply influenced by her favorite literary character, Jo from *Little Women*. *If only*, Laura thought, *I could write stories, too*. Many years later, after a twenty-five-year career as a high-school English teacher and independent school administrator, Laura's ambition was unexpectedly realized. When she and her husband took early retirement and built their dream home on Beaver Lake outside of Eureka Springs, Arkansas, he bought her a new computer and uttered these life-changing words: "You always said you wanted to write. Now sit down and *do* it!" Happily, she sold her first attempt to Harlequin Superromance, a success followed by fourteen more sales to the same line.

Other professional credentials include serving as an educational consultant and speaker. Active in her church, Laura is a licensed lay preacher. Her greatest pride, however, is her children—all productive, caring adults and parents—who have given her eleven remarkable, resilient (but who's prejudiced?) grandchildren, including at least three who show talent in writing and may pursue it as a career. Jo March, look what you started!

Laura enjoys corresponding with readers. Please write her at LauraAbbot@msn.com, referencing the book title in the subject line.

❧ ❧ ❧ ❧ ❧ ❧ ❧ ❧ ❧ ❧ ❧ ❧ ❧ ❧ ❧ ❧ ❧ ❧ ❧

HARLEQUIN HEARTWARMING

Laura Abbot

Change of Heart

TORONTO NEW YORK LONDON
AMSTERDAM PARIS SYDNEY HAMBURG
STOCKHOLM ATHENS TOKYO MILAN MADRID
PRAGUE WARSAW BUDAPEST AUCKLAND

If you purchased this book without a cover you should be aware that this book is stolen property. It was reported as "unsold and destroyed" to the publisher, and neither the author nor the publisher has received any payment for this "stripped book."

Recycling programs
for this product may
not exist in your area.

ISBN-13: 978-0-373-36426-8

CHANGE OF HEART

Copyright © 2011 by Laura A. Shoffner

Originally published as THE WRONG MAN © 2004 by Laura A. Shoffner

All rights reserved. Except for use in any review, the reproduction or utilization of this work in whole or in part in any form by any electronic, mechanical or other means, now known or hereafter invented, including xerography, photocopying and recording, or in any information storage or retrieval system, is forbidden without the written permission of the publisher, Harlequin Enterprises Limited, 225 Duncan Mill Road, Don Mills, Ontario M3B 3K9, Canada.

This is a work of fiction. Names, characters, places and incidents are either the product of the author's imagination or are used fictitiously, and any resemblance to actual persons, living or dead, business establishments, events or locales is entirely coincidental.

This edition published by arrangement with Harlequin Books S.A.

For questions and comments about the quality of this book
please contact us at Customer_eCare@Harlequin.ca

® and TM are trademarks of the publisher. Trademarks indicated with ® are registered in the United States Patent and Trademark Office, the Canadian Trade Marks Office and in other countries.

www.eHarlequin.com

Printed in U.S.A.

Change of Heart

For Marcia, my "forever" friend,
with love and appreciation for a lifetime
of rare and enduring friendship and for
teaching me what grace under adversity looks like

CHAPTER ONE

CHURNING WHITE-WATER rapids, treacherous black slopes, amateur bronc riding. Until recently, Trent Baker had dared much, accustomed to triumphing over obstacles. Nothing, however, had prepared him for the reality of being a single father.

"Kylie, honey, you'll be late for school."

"I've got to find it, Daddy. Mommy said it looks pretty."

Curbing his impatience, Trent slumped against the wall of the pink-and-white bedroom while his seven-year-old daughter emptied the contents of her musical jewelry box, hunting for the elusive barrette she insisted was the only one that matched her outfit—pink leotards and a purple-and-pink flowered turtleneck. They'd already searched her dresser drawers, the floor of her closet and the bathroom cabinet.

"Here it is!" She pirouetted to face him, her cornflower-blue eyes alight. She handed him her hairbrush, then plopped onto her bed. "Fix me."

Her innocent words stabbed him. Doing his daughter's hair was challenge enough. Other things, regretfully, went far beyond "fixable."

Kylie sat quietly as he drew the brush through her straight, silky blond hair, so like her mother's. Fumbling with the barrette clasp, Trent wished for the umpteenth time that little girls came with instruction manuals. His clumsy fingers could scarcely wrap around the purple plastic bow. "How's that?" he said at last.

She jumped up to inspect herself in the mirror. "It's crooked."

Trent sighed. Ashley would have done it perfectly. "Get your coat, honey."

Her look let him know he'd failed as a hairdresser, but to his relief, she walked to the hall closet, where he helped her into her parka, careful not to disturb the all-important barrette.

Dragging her book bag behind her, she followed him from their first-floor condominium to his extended-cab pickup, engine and defroster already running. After settling Kylie in the backseat, Trent scraped the remaining ice and snow from the windshield. "Warm enough?" he asked as he climbed behind the wheel.

Kylie merely shrugged, folding her arms around her body and ducking her head, her lower lip thrust out.

With slight variations, the same thing

happened each morning. Today the delaying tactic was the lost barrette. Other times she complained of a stomachache, refused to eat breakfast or gave him the silent treatment, as she was doing now. He fought the familiar panic. He had no idea what to do for her—with her.

Ashley had always known. But Ashley wasn't here. Would never be here. And back then... Kylie had been a model child.

Her behavior was natural, the school counselor had told him. Children handled grief in different ways, an aversion to school being one of them. Or withdrawal. Controlling behavior. Acting out.

Trent glanced in the rearview mirror. Eyes downcast, Kylie stared at her clasped hands. She looked fragile, defenseless, lonely.

His grip tightened on the steering wheel. It wasn't fair. Vibrant, beautiful Ashley wasting away, ravaged by the relentless leukemia he'd been powerless to stop. Nearly a year had passed, and still their condo echoed with her absence. The leukemia had sent a message loud and clear. Trent Baker no longer controlled his life. Man, he couldn't even find a way to help Kylie. Some kind of father he was.

A sullen voice from the backseat jarred him. "I'm not going."

He struggled for a neutral tone. "We've

discussed this, Kylie. You *are* going. It's the law."

"I hate you!" He couldn't bring himself to glimpse in the mirror once more and see the belligerence that he knew sparked in his daughter's eyes.

"That's too bad. I *love* you." Pulling in to the driveway of the school, he noted that most of the children had already been dropped off. While Kylie unbuckled her seat belt, he spoke soothingly. "Try to enjoy yourself. Give school a chance. You just might like it." He mustered a grin, which was met with the withering scorn of a pint-size cynic.

Kylie scrambled from the car, and without a backward glance trudged toward the school entrance. By afternoon, her teacher had told him, Kylie would be fine, but with a fatalism born of experience, he knew that the cycle would repeat itself tomorrow morning.

It didn't help that after school she would be bussed to a day-care center and then picked up by her grandmother until he got off work. Or that the cold Montana winter kept her confined to the condominium much of the rest of the time. Or that his rental agreement prohibited pets.

But even if he could have addressed all those

issues, he still wouldn't be able to provide the one thing she needed most—her mother.

LIBBY CAMERON shrugged into her goose-down coat, gathered the tote bag loaded with graded papers, locked the door and carefully made her way down the ice-covered steps of her house toward the Suburban SUV waiting at the curb. "Brr," she said as she climbed into the passenger seat. "Cold morning in Whitefish."

Doug Travers grinned. "What's a little bracing Montana air?" He picked up her gloved hand. "Especially when I'm with such a pretty woman."

The scent of expensive aftershave and new-car leather mingled with the welcome warmth from the heater. "Thanks for taking me to work. One of the other teachers will drop me off at the garage after school to pick up my car."

"Sure I can't help?" The eagerness in Doug's voice was unmistakable.

She studied his profile—firm chin, full lips, Roman nose, high forehead, prematurely receding hairline. Handsome in a successful-executive kind of way. A good man. Dependable. Family-oriented.

Libby had been surprised when Mary Travers, principal of the elementary school where she taught, had suggested the blind date with her son. Initially Libby had resisted, reluctant to consider dating after several dead-end relationships. And she most certainly did not want to entertain that ridiculous fantasy called romance. In fact, living alone was a bargain compared to being with the wrong man. She was no fool, and experience had been a powerful teacher. Yet slowly but surely, Doug had ingratiated himself with her. He had been a total gentleman in the six months they'd been dating, and much as she hated to admit it, having an escort for movies, community functions and faculty parties was pleasant.

"Lib, I was able to get tickets to the symphony in Missoula this weekend. I thought we could run down there, have a fancy dinner, take in the concert, maybe stay at this new bed-and-breakfast I heard about."

Her palms moistened in her suddenly over-warm gloves. Was it her imagination or had he deftly slipped in that last part about the B and B? She found herself stammering, "I...the concert... Who's the guest artist?"

He gave her a puzzled look before answering. "A cellist from Prague."

"Oh." *Say something,* she urged herself. "Which night?"

"Saturday," he said evenly as he pulled into the faculty parking lot.

She scrambled to hook her arm through the handles of her tote. "Let me think about it."

He stayed her departure with a hand on her forearm. "Lib, are you worried about the B and B?"

Her mouth went dry as week-old chalk dust. "I didn't quite know what to think." She must sound ridiculous. Any thirty-plus woman in northwest Montana would jump at the chance to spend a weekend with Doug Travers. By any standards, he was a catch. A successful insurance agent accustomed to nice things, generous with his money, a doting son and uncle. She wished...

"I can book separate rooms," he said.

Libby swallowed. "That would be nice." She stepped from the car. "All right, then. I'll look forward to it."

As she stood in the overcast early morning watching him drive off, an unsettled feeling lodged in her stomach. Up to now their relationship had been...comfortable.

The cold December wind whipped the ends of her scarf, mocking the word. What normal, red-blooded man wanted to settle for *comfortable?*

Why couldn't she offer more?

She knew the answer. *Don't go there,* she muttered as she sought the sanctuary of her brightly decorated classroom, where the giggles, hugs and infectious enthusiasm of second-graders made her come alive in a way nothing else had since…

Idiot! Absolutely do not *go there.*

TRENT RESTED on his haunches, surveying the French doors he'd just installed in the monstrous family room. Through the glass he could see the city of Billings, then, across the Yellowstone River, the sweep of prairie shadowed by dark, heavy clouds. Behind him in the kitchen, his father-in-law conferred with the demanding home owners, who were belatedly requesting yet another change in the specifications. Trent groaned. He didn't understand how Gus stood it, but as his father-in-law frequently reminded him, building a custom house meant exactly that—fulfilling the customer's expectations, no matter how inconvenient or frivolous.

Tool chest in hand, Trent moved to the guest bedroom, out of earshot. Plugging in his sander, he worked on shelves for a built-in bookcase. Even before his friend Chad's phone call last week, he'd wondered how much longer he could last as a home builder. Not that he hadn't appreciated Gus Chisholm's employment offer at the time. When Trent had met Ashley, he was coming off a series of jobs that included ski instructor, rafting guide, ranch hand and carpenter. He'd known he had to settle down if he wanted to marry her. Up to that point, though, he'd concentrated on fun and adventure, unwilling to commit to the hazy notion of "career."

But soon after they got married, she'd discovered she was pregnant, catching both of them off guard.

Gus's offer to have Trent join him in his business building luxury homes had been a gift, and he didn't want to think about what he and Ashley would've done without the company medical insurance when Ashley got sick. But more and more lately, Trent realized he didn't have the patience for the construction business or the diplomacy to massage the egos of wealthy, demanding clients.

Was now the time to make a change? Chad Larraby, his best friend since boyhood, needed a partner in order to buy out Swan Mountain Adventures, an outfitter in their hometown of Whitefish that offered seasonal excursions—rafting, hunting, fishing, hiking, backpacking and mountain biking. It was the perfect job opportunity. He and Chad had always made a great team, whether it was pulling off a spectacular high-school prank or combining their scoring talents to win the league basketball championship. There was no one Trent trusted more.

He pinched his nose, permanently crooked from an opposing center's elbow. Back then, he and Chad were convinced the world had been invented for pleasure, and they had taken every opportunity to test that belief. Now? Chad was married with a son and a daughter, and both men took fatherhood seriously. Although miles apart, they'd tried to stay in touch, but since Ashley's death, Trent had especially missed his friend's ready laugh and common sense. Chad's was an offer he had to consider. The work would satisfy both his zest for adventure and his need to secure the future.

But what would a move back to Whitefish—or anywhere for that matter—do to Kylie? Was it fair to uproot her from her grandparents?

It wasn't a question of finances. He and Ashley had set aside considerable savings, hoping to buy a house, and Gus had been generous with bonuses. There was also the money from Ashley's life insurance policy, which he hadn't been able to bring himself to touch. But if it bought him and Kylie a better future?

With the palm of his hand he tested the newly sanded shelf, then nodded with satisfaction. Chad's offer seemed perfect for him.

Except for one thing.

If he moved back to the Glacier Park area of Montana, inevitably he would run into Libby.

Why subject himself to a past he'd moved beyond?

Liar! You haven't moved beyond anything.

Ever since Chad's call, Trent could hold back neither his thoughts of Libby nor the powerful emotions those memories churned up. What did philosophers say about first love? You never quite get over it? Trent leaned against the wall, wishing life could be simple. Yet the mental pictures of Libby—her dark, thick ponytail flying behind her as she skimmed over a mogul or firelight turning her skin to flame—halted him in his tracks. *Stop it, Baker.* He ran his fingers through his hair. Why was he thinking of Lib? That was in the past and needed to stay there.

Yet despite his resolve, he had another sudden image of Libby, who nurtured every small creature she met, enfolding his daughter in her arms.

Man, when you lose it, you go all out.

From the hallway he heard Gus call his name.

"Coming," he said, gathering up his tools. Even if he couldn't picture himself as a career home builder, did he dare leave a secure job? Move Kylie? Bet on a future that held a great deal of promise but no guarantees? The alternative was spending a lifetime doing work he didn't enjoy. The last thing Kylie needed was an unhappy father.

At Gus's direction, he moved to the dining room to install wainscoting. Yet as he worked, his thoughts were a million miles away.

Chad needed an answer. Soon. Trent could rationalize all he wanted, but the truth reverberated with every blow of his hammer. His decision was a resounding "Yes!"

BY THE END OF THE DAY, Kirby Bell had mastered addition of two-digit numbers, Heather Amundsen had gum snarled in her hair, and Josh Jacobs had upchucked his lunch. Libby had a kink in her back from helping little feet into boots, but as the last second-grader left the room, throwing his chubby arms around her waist in a fleeting hug, she smiled with satisfaction and relief.

Straightening the rows of desks, she relished the smells of glue, markers and modeling clay that lingered in the classroom. Almost daily she thanked her lucky stars that she had found the work she was born to do and that it paid enough for her to live simply and comfortably in one of the most beautiful places in the world.

In preparation for the upcoming visit from master storyteller Louise Running Wolf McCann, Libby removed the photographs of plants of the Northwest from the bulletin board, replacing them with those of indigenous animals. "Weezer," as the Blackfoot woman was known to generations of Whitefish children, would share Native American animal legends with the class.

Returning to her desk, Libby gathered the day's worksheets. She frowned when she noticed that little Rory Polk had left half the answers on his reading sheet blank. Bless his heart, he'd been trying so hard to hide during class, burrowing into his desk and making himself even smaller, hoping to escape observation. Libby couldn't shake the nagging sensation that something might be wrong at home.

A glance at her watch told her it was time to meet Lois Jeter, her best friend and colleague, in the office if she wanted a ride to the garage.

She hurried down the hall, noting with pleasure the red and green links of construction paper making a merry border for various holiday art projects. Mary Travers stood outside the office, her hands resting on the shoulders of a scrawny fourth-grader. "Jeffrey, we've talked before about snowballs. Are we going to have to have another conversation?"

The boy hung his head. "No, ma'am."

"Good. I know throwing snowballs is fun, but it can also be dangerous, especially with so many little ones in the area."

Libby watched Mary turn the boy around, pat his back and send him on his way. The principal, a short, bouncy woman with youthful skin and salt-and-pepper hair drawn back into a simple chignon, ran a tight but loving ship and was universally respected.

Libby approached her. "That went well."

Smiling, Mary shook her head. "Boys. It's so hard for them to resist temptation." She accompanied Libby to the office. "How was your day?"

"Almost perfect. Just like all of them."

"You can say that even after the Josh Jacobs caper?"

"That goes with the territory. Poor little guy. He was so embarrassed."

Mary's voice lowered. "We couldn't reach his mother until just before school was out."

"Let me guess. She was irritated he was sick?"

"That would be an understatement. Some people should simply never have children."

Libby winced. Why were people like Mrs. Jacobs given the gift of children when she wasn't? Quickly, she controlled her emotions. "That's one reason we're here. To pick up the pieces."

"Lib," a voice rang from down the hallway. "I'll be right there." Redheaded Lois Jeter, the physical education teacher, scrambled into her all-weather coat and hurried toward them. "Sorry, the gym was a disaster area today. I just now got the mats hung up."

"We really appreciate you," Libby assured her with a grin. "On these wintry days, the kids need to work off all the steam they can."

Mary turned toward Libby. "I understand you and Doug are going to Missoula this weekend."

Butterflies converged in Libby's stomach. It didn't help that Mary was beaming approval that had nothing to do with Libby's skillful handling of a second-grader's intestinal upset.

"Missoula?" Lois cocked an eyebrow.

"We're going to the symphony."

Lois threw up her hands in playful despair. "And here I thought you were going to hit the wild club scene."

Libby did her best to match the mood. "What? And miss Mozart? I'm looking forward to a bit of culture."

"So is Doug, my dear." Mary patted Libby's shoulder. "So is Doug."

On the ride to the garage, Libby was grateful that Lois's chatter prevented her from dwelling on the expectant look in Mary Travers's eyes. Worse yet, she didn't want to consider why Mary's approval bothered her.

TRENT SAT at the table in the kitchenette alcove, poring over figures. In front of him was Chad's printout of estimated start-up costs, profit-and-loss statements from the last three years, and a breakdown of income generated by the various services Swan Mountain Adventures offered. Because of recent forest fires in the area, the current owners were making them a great deal. Chad had the people skills and the business background to handle accounting and marketing, and Trent knew equipment and maintenance. They shared knowledge of the outdoors and expertise in guiding. With hard work and a bit of luck, the venture looked like a winner.

Setting down the pencil, he stared into the living room, where Kylie sat on the floor, Barbies positioned around her in a protective circle. She mumbled dialogue as she picked up first one and then another. "Mommy doesn't want you to wear orange with red," he heard her chide the platinum-blond figure. She shook her head disapprovingly. "They don't match."

He closed his eyes briefly. Ashley had been a clotheshorse, occasionally straining their finances with her need to look bandbox perfect, but he had to give it to her. Heads had turned when she walked into a room. Kylie's prissiness, on the other hand, worried him. It was as if she'd seized on her appearance as a means to...what? Control her world? Keep Ashley's memory alive?

"Daddy?"

Trent's eyes snapped open. "What, baby?"

"Are you doing homework?"

"I guess you could call it that."

She set down the doll and approached him, her forehead wrinkled. "You don't go to school."

"No, but I work."

Sidling up to him, she put her thin arm around his neck. "With tools. You're a carmpenter."

Her mispronunciation of the word never failed to amuse him. "Car-pen-ter." He ruffled her hair, then drew a deep breath before launching the subject he'd been avoiding. "What if I didn't want to be a carpenter any longer?"

Eyes widening, she looked at him as if he'd just emerged from a UFO. "Not be a carmpenter? What would you be then?" Before he could begin his carefully reasoned explanation, she hurried on. "I know! You could be the boss, like Grandpa Gus."

He pulled her up on his lap, snuggling her against his chest. "No, honey, I couldn't. Even if I were the boss, I would still miss doing all the things I love."

"You don't love carmpentry?" She sounded surprised, as if fathers weren't supposed to change—ever.

"No, honey, I don't. I love hiking and skiing and fishing and being out-of-doors."

"Oh." She nodded her head in understanding. "You want to play, not work."

Play? Was that what this was? An immature need to recapture his adolescence?

"What if my work felt like play?"

She giggled. "That's silly, Daddy."

"What if I could be—" he hesitated, his mouth dry "—happier?"

Lifting one small hand to his cheek, she studied him. "We're sad, aren't we? We miss Mommy, right?"

"But Mommy would want us to be happy again, to laugh and play."

"Okay," she said, as if the matter was settled.

Okay? If only it could be that simple. He had gone back and forth about the best way to break the news to Kylie, but now that the time had come, the words stuck in his throat. He licked his lips, cuddled her closer, and then, with a deep breath, began, "I have something important to tell you, and I want you to listen carefully."

"It's about Mommy, isn't it?"

"Not exactly."

She rubbed her nose. "I know. About your carmpentry."

"Yes. Yesterday I told Grandpa that I won't

be working for him anymore." Much as he'd dreaded telling Gus his plans, Trent had been relieved when, despite his obvious disappointment, his father-in-law had claimed to understand. Now he said to Kylie, "I've accepted a job in a place called Whitefish that will make me much happier. I think you'll really love it there."

"We're *moving?*"

Swallowing hard, he nodded.

She jumped from his lap and stood glaring at him, her fingers working the lace trim of her sweater. "No!"

"But, honey—"

"I'm not going." Her protruding lower lip sent a powerful message.

"Just now you said it would be okay for us to learn to laugh and play again."

She stamped her foot. "But right here."

Tension knotted Trent's gut. "You'll like Whitefish. It's where I went to school."

"I don't like fish!"

"There are lakes and mountains. You can learn to ski and snowshoe and—"

"No." She shook her head back and forth, her straight blond hair fanning the air. "We can't leave."

Trent tried desperately to see the situation from his daughter's point of view. She'd had too many changes lately. Did he have any right to inflict one more on her, even one that would free him in ways that made him light-headed with relief? "Why not?"

Kylie stood stock-still, looking at him as if he had just asked the world's most ridiculous question. "Because Mommy's here."

His chest ached. "Sweetie, we've been over this so many times. Mommy is in heaven. Even though she is never coming back, she is always with us in spirit, but she isn't in Billings."

He watched, thunderstruck, as Kylie's face screwed up into a red ball before she screamed at him, "She is too! She's at that place with the stone. The c-cem-cementery!"

"Oh, honey." Although Kylie struggled against him, he gathered her back into his arms, where she remained stiff and unmoving. "The decision has been made."

She stared at the far wall. "I'm *not* going."

This was harder than he'd imagined. "Where else would you live except with me?"

"With Grandma Georgia and Grandpa Gus."

Trent bit his lower lip, knowing full well his in-laws would welcome that plan. "Wouldn't you miss me?"

She shrugged, unwilling to meet his eyes. "You could visit me."

It was time for a dose of reality. "I wouldn't be able to visit very often. I'll be working."

She didn't move.

"I'd really like you to come with me. In Whitefish there's a big lake and a ski slope. You could go to the same school where I went as a little boy."

Her lips quivered and she wrung the hem of her sweater.

"Looks like we have a problem, doesn't it? I'm not happy being a carpenter. You don't want to leave Billings. What do you think we should do about this?"

"What would you do there—in that place?" she mumbled.

Patiently he explained about the adventure-outfitting business. About his love of the out-of-doors, which he wanted to share with her. About how lonely he would be without her.

"Where would we live?"

"To start with, in Weezer McCann's guest cabin."

She wrinkled her nose. "Weezer? Who's that?"

"I've told you about her. Remember, she's the lady who helped Grandma Lila and me when I was a little boy. She was like my second mother. You'll love her. She tells the most wonderful stories."

Kylie twined her fingers around his wrist. "What about?"

Wow, had he actually succeeded in capturing her interest? "Native American legends about birds and fish and animals. Why they're named what they are. Why they do what they do."

"Like beavers and bears and stuff?"

"Exactly."

Just when he thought he'd convinced her, she scowled. "No," she said, adamantly shaking her head. "I have to stay here."

Gently he ran a hand over her soft hair. "Can you tell me why?"

She sniffled against his shirt. "Mommy."

He held her close, feeling her fists curl against his chest. "Mommy is in heaven," he said again. "Don't you suppose she wants us to be happy?"

Seconds passed. Then she looked up at him. "I 'spect so."

"Our love for Mommy and our memories of her can go with us anywhere in the whole wide world, right?"

A teary nod.

"So whaddya say we take Mommy with us to a place where you and I can be happy? She would love it. It's beautiful country filled with wildflowers, big green trees and gurgling streams."

She squirmed to the end of his knees and regarded him thoughtfully. "Did you say mountains?"

"Spectacular mountains."

"Ice cream?"

The non sequitur made him laugh. "Scoops and scoops of it!"

She looked directly into his eyes. "Daddy, I like it when you laugh. Do you think you can laugh again when we go to that fish place?"

Laugh *again?* Had he been that out of touch? He reached for her and enfolded her in a huge bear hug. "Yes, sweetie, I'll laugh again—lots more. And so will you."

"Okay, then."

He kissed the top of her head. "I'm glad you're coming with me."

"But there's one thing."

At this point he would gladly have presented her with the entire state of Montana had it been within his power. "What's that?"

"I know Mommy's with us in spirit, like you said, but what about that cementery? Could we go say goodbye before we move?"

Trent's heart shattered. "Tomorrow, honey."

With the wisdom given only to children, she had hit upon the one act he now realized he, too, needed to perform.

LIBBY DUCKED her head as she and Doug climbed the steps of the bed-and-breakfast following the symphony. Brahms and Mozart had done little to soothe her nerves. Instead, she'd spent most of the concert thinking about whether her insistence on two rooms had jeopardized her best chance for love and family.

"Feel like a nightcap?" Doug asked in the lobby as he removed her coat. "There's a wonderful gas fireplace in my room—and a bottle of Amaretto."

Doug, always considerate, deserved her enthusiasm. "It's hard to turn down a cozy fire and an after-dinner drink." She smiled. "Not to mention one very nice man."

"Good," he said, his eyes warm with affection.

The fireplace cast light and shadow over Doug's room, which was decorated in deep burgundy and green tones. Settling her on the love seat, he filled two goblets, then sat beside her, raising her glass in a toast before handing it to her. "Here's to you, Libby."

The toast was definitely more than a casual "Here's to ya." Libby watched him sip from his glass, then sit back in satisfaction, before she took a swallow, letting the almond sweetness linger on her tongue.

To fill the silence, she started a discussion of

the concert. She'd always loved music, even as a tiny child. A dim memory returned, a long-lost vignette. Her mother sitting in the corner of the high-ceilinged living room, the sun falling on her dark curly hair as she bent to the harp, the melody of the plucked strings sending a thrill through Libby's small body. How old had she been? Four? Five? Gazing now into the dancing flames, she treasured the immediacy of the image before recalling the dark days that followed. When she was six, her mother died, and the silenced harp gathered dust in the corner until her stepfather had finally sold it.

"You're awfully quiet all of a sudden," Doug said, taking her half-empty glass and setting it on the coffee table beside his.

"Just remembering." His arm settled around her shoulder. "Music does that for me."

"Evocative," he said quietly.

"Very."

"Feel like telling me about it?"

She shrugged.

"You don't talk much about the past."

What was the point? Talking didn't change anything. "No." She tried a cheery smile. "The present and future are so much more compelling."

She observed a question in his eyes, but he didn't press her, for which she was grateful. "I could get interested in discussing the present and the future," he whispered, drawing her into his arms. "Starting with tonight." He lowered his head and began kissing her lightly.

Libby's awareness hovered somewhere above and beyond the pressure of his mouth, the tingle of his fingers running through her hair. He'd kissed her before, of course, but this was different. Not unpleasant, but no longer merely platonic.

She tried to relax, to give in to the sensation of being held. He cupped the back of her head, enjoying the kiss. Involuntarily, a response flared within her, irritating her. She didn't want this, yet at the same time, she did. It was the best thing that could happen. Doug made her feel cherished. Safe.

When he withdrew, he framed her face with his hands, and his eyes sought hers. "Libby?"

"I'm sorry, but…"

She ducked her head. She wanted a husband. A home. Tears darted to her eyes. Children. Especially children. And Doug would make a wonderful father. Sadly, she knew from bitter experience that the same could not be said about some men. So why was she pulling away from him?

From somewhere outside her, she heard

Doug's voice. "I care about you, Libby. I can be patient."

She dissolved against him, feeling the steady beat of his heart, his body radiating a heat that slowly thawed the chill in hers.

It was well after midnight when she finally roused from his embrace and went to her room.

Alone.

GEORGIA CHILSOLM PAUSED in the doorway of her immaculate living room. A single dust mote fluttered and settled on the polished surface of the sofa table. She moved forward, wiping the cherry wood with the tissue she held in her hand. Then, walking briskly across the room, she aligned the pillows on the damask sofa, which were off by a fraction of an inch. The latest issues of *Architectural Digest* and *Style at Home* lay fanned on the coffee table. She checked to see that the large crystal vase of carefully arranged gladioli held sufficient water. Satisfied that all was in order, she permitted herself to stand before the fireplace, studying the pastel portrait hanging above the mantel. Ashley.

Every afternoon she spent time with her daughter, studying the serene blue gaze that followed her wherever she sat in the room. Remembering the silky feel of those white-blond tresses. Hearing in her mind Ashley's laughter, bright and sparkling. She longed to trace once more the smooth, pale pink skin of her daughter's cheek, to watch her lips form a small O of surprise and delight.

It was cruel, too cruel.

Georgia stepped backward, then eased into an armchair, her eyes never leaving the portrait of her daughter, frozen in time at twenty-three. Just before she met Trent Baker.

It was too late for if-onlys. Georgia had entertained such grand plans for her daughter. She closed her eyes now and pictured the shabby shotgun house in the company mining town in which she'd grown up. She could still remember how her mother hoarded the few dollars she could cajole from Georgia's miner father before he headed for the tavern. Georgia steeled herself against the memories of nights she went to bed cold and hungry. When she'd married Gus, his thriving construction company promised a better life and a respectable standing in the community. Because of that, Ashley could have married any number of young, attractive, professional men.

Georgia worried the arm covers of the chair with her restless fingers. So why Trent? It had made no sense. A rough-and-tumble young man, no more at home in a museum or theater than a lumberjack would be. He was handsome, she'd give him that. But she'd raised Ashley to be more discriminating than to be won over by physicality and raffish charm. A twinkle in the eye was scant measure of a man's ability to provide and protect.

Ashley had been a delightful, tractable child. A thoughtful and affectionate teen. Nothing in her experience as Ashley's mother had prepared Georgia for her daughter's reaction to Trent Baker. Ashley had dug in her heels, deaf to her mother's pleas, determined to marry the man.

Not wanting to alienate her daughter, Georgia had done her best to coexist with Trent. He knew she didn't like him and would have preferred someone else for Ashley. Only the birth of Kylie had softened her stance. He was a loving father to the child, who slowly and inexorably grabbed hold of Georgia's heart in a way no one except her daughter ever had. Georgia could almost forgive Trent as she marveled over the exquisite little girl.

Then had come the diagnosis. Abrupt. Devastating. Terminal. Georgia lifted her eyes to the portrait, where Ashley sat poised as if to speak, a smile softening her features. *What would you tell me if you could, my darling daughter?*

Through the long months of Ashley's illness, Trent had remained devoted, exhausting himself with the care of both his wife and daughter. It was as if he'd wanted to graft himself to them in a desperate attempt to stave off the inevitable.

Now he was taking her granddaughter away. It would have been kinder had he taken a knife and carved out a section of her heart. This loss, on top of the other, was unbearable.

The shadows lengthened on the thick Persian rug, but Georgia was oblivious, her eyes trained on the portrait, where Ashley seemed to nod her head imperceptibly as she always had when her mother overstepped her bounds with Trent. Whether Georgia understood it or not, Ashley had loved Trent to the end. And, in his own way, he had loved her.

How could he even think of taking Kylie and moving away?

It was when she turned her thoughts to her granddaughter that the tears began to trickle in earnest down her powdered cheeks.

CHAPTER TWO

"WEEZER!" Libby greeted the leather-skinned woman with the single silver braid of hair who was walking toward her classroom. Her legs were encased in worn jeans, her feet clad in knee-high moccasins, and around the neck of her colorful Western shirt, she wore a thong of beads, stones and feathers. But it was Louise McCann's dark eyes and wrinkle-encased smile that captivated people. A member of the Blackfeet tribe, the longtime widow owned the Kodiak Café, a Whitefish institution.

"Greetings, little one. Ready for me?"

Libby moved into the hall. "Oh my, yes. The kids can't wait."

"With the Christmas vacation so close, I imagine they're more restless than usual."

Libby rolled her eyes. "You have no idea." Grinning, she ushered Weezer into her classroom. "You'll make their day."

"I'm just a storyteller." Weezer moved to the back wall to examine the construction-paper

Santa Claus figures plastered there. "Are you going home to Muskogee for Christmas?"

Home? "No. My stepfather is staying in D.C., and I'm not excited about presenting him with a holiday photo op." Weezer turned to face her, but said nothing. Libby knew people didn't understand why she avoided her stepfather, the Honorable Vernon G. Belton, United States senator from Oklahoma. But neither Washington, D.C., nor Muskogee, Oklahoma, had been home for a long, long time. And "Daddy" Belton, as he'd insisted she call him after he married her mother, had always been far more interested in politics than in his albatross of a stepdaughter.

"We're having a community Christmas dinner at the café. You could pull up a chair with us."

"Thanks, but I've been invited to the Traverses'." Libby warmed at the thought. She'd spent Thanksgiving there, too, surrounded by Doug's parents, siblings, cousins, aunts and uncles. Norman Rockwell couldn't begin to do justice to the gathering.

"I'm glad. You won't be alone, then."

Weezer didn't have to complete the thought. *Like you were that awful Christmas twelve years ago.* Libby willed away the painful memory, then cupped her ear. "Hark! Is that the prancing and pawing of little feet?"

In trooped the second-graders, flushed from

recess, and the room filled with excited chatter and the odor of damp mittens. "Weezer, will you tell us about Brother Moose?" "No, I wanna hear 'bout Winter Wolf." The children hurriedly removed their coats and boots, then clustered around the old woman, who calmed them with one raised hand and a softly spoken, "Once, many moons past, Old Man made…"

Libby sank into her desk chair, drawn into the legend by the gentle cadence of Weezer's voice, the expressive gestures of her hands and the sense of something ancient, unchanging and enduring. She envied the woman her roots and traditions.

What were her own legacies? Libby closed her eyes, weariness suddenly overcoming her. They didn't bear thinking about.

TRENT ROLLED OUT of the unfamiliar bed and moved stealthily to the window. He glanced back at the other twin bed where Kylie slept, one hand curled beneath her chin, the other clutching a white plush polar bear with a red plaid neck scarf. Though it was still dark, a glaring street lamp had awakened him from a restless sleep.

The Chisholms had invited Kylie and him to spend the night of Christmas Eve with them. Holidays were for family, they had insisted.

Trent could hardly refuse. As the day of their departure for Whitefish neared, his in-laws had become increasingly protective of Kylie, and while Gus maintained a stiff upper lip, Georgia, saying little, targeted Trent with accusing eyes. In fairness, he could hardly blame them. Since Ashley's death, the two of them had grown even more attached to Kylie and she to them. He couldn't expect jubilation when he was moving their only grandchild nearly five hundred miles across the state.

Their Christmas Eve dinner had been formal, even pretentious, complete with china, crystal and enough forks to confuse Martha Stewart. Ashley's place was conspicuously vacant, and the conversation among the three adults was forced, at best. Gus had talked business, then switched to sports until Georgia, a distressed look on her face, objected. Kylie had kept silent, picking at her food, occasionally casting worried glances at her grandmother, who addressed the girl's nervousness by slipping her after-dinner mints.

Trent returned to his bed, lying on his back, his hands cradling his head. Gus was all right, a fair person. But Georgia's disapproval of him had been obvious from the get-go. He was the man who had married their little girl. The one who wasn't worthy of Ashley, who, as Georgia had taken pains to inform him, had been destined for marriage to a white-collar professional, not a jack-of-all-trades with a limited future. Even Kylie's birth had failed to mellow her at first, as if the baby had symbolically represented Georgia's failed hopes for Ashley. But soon the infant had won her over, and from that time on, the challenge had been to keep her from spoiling Kylie rotten. A fussy, particular woman, intent on overcoming her humble origins, Georgia fixated on appearances, sometimes failing her granddaughter in fundamental ways, although she would vigorously have denied that assessment.

Trent turned onto his side, watching the gentle rise and fall of his daughter's chest. She needed a warm, cuddling grandmother who smelled of cinnamon and flowers and read stories and played Pretend.

As for his own mother… Lila did her best on her infrequent visits from Las Vegas, where she worked as a cashier at a casino, but even her best was questionable. Always so busy making a living, she'd had little opportunity to exercise her maternal instincts. She had the ready laugh of a survivor, but she would never be one to sew doll clothes or bake cookies. Teaching Kylie Crazy Eights was about as good as it got.

Was this one reason he couldn't stop thinking

about Libby, the most selflessly loving person he'd ever met? She would be so good for Kylie.

He forced himself to derail that train of thought. He couldn't imagine she would ever give him another chance. Not after what had happened.

Flopping over on his back again, he struggled to think about St. Nicholas, reindeer, even visions of sugarplums dancing in his head, whatever that meant.

But all he could think of was Lib, and how she'd be good, all right. Not only for Kylie. For him.

THIS WAS A PICTURE-BOOK Christmas. Libby glanced around the living room of the Traverses' large chalet-style home. Through the floor-to-ceiling windows was a breathtaking view of Whitefish Lake. In one corner stood a nine-foot-tall spruce, decorated from base to top with ornaments made through the years by Doug and his brother and sisters. Aromas, savory and tantalizing, wafted from the kitchen. Doug sprawled on the floor, helping his brother and nephew lay track for an electric train, while his sister Melanie's four-year-old twin girls cuddled on either side of Libby as she read Dr. Seuss's *How the Grinch Stole Christmas*.

Bedecked in green tights with a long red-knit sweater, Mary Travers entered the room carrying a bowl of frothy nonalcoholic eggnog, which she set on the buffet. Smiling from one twin to the other, she addressed Libby. "You look like a natural."

"I've had plenty of practice at school."

Mary shook her head, an impish smile playing across her lips. "That's not what I meant. You look like a mother."

The illustration of the Whos down in Whoville blurred. "Maybe someday," she managed to say.

Slanting her head toward Doug, Mary winked and said, "I'll work on it. Meanwhile, after you get that mean old storybook Grinch in the Christmas spirit, come have a glass of eggnog."

"You gonna drink eggs?" Margot, the twin dressed in green, stared up at Libby. "Yuck."

Maddy, the more serious of the two, shook her head. "Not eggs. Nog." The triumphant look slowly faded from her face. Finally she got up on her knees and whispered in Libby's ear, "What's a 'nog'?"

Giving her a quick hug, Libby answered. "It's what the Grinch drinks to remember how much he likes Christmas."

Across the way, Doug caught her eye, a

sappy grin on his face. "You gals make a nice picture."

Brushing aside the implications of the compliment, Libby quickly finished the story, then moved to the buffet and helped herself to the nonalcoholic eggnog. Doug came up beside her and put his arm around her. "Having a good time?"

"Yes, I am." It was the truth. The easy give-and-take of this family and her overwhelming sense of welcome, especially from Mary and her adorable husband, felt heady for a woman accustomed to living alone with her cat.

"Feel like a walk before dinner?" Doug asked.

"Do we dare sneak off?"

He tightened his grip on her waist, then grinned wickedly. "Dare? I think it's expected."

"Let's go, then."

Outside the air was crisp, and the sun shone weakly through the snow-dusted trees. Doug tucked her arm through his as they started briskly down the road. "I'm glad you're here with us for Christmas. That's the best present you could give me."

"Your family has made me feel very welcome."

"They're crazy about you."

Flustered, she stopped to adjust her scarf. "I,

uh, I like them, too. Your sister Melanie is such fun, and your brother makes me laugh."

"And don't forget Izzy."

Isabelle, Doug's other sister, had been busy in the kitchen all day. A chef at a pricey Seattle restaurant, she was cooking the Christmas dinner. "How could I forget her?" Libby rubbed her stomach. "I've gained five pounds just smelling that food she's preparing. And I haven't even eaten."

Doug gently held her by the lapels of her coat, his expression turning serious. "And what about me?"

"You?"

"Yeah. Do I rate as highly as my siblings?"

She fumbled to keep her answer light. "Well, you're fun like Melanie and your brother, but as for your cooking…"

He laid his forehead against hers. "I'm not talking about cooking." He hesitated, his breath forming small clouds in the frosty air. "I guess I'm asking…could you love me, Lib?"

His eyes were close, so rich and deep a brown they took her breath away. Could she? Love him? Suddenly, in that moment, she thought perhaps she could. "I think maybe so, Doug."

"Good," he murmured, pulling something from his pocket.

Libby didn't know what she'd expected, but

not the sprig of mistletoe he now held over her head.

"Merry Christmas, sweetheart," he whispered, before tossing the mistletoe in the air and kissing her in a way that would have delighted the reformed Ebeneezer Scrooge.

AT HOME LATER that evening, Libby sat, pensive, in the rocker she'd brought from Oklahoma, the only piece of furniture she'd moved. It was the chair in which her mother had cuddled her before bedtime. Mona, a sleek gray cat with a white, diamond-shaped mask, sat in her lap, purring with contentment. The occasional crackle of a log settling and the ticking of the cuckoo clock were the only other sounds.

The perfect Christmas.

Convivial company, delicious food, laughter, plenty of hugs. It was the Christmas she'd always dreamed of—and a far cry from those girlhood holidays after her mother died. Oh, there had been no shortage of gifts. To the contrary. Everything she'd ever wanted had been provided. And that was the operative word: *provided*. Not *given*.

At that time Daddy Belton was serving in the Oklahoma legislature. His secretary bought and wrapped Libby's presents. Christmas Eve at their Muskogee home was traditionally celebrated with a huge open house for her stepfather's influential constituents and political allies. On Christmas Day, the two of them opened their gifts, Daddy made obligatory phone calls, and then they were served a late lunch by the housekeeper in the drafty old dining room. Libby spent Christmas afternoons alone in her bedroom.

In her youthful naiveté, she had dreamed of creating a real family, complete with a loving husband and a houseful of children. Life, however, had taught her the folly of such dreams.

She nestled Mona closer, drawing her fingers up and down the cat's ridged back. Today had been both perfect and disturbing. It scared her how badly she wanted to be part of a family like the Traverses. This afternoon she had sensed Doug was on the verge of offering her the fulfillment of her fantasies.

Could you love me? he'd asked. She had been taken aback by the directness of his question. A marriage without love would be empty. Ruefully, she bent her head and nuzzled Mona's neck. Had she committed herself by giving Doug a definite "maybe"? And what kind of cowardly answer was that?

On the wall, the cuckoo clock repeated its call twelve times—each syllable taunting her. She was "cuckoo," all right. Doug hadn't asked the one question she would ultimately have to answer.

Not *could* she love him, but *did* she love him?

WEEZER RUBBED her gnarled hands in anticipation. Dark, and still no sight of them. She checked the mantel clock. No point standing at the window fretting. She strode to the fireplace, picked up the poker and jabbed at the bottom log, sending sparks up the chimney. Trent knew how to drive in these conditions. He'd be careful. Yet what if…

Despite Trent's eagerness to get back to Whitefish, Weezer had picked up on his concerns. Kylie's aversion to school. Separation from her grandparents and her familiar surroundings. Beyond that, the child had to still be grieving her mother, probably struggling to mask her pain.

Trent ought to know all about that. He'd been skilled at it. From the day that worthless cowboy Charlie Baker walked out on Lila and Trent, the boy had acted as if he didn't care, practically daring the gods to zap him, be it on a skateboard, bicycle or snowboard. Then later in a two-man raft shooting rapids, or rappeling from precipitous cliffs. Whenever Lila or Weezer had asked him if he thought he was invincible, he had merely laughed and said, "A guy's gotta have some fun."

By now, Weezer suspected, he'd learned the hard way that life was about more than fun.

She shook her head sadly. Kylie's mother's illness and death had been tragic. It seemed as if every time Trent risked love, something happened to steal it from him. Or he did something to sabotage it.

Lights flared against the spruce and pine trees lining the driveway. Beside her, Scout, her German shepherd, thumped his tail, then ran to the entry hall, looking expectantly back at her. Weezer hurried to the door, fumbling with the knob—awful arthritis—then stepped out onto the porch.

When the pickup pulled to a stop, she peered through the darkness, but couldn't see the child. Trent stepped out of the truck, a crooked smile on his face. "We made it. I hope you weren't worried. A semi jackknifed near Lakeside, blocking the highway."

Weezer took the porch steps carefully, then moved into Trent's hug. "Glad you're here safely." She stepped back. "Now, where's that daughter of yours?"

Trent took her hand and led her to the truck. He opened the door and pointed. Lounging against the backseat, sound asleep, was the rosy-cheeked child Weezer hadn't seen since she was tiny.

"Poor little thing."

Trent sighed. "It's been a long day."

Just then, Scout threaded his way between them and climbed into the backseat.

"Scout!" Before Weezer could restrain him, he stood over Kylie, gently licking the girl's face.

Kylie's eyes fluttered opened. "D-Daddy?"

"Don't be frightened, honey. It's just Scout."

Rubbing her eyes, Kylie sat up straighter. "A dog? I love dogs." She wrapped her arms around Scout's neck.

Weezer nodded sagely. "I think your little girl has made her first friend in Whitefish."

Through dinner and unpacking, Kylie never let Scout out of her sight. Although the child didn't say much, she seemed to keenly observe her surroundings.

Finally, after Trent had unloaded the truck and seen to Kylie's bath, the three of them settled in the guest cabin's living room for hot chocolate. In her footed flannel pajamas, Kylie curled up on the sofa with Scout. She seemed overcome with shyness, but finally, she turned to Weezer. "Is this a real log cabin like *Little House in the Big Woods?*"

"Well, we have more modern conveniences

than Mary and Laura Ingalls did, but, yes, little one, this is as real as it gets."

"Good," Kylie said. "I can pretend I'm Laura. Or Mary."

It was an innocent enough remark, but Weezer felt a chill pass through her. Would Kylie deal with her problems by retreating to a make-believe world the same way Trent had lost himself in derring-do?

"It's about time for bed, sugar," Trent said. "I can't wait to show you this beautiful place in the daytime." He set down his mug and held out his arms. "How about a good-night hug?"

Kylie nudged Scout's head from her lap and joined Trent in the big recliner. Lacing her fingers together, she gazed up at him, then said softly, "I'm trying not to be scared, Daddy."

"I know. It's natural for things to seem strange at first. But you'll soon feel at home." He wrapped his arms protectively around his daughter.

The love on his face, commingled with sadness and concern, tore Weezer's heart. But then came Kylie's response, plaintive and wistful, and Weezer had to turn away so neither father nor daughter would see the tears gathering in her eyes.

"Please, Daddy," the child whispered, "be happy."

ALTHOUGH THE HOLDIAY break had been more than welcome after a challenging first semester, Libby was glad to get back to her second-graders. To settle them on this first day of class, she'd put them to work making models of trains, boats, planes or any other form of transportation out of old cereal boxes, empty toilet-paper rolls and assorted odds and ends from her crafts bin. Now, as she helped Rory pour glue onto a Popsicle stick, she concluded she must have lost her mind. This was *not* a good idea. No sooner would she assist one child, than another would call out, "Miz Cameron, help!" She needed the legs of a centipede and the wits of Machiavelli.

"It's ruined." Behind her, ginger-haired Lacey Ford began to cry. "He did it!" The girl pointed her finger directly at Bart Ames, the class bully, who stood with his arms folded over his chest in imitation of a superhero.

"Did not!" Bart shouted. "It was just a stupid ole submarine."

Libby mentally counted to five—ten was clearly out of the question—and took hold of Bart's arm, directing him to a chair at the reading table. Then she returned to Lacey, who was in dire need of a tissue. "Calm down, honey, and tell me what happened."

After Lacey told her story, Libby joined the

sullen-faced boy and squatted beside him. "Did you smash her submarine?"

Bart looked up at the ceiling, then shrugged. "Didn't mean to."

"What do you think you should do now?"

Another shrug.

"How would you feel if someone destroyed your helicopter?"

"Mad."

"Do you think you could tell Lacey you're sorry, and that you'll help her build another sub?"

The boy's hands moved nervously over his corduroy-clad knees, belying his tough-guy exterior. "I guess."

Libby patted him on the shoulder. "Scoot, then."

She remained hunkered down, trying to take a little breather. Then she heard the classroom door open, and out of the corner of her eye she spotted three sets of feet—Mary Travers's Birkenstocks, a pair of scuffed cowboy boots and a small pair of white tennis shoes laced with pink. *Please,* she implored the patron saint of elementary-school teachers, *not another new student.*

"Miss Cameron?" Mary's voice carried across the room. "I'd like you to meet someone."

As she swiveled around, Libby took in the

slightly built girl with downcast eyes and shoulder-length straight blond hair. Immediately she reprimanded herself for her insensitivity. The poor kid was practically shaking with fear. The class had quieted of its own accord, intently scrutinizing "the new girl."

Libby rose to her feet to meet the girl's father and welcome the child to her class. But as her eyes traveled up the long, muscled legs, past the tapered waist to the broad shoulders, her heart caught in her throat. It couldn't be. And then the face, each contour so familiar that her fingers twitched to touch the closely shaven skin once more. Her gaze took in his sensual lips, crooked nose, thick eyebrows and curly sand-blond hair, and then she could no longer put off the inevitable. She had to look into those intoxicating deep blue eyes. "Trent," she said, stumbling against the reading table.

He took a step forward, then stopped. "Libby." The one-word acknowledgment halted time.

For a moment the walls blurred in a kaleidoscope of primary colors. Then, to Libby's great relief, Mary bridged the awkwardness by taking the girl by the shoulders and urging her toward Libby. "Kylie, this is your new teacher, Miss Cameron."

Struggling to ignore the cascade of emotions that threatened to drain her of all sense, Libby approached the child. "Kylie, what a lovely name. Welcome to second grade." She put her arm around the girl's thin shoulders and turned her to face the class. "Boys and girls, isn't this exciting? It's a new year and we have a new student. Could you say hello to Kylie?"

The girl blushed painfully as the chorus of voices greeted her. "Hello, Kylie."

Mary handed Libby Kylie's transfer-student folder, then smiled from Trent to Libby. "I gather you two know each other?"

With effort, Libby forced herself to look at Trent again. The features were all there, just as she remembered them. Yet sadness weighed down his eyes, and the worry lines and Norse-blond hair, now darker with the passage of time, made a stranger of the happy-go-lucky man who had once been her husband.

"Yes, we knew each other," Libby said. "A long time ago."

"Good, then. Shall we leave now, Mr. Baker?"

Mary turned to go, but Trent stood his ground, his eyes never wavering from Libby's. His voice caught. "Take good care of her, Lib."

Libby wanted to look away, to be anyplace but here, doing anything but this. "I will," she said quietly.

They left the room, and when Libby caught up a tissue for Lacey, she also took one for herself.

TRENT SLUMPED BACK against the leather seat of his truck. Of all the crazy things! He'd known Libby was teaching in the area, but what were the odds of her being in the same school—the same grade—where Kylie was enrolled? Last he'd heard she was the kindergarten teacher in Polson, at the far end of Flathead Lake.

Not that he'd heard much about her in recent years. After their divorce, he'd gotten out of Dodge and made a new life for himself in Billings. Weezer and Chad had known better than to mention Libby. When he'd left northwest Montana, he'd erased that slate. Or so he'd thought.

Miss Cameron? It sounded somehow like a missed chord. He'd known she'd taken back her maiden name, but still… Hearing it like that hurt.

On some level, he'd anticipated that returning to Whitefish would resurrect old memories, but seeing her today had knocked him for a loop. Just like that first time he'd clapped eyes on her coming out of the administration building at Montana State. When he was a little kid, his mom had taken him to see Disney's *Snow White*, so when he'd spotted Libby walking toward him across the campus, all he could think was that here, in the flesh, was his own personal Snow White—the same dark, wavy hair, high color in her cheeks, rosebud lips. The only difference was that Libby had sparkling blue eyes instead of brown.

He blew out a puff of air. Man, she wasn't older, she was better. The same trim figure, but now with more generous, womanly curves. When she'd smiled at Kylie, he'd had to force himself not to reach out to touch her.

Pull yourself together, Baker. The woman was going to be Kylie's teacher. He was grateful for that. If anybody could ease Kylie through this transition, it would be Lib. His own confused emotional state was a small price to pay.

Checking his watch, he started the truck. He would be late meeting Chad at the bank. However, as he drove the familiar streets, his thoughts were far from business loans. He could fantasize all he wanted about getting back together with Libby, about providing Kylie with a loving stepmother. But that's all it could ever be. Fantasy.

Libby would never forgive him. He'd had a tough enough time trying to forgive himself. He'd been a complete idiot.

And if she did?

Things would have to be very different. *He* would have to be different.

And yet?

He thought about Ashley and those last few days when he'd sat by her bedside holding her hand. And the important things they'd had just enough time to say to each other.

He knew a lot more about love now. And loss. Especially loss.

TRENT? Here in Whitefish? Nothing could have prepared her for the onslaught of emotions, everything from shock, grief and anger to joy, hope and confusion. And of course regret. Somehow Libby pulled herself together enough to settle little Kylie. She paired her with Lacey, who seemed pleased to be singled out to help and relieved that Kylie, not Bart, was now assigned to help repair the damaged submarine. Kylie, however, sat mute, turning the glue stick over and over in her hand.

She blushed furiously when Bart pulled on her hair and said, "Hey, new girl, where'd you come from?"

She didn't look at him, but merely whispered, "Billings."

"You prob'ly don't even know how to ski," the boy scoffed.

"Kylie will learn," Libby said, deftly steering him to his seat.

Then it was time to put away the craft projects. Amid the clatter of drawers and bins opening and closing, Libby had a moment to study Kylie. She had Trent's square face and generous mouth, but the hair must be her mother's. Trent's was curly. A hitch caught in her chest. She remembered the springy feel of those curls that refused to be tamed. When the bell for recess rang, Libby felt relieved. She didn't want to think too much about what Kylie looked like. Whom she resembled. Whose child she could have been…

Libby threw on her coat. *Stop it!* But the unfairness burned in her throat like bitter medicine.

On the playground, the girls headed for the swings while the boys clustered around a soccer ball, dividing up into teams. Kylie, however, stood just outside the door, hands thrust deep into the pockets of her pink-flowered parka. Every so often, her eyes darted around the playground before settling back on her boots. Weezer had told Libby that Trent's wife had died within the last year. Her heart went out to Kylie Baker. Libby understood what it was like to lose a mother, to have the idyllic world of childhood shattered, replaced by emptiness and uncertainty.

Libby approached Kylie. "Did Lacey invite you to play with the girls?"

"Yeah. But I don't want to."

The thrust of the child's chin was hauntingly familiar. "Why not?"

Kylie merely shrugged.

Libby put her arm around the child. "It's hard being new, isn't it?"

The answer was a sniffle.

Pulling her closer, Libby said, "Moving involves lots of changes. Everything seems unfamiliar, I'll bet. We all want to help you, though. Will you let us?"

When Kylie turned her face into Libby's coat, Libby could feel her shoulders shaking with sobs she didn't want her classmates to observe. Digging out a tissue, Libby knelt with her back to the playground, shielding the girl from view. "Here, sweetie." She handed her the tissue.

"That's what—" sniff, sniff "—my daddy calls me sometimes."

"Daddys are nice that way."

"I guess. But I don't have a mommy."

"You miss her a lot, I imagine."

Eyes streaming, she nodded vigorously.

Libby helped dry her tears, then stood. When Kylie shyly slipped her hand into Libby's, a satisfying warmth traveled through her. This little girl was so desperate for love. But she was Trent's daughter. Libby mustn't get too involved.

"Can I tell you something?" Kylie said, adoration in every feature.

"Certainly."

The little girl gripped Libby's hand more tightly. "I think you're beautiful, Miss Cameron."

"Thank you, Kylie." Libby blinked furiously, blaming the cold wind when she knew perfectly well why she was really in danger of blubbering.

Throughout recess, Kylie remained by her side. Libby drew her out about the move and learned that Trent and his daughter were living at Weezer's, and that Kylie loved dogs and Barbie dolls. Libby told her about Mona, inviting her to come see the cat someday, then reassured her that she would learn to ski in no time. But it was the girl's answer to her final question that lanced the emotional scar Libby had thought was forever sealed. "Why did you move to Whitefish, Kylie?"

The wistfulness of the whispered reply explained everything. "So my daddy could be happy."

Of course. Wasn't that just like the Trent she'd been married to? His happiness, his comfort. That was all that mattered.

CHAPTER THREE

BY THE LAST PERIOD, Kylie seemed slightly more relaxed. She still avoided contact with most of the other children, and even when they found something uproariously funny, she remained glum, detached.

Libby dreaded the end of the day when she'd have to usher the children to the buses and carpools. It would be impossible to avoid Trent, so she'd better get used to the idea of seeing him. Well, she could do that. After all, she had her own life, which included a job she loved, a budding relationship with Doug and a host of friends. The only thing lacking was children. She loved each and every one of her second-graders, but someday, before it was too late, she wanted her own child with a longing that was almost visceral. Maybe it would happen. Doug was perfect father material.

She lined up the children, then led them to the circle driveway in front of the school. After directing the bus riders to the appropriate vehicles, she stood with the remaining children as cars, trucks and SUVs pulled into the pick-up area. And then, there he was, his forehead creased with concern. Libby took Kylie by the hand and helped her into the backseat of his truck. "Did you have a good day?" Trent asked uncertainly.

Kylie shrugged. "Miss Cameron has a cat named Mona."

Trent looked puzzled by the abrupt change of subject. "She does?"

"She said I could meet her someday. Can I, Daddy? Soon?"

When Trent looked helplessly at Libby, she inwardly berated herself for ever having made the suggestion. Yet much as she wanted to retract her ill-considered invitation, she couldn't ignore the happily expectant expression on Kylie's face. "Perhaps you could bring Kylie by the house sometime."

"How about tonight?" Trent asked, his eyes silently beseeching her. "Kylie could use a friend named Mona."

"Trent, I..."

"How do you know Miss Cameron, Daddy?"

"Um..."

Determined to avoid discussion of that topic, Libby jumped in. "Tonight would be fine."

"What if we bring a big pizza and come around six?"

How had this gotten out of hand so fast? Libby's stomach buzzed. "I don't think that's a good idea."

"Please, Lib."

After one glance at Kylie's dancing eyes, Libby reluctantly gave Trent her address, then stepped back, closing the door gently.

How had he worked his way with her already? Using Kylie, that's how. Poor kid. Innocently stuck in the middle of a situation that could only go from awkward to hostile. One pizza. One cat meeting. That was it!

Back inside, she sat at her desk studying Kylie's transfer file. Both achievement records and teacher comments had become increasingly negative over the past year. In early reports Kylie was described as a bright, sunny child by the first-grade teacher, but later comments suggested apathy and unhappiness. Then there were the principal's remarks, which revealed a recent history of aversion to school. Libby closed the folder, then sat back, staring out the window. What in the world had Trent been thinking? There couldn't have been a worse time to move Kylie.

But when had Trent ever been known to think about others first? He was all about fun and frivolity, not responsibility. Oh, he was charming, all right. She had to give him that. The heady first months of their marriage had been a whirlwind of laughter and new experiences. But Trent had never been cut out to be a husband. At least, not hers.

When, at last, Libby flipped off the lights to her classroom and started down the hall toward the parking lot, Mary stepped out of the office. "How did it go with Kylie Baker today?"

Libby held out her hand, palm down, and waggled it. "Given her history, it could've been worse."

Mary nodded sagely. "Poor little tyke. She's having to deal with an awful lot. That's one reason I placed her in your class instead of John's. She desperately needs a woman's touch. John is a good teacher, but not the one for Kylie right now."

If Libby had been given a choice in the matter, would she have accepted Kylie in her class? She chided herself. It was Kylie's welfare that was important, not hers or Trent's. "She's very lonely."

"I know. With time, we'll fix that. I have every confidence in you."

Libby hoped that confidence wasn't misplaced.

"By the way," Mary continued, "how are you and Trent Baker acquainted?"

It was all Libby could do not to flinch. But the

question was not only natural, it was inevitable. Mary knew she had been married before and had resumed her maiden name, but Libby had never found it necessary to go into detail, even with Doug. That chapter of her life was closed. Or so she had thought. "He's my ex-husband."

"Oh." The syllable dropped into the silence like a stone in a deep well. Libby could almost see the wheels turning as Mary processed the information and its implications.

"We haven't been in touch since the divorce."

Recovering quickly, the principal laid a hand on Libby's shoulder. "Dear, if this will be awkward for you, having Kylie in your class…" She trailed off, the alternative obvious.

The offer was tempting. At least then, Trent would be one step removed from her.

But there was Kylie to consider.

Like it or not, the child had tapped into the main reason Libby was a teacher. Love.

"Thank you, Mary, but I agree with what you said earlier. I think Kylie needs me."

Libby fervently hoped she was being honest with herself, and that a student's welfare was her only consideration for keeping Trent's daughter in her class.

WEEZER WATCHED TRENT and Kylie stomp snow off their boots before they entered her cabin.

Kylie immediately looked around. "Hi, Weezer. Where's Scout?"

"In the kitchen," Weezer told her, ruffling the girl's hair. "You two ready for some fresh-baked cookies?"

Trent removed his coat, then took Kylie's. "You bet."

Kylie followed Weezer into the kitchen. There by the woodstove lay Scout, fast asleep.

"He's not much of a watchdog, is he?" Weezer said. "Otherwise he'd have known you were here." She nudged the dog with her foot. "Wake up, sleepyhead, and let's hear about Kylie's school day."

Trent lounged against the doorjamb, an inscrutable expression on his face. "Go on, sugar. Tell Weezer and Scout all about it."

Kylie sat down beside Scout, scratching his ears. "The kids were mean."

Ignoring her uncooperative knees, Weezer knelt on the floor beside the girl. "Tell me about it."

Slowly Kylie began. "This one boy made fun of me. He said I didn't know how to ski."

Weezer nodded. "We can do something about that."

"And the girls all ran off at recess."

"Did they invite you to join them?"

Kylie concentrated on burrowing her hands deep in Scout's fur.

"Kylie? Weezer asked you a question."

"Uh, yeah."

Weezer made a show of examining the dog's paw. "Why didn't you play with them?"

"I don't know them."

"But—" Trent began.

Holding up her hand, Weezer forestalled him. "Let me ask a question. How will you ever get to know them if you don't give them a chance?"

Kylie's cheeks reddened. "I dunno."

Weezer let that sink in before continuing. "If you think really hard about it, I bet you can come up with one or two bright spots in your day."

"Well, maybe." Kylie sat back, deep in thought. "Lacey was okay, I guess."

"What about your teacher?"

"Oh, she's so pretty, and really, *really* nice."

"See? There's a big plus. What's her name?"

"Miss Cameron. And we're going over there tonight for pizza and she has this cat named Mona and she invited us."

Startled, Weezer glanced up at Trent, who shrugged helplessly. What in the world was going on? Trent and Libby's divorce, though mutually agreed upon, had been far from amicable. So far as Weezer knew, the two hadn't had any contact in years.

Finally Trent spoke. "What was I to do? My daughter wanted to meet Mona."

"Miss Cameron says she's a beautiful gray cat. I'm so excited."

At least the child was showing enthusiasm for something, a vast improvement from the beginning of this conversation. But Trent had moved to a kitchen chair and sat tensed like a cougar waiting to pounce.

Weezer seized on a diversionary tactic. "Kylie, why don't you help yourself to a couple of cookies, put on your coat and boots and take Scout outside to play."

"Can I?" The girl leaped to her feet, grabbed two snickerdoodles and her parka and headed for the door. "C'mon, Scout." Tail wagging, the dog joined her, and the two of them exited in a gust of frigid air.

Weezer pulled two cups from the cupboard, then poured coffee. When she placed Trent's in front of him, she tilted his chin. "Out with it. What's this all about?"

He brushed a hand through his hair. "I don't know."

"Dinner? Pizza? I practically raised you, boy. I think you *do* know." She sank into the chair across from him.

"I wasn't aware Lib taught in Whitefish."

"You could've asked me. But you made it clear a long time ago that she was off-limits in our conversations."

"When I left for Billings, I never intended to return. I was happy with Ashley." His voice sounded tortured.

"I know you were. But you were running, too. When you do that, the past has a way of circling and nipping you in the behind."

He stared into the depths of his coffee. "Tell me about it."

"So how come the meeting tonight?"

He sighed. "Kylie." Weezer waited for him to continue. "It's the most excited she's been since I decided to move here. I don't know, the bit about the pizza just popped out of my mouth."

"You're sure this is only about Kylie?"

Trent slumped back in his chair. "No."

"I see." Weezer stalled by taking a sip from her cup. "Be very careful, son. You and Kylie don't need any more hurt and disappointment."

"Neither does Lib."

"Good. I hope you remember that."

"It'll be just this once."

Just this once? Weezer doubted it. Even when he was a youngster, Trent's expressions had been transparent. And right now what she saw on his face was longing, pure and simple.

LIBBY RESISTED changing her clothes. She didn't want to give Trent the impression that anything special was going on. In fact, part of her didn't want him to step foot in her home. After their divorce, she had sold or given away the few belongings they'd owned jointly and had haunted antiques shops and estate sales, gradually accumulating enough to furnish her modest house. She loved the wood grain of her oak coffee table, the high back of the armchair, the prints of native flora on the wall, the faded Persian rug she'd bid too much for at an auction. The place wasn't fancy, but it was hers. Her sanctuary.

Trent's presence here would feel invasive.

Furthermore, she was having difficulty picturing Trent as a single father. He'd never shown the slightest interest in parenthood. Instead, he'd always laughed and said, "Lib, I'd be a lousy father." His rationalization was that since his own father had walked out on him when he was four, he'd had no role model. He'd then go on to say by way of justification, "A baby deserves a daddy who knows a little something."

Hindsight suggested he'd been right.

Oh, why had she ever agreed to let them come?

Yet even as she asked the question, she continued laying her silverware and colorful plates on the sunshine-yellow tablecloth.

How could she have let Kylie tug at her heart-strings like that? Was it because she was Trent's daughter—the child they'd never had together? Or was it because Libby was motherless, too, and identified with the little girl? Seeing Kylie reminded her so powerfully of the day she her-self had come home from school to the news her mother would never return from the hospital.

Libby needed to be on her guard to keep this relationship professional. She was a teacher ex-tending kindness to an emotionally needy stu-dent. Her previous relationship with the girl's father was irrelevant.

Just get through this evening.

Precisely at six, she heard a vehicle pull into the driveway, then doors slam. She stood, smoothing her skirt, willing indifference. "Hello," she said, holding the door open. "Smells good," she mumbled as Trent stepped by her with the pizza box, trailing a scent of tomato sauce and oregano. "Let me take your coats."

Kylie quickly shrugged out of hers, then Trent handed Libby his parka. "I imagine you're eager to meet Mona," Libby said as she hung their coats in the hall closet.

"I can't wait!" Kylie cried, bouncing on her toes.

"Cats aren't as friendly right away as dogs

are, you know. It takes them a while to warm up to strangers."

"Weezer told me that. She said I have to be patient. Let Mona come to me."

"That's good advice."

Libby was marginally okay so long as she was dealing with Kylie, but then she made the mistake of glancing up. Trent stood silhouetted against the fireplace, looking far too handsome in formfitting jeans and a Black Watch plaid flannel shirt. He held up the box. "The pizza?"

"Oh, I'm sorry. Here, let me take it." Kylie had already climbed into the big chair and sat, a forefinger to her lips, quietly awaiting the elusive Mona. Trent followed Libby into the kitchen. "Nice place," he murmured.

"It's home," she said, setting the box on the counter near the oven. "Should we heat this up yet?"

"Kylie won't eat a thing until she meets Mona. Let's wait a few minutes."

"Uh, would you like a drink?"

"Soda will be fine."

After handing him a soda, she selected one for herself.

She peered around him into the living room. "Look."

They both moved to the doorway. He was

standing too close, his body only inches from hers.

"She looks so happy," he said huskily.

Kylie sat, dwarfed by the big chair, while a contented Mona kneaded the girl's chest with her paws. Oblivious to her audience, Kylie was whispering something in the cat's ear.

Trent nodded at Libby. "Thanks. I hope this visit isn't too awkward for you."

Too awkward? It was nothing short of bizarre. "I'm doing this for Kylie."

"I know."

"Daddy, isn't Mona pretty?"

"She sure is."

"We're getting acquainted. You guys can go back to the kitchen."

Trent grinned down at Libby. "Sounds like we've been dismissed."

"Suits me. I need to preheat the oven anyway."

In the kitchen, Trent pulled one of the chairs out from the table and straddled it, leaning his arms across the back. Just as he used to do. Libby bit her lip at that last thought. She didn't welcome these reminders. Instead, she needed to focus on getting through the evening. "What brought you back to Whitefish?"

Fortunately his explanation about going into business with Chad Larraby permitted her to warm the pizza and toss the salad she'd made earlier, keeping her so busy she almost succeeded in ignoring the way his voice brightened with enthusiasm and his eyes following her every move. When he finished with an explanation of their upcoming season's advertising campaign, he asked her about herself.

She gave him the short version. She'd gotten her first job in Polson, where they'd lived at the time of the divorce, and completed her master's degree in the summers. She'd moved to White-fish three years ago.

There was nothing easy about the conversation. She walked around the kitchen, making busywork. Fixing glasses of ice water, grating the Parmesan cheese, digging out a platter for the pizza, anything to delay sitting down across the table from her ex-husband. But there was one question that had to be faced. "Have you told Kylie we were married?"

He ran a hand through his hair. "No. It's too early."

"What do you mean?"

His eyes displayed anguish. "She's had so much to deal with. Ashley's death—and the move. She likes you. I don't want to do anything right now to rock her boat."

"She'll have to know sometime."

"Please, Lib, just not yet. Let her settle in first."

Libby wasn't sure withholding the information was a good idea, but Trent was the girl's father and presumably knew her better than anyone.

"You're the parent. I'll abide by your wishes."

He nodded. "Thanks. I appreciate that."

In the awkward silence that followed, she busied herself at the counter.

Just before the oven buzzer went off, Kylie appeared, the large cat draped over her shoulder. "Miss Cameron, I think Mona likes me."

Libby smiled. "No doubt about it. She doesn't let very many people pick her up."

"Can she eat with us?"

Trent laughed. "Do you think cats like pepperoni?"

"Oh, Daddy, you're funny. I mean, can she sit on my lap while I eat?"

Trent caught Libby's eye and she nodded. "Just don't use her as a napkin," he said.

To Libby's amazement, Mona remained in Kylie's lap while they ate, only occasionally pawing the tablecloth as if to say, "How about me?"

"Good salad," Trent said appreciatively.

"Thank you."

Kylie ate with gusto. "This is the best pizza."

Trent picked up his napkin and wiped the corner of his daughter's mouth. "Whitefish's finest."

"Whitefish. I hate that name." A shadow fell across Kylie's face. "Do I have to go to school tomorrow?"

"Of course. You know that." Trent shared a look of concern with Libby.

Kylie said nothing, but pushed her plate away.

"I'd be disappointed if you weren't in my class," Libby told her.

Kylie's eyes filled with tears.

"What is it, honey?" she asked, leaning forward.

Sensing the tension in the girl, Mona wagged her tail slowly from side to side. "They'll laugh," Kylie confided.

"Who?"

"The kids."

Libby stole a quick glance at Trent, whose expression was anguished. "Why?"

"Be-be-cause." Silently, tears oozed down the little girl's cheeks. "I...I'll have to read."

Libby's stomach plummeted. Bless her heart, the poor thing was terrified. "I'll be sure they don't laugh. Don't you like to read?"

"I used to."

"When was that?"

"Before Mommy went to the cementery."

Trent turned his head away and Libby picked up the girl's hands. "Honey, did you read to your mommy?"

"Yes."

"And was she proud of you?"

"Uh-huh."

"Do you think she'd want you to give up?"

Kylie swiped an arm across her nose. "No," she said in a little voice.

"I have an idea. Can you come to school early tomorrow?"

Trent nodded quickly.

"I guess," Kylie said.

Hoping her idea would work, Libby grasped Kylie's hands even tighter. "We'll practice reading together before the other children come— just the way you used to read to your mommy. Could you do that?"

In the silence that followed, Mona jumped from Kylie's lap onto the table and began sniffing at the leftover crust. Libby never took her eyes from Kylie's. Trent scooped up the cat.

Finally the girl spoke. "I think so. I don't have a mommy now, but if I ever get a new one, I want her to be just like you, Miss Cameron."

Libby caught Kylie to her in a hug she wished

would last forever. She didn't dare examine her feelings—or look at Trent.

Setting Mona on the floor, Trent stood, clearing his throat. "I'll have her there at seven-thirty."

"Daddy, do we have to leave?"

"Sure do, sweetie. I need to get you to bed if you're going to be bright-eyed at the crack of dawn. What do you say to Miss Cameron?"

"Thank you for letting us come, and 'specially for Mona. She's a super cat."

"Why don't you tell her goodbye while I get your coats?"

Kylie dashed off to the living room, where Mona had scampered. Libby moved quickly to the closet, extracting their parkas. When she turned around, Trent laid a hand on her shoulder. "You're great with her, Lib. I appreciate that."

"She's easy to like."

"I, uh…" He paused, his eyes clouded. "I know this probably isn't the time or place, but here goes. I'm sorry for the pain I caused you back…well, you know when. I wasn't there for you the way I should've been. I said some terrible things."

Libby's knees shook and she felt hollow inside. "What's done is done. We've both moved on." She was pretty sure he wanted her to tell him she'd forgiven him, but the words stuck in her throat. Instead, she said, "I'll take good care of Kylie."

"I know you will." He was staring at her with an intensity that aroused feelings she was reluctant to identify, then finally turned away. "Kylie, time to leave."

After they'd left, Libby couldn't move. Rooted to the spot, resting her forehead against the closed door, she thought she might be sick. Sorry? He'd said he was sorry? Was he seeking forgiveness *now?*

Entwining her arms around her abdomen, she finally made it to the rocking chair, knowing that nothing—nothing at all—could salve the wound he'd opened up.

She couldn't have said how long she sat there. It might have been mere minutes—or hours. The repetitive to-and-fro of the rocker failed to soothe her. She was way beyond soothing.

She should have been rocking a baby. His baby.

Impelled by a force beyond herself, she rose and moved toward her bedroom, knowing on the one hand the act was masochistic, but on the other, inevitable. She knelt on the braided wool rug, her heartbeat a mournful thud, then, with trembling hands, raised the lid of the cedar chest. The aromatic fragrance nearly gagged her.

She could stop now. She didn't have to do this. But instinct was deaf to reason. Burrowing beneath sheets, tablecloths and out-of-season clothing, she found the hardcover volume, long buried.

Blind, futile rage enveloped her as she wrested the book from the depths of the cedar chest, oblivious to the disorder left behind.

By the soft light of the bedside lamp, she forced herself to read the title that her fingers involuntarily traced. "My Baby Book."

Clasping this journal of dashed hopes to her chest, she carried it to the bed, where she perched on the edge like a sleepwalker recently aroused. She flipped to one of the first pages, filled with her own handwriting. "How Mommy Told Daddy About Me." Then, "Mommy's First Visit to the Doctor." And finally to the stark white, blank pages—screaming loss—after "Mommy's Third Month."

Her throat worked in spasms but she refused to cry. She had shed enough tears to last a lifetime, and they had changed nothing.

How dare Trent reenter her life? How dare he bring that precious, beautiful daughter of his to break her heart? And how dare her traitorous heart feel something for him?

She stared at the book in her lap, knowing that from this moment on, it would serve as a potent reminder. Trent was not part of her life. He had long ago given up any claim on her.

He had never understood how she felt. He'd even been cavalier. To him it was "just a miscarriage." To her, a loss beyond bearing.

Now he had his child. She had no one.

For him, it had been a simple matter. She would never forget his words that awful day when she couldn't stop sobbing, when nothing could stanch her pain and grief. "It's not the end of the world, Lib. We can always have another baby."

No, he hadn't been there for her. That same day, love died.

CHAPTER FOUR

TRAPPED IN AN UNDERTOW of guilt, Trent concentrated on his driving, focusing on every intersection, each curve in the road.

"Daddy, did you see how Mona curled up in my lap? She has the softest fur and I love petting her. 'Course, I love Scout. Dogs are my favorites, but cats are…"

Kylie had jabbered nonstop ever since they left Libby's. His role, limited to nodding occasionally or muttering a well-timed "Uh-huh," left him too much time to think. To remember.

Libby's euphoria when the home pregnancy test had turned up positive. The way she had welcomed morning sickness as a harbinger of the new life within her. Her ecstatic plans for turning their tiny second bedroom into a colorful nursery. How nearly every conversation had revolved around possible baby names.

That wasn't all he remembered.

With a shame that tightened his stomach, he also recalled his own panic.

A baby? No way was he prepared—not

financially and certainly not emotionally. He was a young man, for cripe's sake, enjoying his free lifestyle. On a whim he could jump in his truck and take off with his buddies to follow the snow or fish a hot section of the river. Then when he got home? Libby would listen to his adventures, laugh at the appropriate moments and applaud his feats.

He had felt that he was being cheated. A baby would spoil everything. He wasn't ready. This couldn't be happening. Libby wanted him to share her excitement, but somehow he could never wrap his mind around the concept of late-night feedings and dirty diapers. It was more fun to escape to the nearest tavern or gather his friends for a poker game.

Yeah, he wasn't proud of his reaction to Libby's pregnancy. After the divorce and his move to Billings, he'd had plenty of time to reflect— and to grow up. Then he'd met Ashley and once again been faced with the prospect of fatherhood. This time he had promised himself things would be different. He would be a loving and responsible parent.

"Daddy, I'm scared." Kylie's last words penetrated his thoughts. "About tomorrow."

"The reading?"

"I, uh, I'm not very good."

"You used to be."

"That was before..."

She didn't have to complete the thought. Before Ashley died. "Yes, but you can be again. Especially with Miss Cameron's help."

Kylie's fear and doubt came out in her voice. "Maybe."

"You like her, don't you?"

"Yes." She was silent a moment, then, with hushed awe, she added her final thought, which totally undid him. "She's wonderful, Daddy."

A horrible thought occured to Trent: What if he'd never had Kylie? Never known the awesome feeling of cradling his daughter in his arms? Libby had every right to hold him in contempt. How could he ever have considered a baby an inconvenience? A burden? His daughter had been the only thing keeping him from going over the edge after Ashley died.

His heart felt heavy. How lame was the apology he'd offered Libby tonight? She should've thrown him out of the house. Yet despite her far-from-cordial feelings toward him, she'd embraced his daughter, offering her the affection and approval she so desperately needed. Libby was obviously a more sensitive human being than he had been.

But could she forgive?

In light of the past, it seemed a huge thing to

hope for. But he was going to continue asking. Begging if necessary.

Because Libby's soulful eyes, her gentle treatment of his daughter, the sense of homecoming that enveloped him the moment he stepped over her threshold—all stirred something deep within him.

She had been his first love. He wanted her to be his last.

"Are we home yet, Daddy?"

"Not yet, sweetie."

No, not by a long shot. They would never be truly home until he could prove to Libby he was a new man. A better one.

AFTER A FITFUL NIGHT, Libby had awakened late, thrown on a pair of wool slacks, a soft red turtleneck, an oversize fleece vest and boots. Racing against time, she pulled her hair into a ponytail and dashed from the house. Despite her misgivings about Trent and all the buried emotions he had brought to the surface, she couldn't be late for her first tutoring appointment with Kylie.

The sun was just peeping over the mountains when she pulled into the faculty parking lot. Suddenly, the thought of facing a day of lively second-graders wearied her. She shrugged. *That's what you get, dummy, for letting Trent Baker turn your world topsy-turvy.* She couldn't tell what had caused her insomnia—the reawakened grief, her anger at his belated apology or her maddening yet undeniable attraction to him.

His words had dredged up a past she'd spent years blocking from her memory. Not just their marriage. But something else, something just as painful. An image of her stepfather caused her to ball her fists. Vernon G. Belton was a politician with the common touch, or so the press portrayed him. A friend to the downtrodden. Yet when his stepdaughter's actions had threatened to embarrass him, sacrifices had to be made. What was one troubled girl weighed against political expediency?

Libby trudged toward the school, determined to clear her mind of such poisonous thoughts. Kylie needed her encouragement, not her bitterness.

By the time Trent and Kylie appeared, Libby had finished her first cup of coffee from the teachers' lounge, written the day's assignments on the board and unearthed the book she intended to use for her reading session with Trent's daughter.

"Good morning, Kylie." Libby pasted on her broadest smile, noticing with chagrin that her lips quivered when she glanced at Trent, who looked as though sleep had eluded him last night, as well. "Have you had breakfast?"

"Cereal."

"Good. It's hard to work on an empty stomach." She gestured toward the reading table. "Shall we?"

She sent Trent a pointed look, but he stood, as if rooted, staring at her.

He shifted from one foot to the other. "I appreciate this, Lib. Can I pay you?"

"That won't be necessary. We're not allowed to tutor our students for pay, though we can offer extra help."

"Oh."

"Bye, Daddy."

Trent bent down to give Kylie a hug. "See you later, sweetie."

Just before he turned to leave, he touched Libby's shoulder. "Thanks," he said, his voice husky.

Libby watched him walk down the hall, that slow, sassy amble of his so familiar to her.

"Miss Cameron, are you okay?"

Caught. Feeling herself flush, she turned back to Kylie. "Sure, honey."

The girl settled into a tiny chair while Libby pulled up her desk chair. Chewing her lower lip, Kylie fingered the book nervously. "You'll laugh."

Libby stilled Kylie's restless hands. "Never." She picked up the reader. "This is a wonderful story about a bear. Why don't we begin with it."

"Okay."

Kylie made a fumbling start, but with Libby's encouragement, she soon began reading with more ease. When they finished, Libby gave her a quick hug. "That was a great beginning. You read with lots of expression."

"That's what my mommy used to say."

"Your mommy was right."

Solemnly, the little girl nodded. "I know." She entwined her fingers nervously. "Could you, uh, help me again?"

"Certainly. Why don't we do this early-morning reading twice a week until you feel ready to give it up?"

"We can talk to Daddy about it, right?"

Libby stifled a sigh. Talking to Daddy was dead last on her list of desirable things to do. "Maybe when he picks you up this afternoon."

Mary Travers poked her head in the door. "You two are quite the early birds." She approached Kylie and laid a hand on her head. "Are you settling in all right?"

Kylie merely shrugged.

Mary smiled reassuringly. "Give us a chance, Kylie. We love having girls like you in our school." She winked at Libby. "Isn't that right, Miss Cameron?"

"Yes, and I'm the lucky teacher who got Kylie in my class."

Outside, Libby heard the roar of a school bus pulling into the driveway. The other children would soon be descending on them, and from that point on, she would have no more time to think about Trent. Thankfully.

"Have a good day," Mary said to both of them, before heading toward the bus-unloading zone.

Mary's presence had a calming effect, not only on Kylie, who had moved to her desk to unload her backpack and arrange her school supplies, but on Libby. And unwittingly, Mary had reminded her of the perfect antidote to Trent.

Doug.

CHAD LARRABY PRANCED down the street toward Trent in imitation of a touchdown-scoring NFL player. "We did it!" he said, extending his palm for a high five. "The insurance is in the bag."

Trent grinned. "You're the man." In truth, Chad *was* the man. He had taken on the formidable challenge of whittling down their liability rates. Trent held open the door of the Kodiak Café and stepped aside. "Coffee's my treat."

"You're on," Chad said, rubbing his hands together.

Weezer waved from behind the cash register where she held court each morning, and one of the waitresses made a beeline for their table with a pot and two mugs in her hand. The aroma of the café's signature cinnamon rolls was impossible to resist. Both men ordered one.

Chad spread his arms along the back of the booth. "How does it feel to be back in Whitefish?"

"Great. I sure appreciate your giving me this opportunity."

"You'd have done the same for me. We're on our way, pal."

Trent hoped so. The business plan looked good on paper, but in the middle of winter it was hard to gauge how many tourists would book their services, especially in light of the recent forest fires. The business had to make it big during the summer season. That meant long hours, seven days a week. He would have to make arrangements somehow for Kylie. But he'd worry about that later. "Are you still on the search and rescue team?"

"You bet. Speaking of which, we're having a training session next week. Any chance you'd be interested in joining us?"

Trent was tempted. It was right down his alley.

While he was in college, he'd been involved with the Bozeman-area group. Simply remembering his role in several harrowing rescues gave him an adrenaline rush. "I'd hate to leave Kylie. Let me think about it."

"If you're interested, my daughter Lisa does quite a bit of babysitting. But back to Kylie. How'd she do yesterday at school?"

"Okay, except for the fact that some midget-size bully made fun of her because she can't ski."

"We can fix that in a hurry."

"That's what I told her. I'm thinking of taking her up to Big Mountain on Saturday."

"You better let old Uncle Chad come along. Nobody should try to teach their own kids how to ski. I had to put mine with an instructor when they wouldn't listen to me."

Trent grinned wryly. "You have a point. Besides, I want the two of you to get acquainted."

"You've got a deal. Lori's taking our kids to Helena this weekend to visit her folks, so I'm free."

After discussing plans for their exhibit at the upcoming outdoor show in Kalispell, Chad looked beyond Trent toward the door, then rose out of his seat, waving his hand. "Chuckers, over here."

A florid, heavyset man approached, a broad smile lifting the tips of his red handlebar mustache. "Well, if it isn't Trent Baker." He grabbed Trent's hand in a knuckle-crunching grip and slid into the seat beside him. "I haven't seen you since that camping trip years ago. Heard tell you've been working down Billings way."

Trent cringed, remembering the results of that trip. He'd been gone for several days and when he returned, Libby had said she'd felt abandoned. In high school, Chad, Chuck and Trent had been part of a group of guys who ran together, but after Trent married Libby, she had become increasingly jealous of the time he spent with them. "I've been living in Billings for quite a few years."

"What brings you back?"

Chad gave him the short version of their new business venture.

"I was sorry to hear about your divorce from—" Chuck struggled a moment with his memory "—Libby? I always thought you two made a great couple."

Chuck appeared oblivious to Chad's warning frown, but Trent faced the question head-on. "Some things just aren't meant to be." Coffee sloshed in his stomach. "I remarried—a Billings woman. She, uh, died about a year ago."

"Oh, man. Sorry."

"I have a little girl. I can't think of a better place to raise a kid than here in Whitefish."

Chuck clapped him on the shoulder. "Me, neither. Glad to have you back." He stood. "Now, if you gents'll excuse me, I'm meeting a fella here. But, hey—" he shot out a forefinger pistol-style "—how about we plan a get-together Monday night at the sports bar?" he said. "Tell a few lies."

Chuck Patterson might be a balding thirty-five-year-old, but his brain was stuck in high school. "Maybe sometime," Trent replied vaguely. "Right now, I'm staying close to my daughter. Everything here is pretty new to her."

"Sure, I understand. Adios." Chuck lumbered off toward the back of the café.

Chad watched him walk away, a bemused smile on his face. "You'd never know old Chuckers had been a wrestling champ, would you? Or that he has five kids." He leaned forward. "Don't think for a minute, though, that he's settled down. He's still a wild man."

Trent took another swig of coffee. "Am I getting old or have I just outgrown him?"

Before Chad could answer, the waitress returned with their piping-hot rolls, gooey white frosting melting on the tops. Chad cut off a bite, but paused before eating to give Trent an answer. "You have responsibilities now."

"Yes. I do." Somehow, at the moment, those responsibilities seemed more burdensome than not. Yet no way did he want to be sitting in some loud bar, watching pro-wrestling and listening to Chuckers regaling him about the "good old days."

Both men concentrated on their food. Finally Chad sat back, patting his stomach in satisfaction. "Bet you can't get anything like that in Billings."

Trent smiled. "There's no Weezer there, that's for sure."

His friend leaned forward, elbows on the table, his expression serious. "Have you seen her yet?"

"Weezer?" Trent asked, pretending to misunderstand.

"Not Weezer. Libby."

The yeasty roll swelled against the walls of his stomach. He'd seen her all right. A lot of good it had done him. "Yeah."

"Well?" Chad inclined his head. "Are you going to tell me about it?"

"There's not much to tell. She's Kylie's teacher."

"You're kidding."

"Nope. What were the odds of that happening?"

"So?"

"Kylie's crazy about her."

His friend fixed his dark eyes on him. "What about you?"

"What *about* me?"

"Feel any of the old vibes?"

Oh, yeah. He'd lain awake most of last night thinking of her. "What if I did? What good would it do me?"

Chad's stare grew even more piercing. "You're no quitter, Baker. If you want her, go for it."

"I did some unforgivable things."

"Twelve years ago. And if you haven't noticed, she's never remarried. Doesn't that tell you anything?"

Trent scooped up the check, then rose to his feet. "We'll see."

Chad stood, too, and put his arm around Trent's shoulder. "Whatever you decide, pal, I'm with you. But if you want her, don't wait too long."

Outside, they went their separate ways. Trent was halfway down the block when he stopped in his tracks, Chad's words thundering in his brain. *Don't wait too long.* Did Chad know something he didn't?

He straightened the brim of his ball cap. Was

there someone else? That was a possibility he'd
never considered. But why not? Libby was a special woman—attractive, fun, compassionate.

His face grim, he started on down the street.
He'd been a jerk before. Why should she give
him the time of day now?

Chad's words mocked him. *You're no quitter,
Baker.*

Fish-or-cut-bait time? He picked up the pace,
lowering his head against the wind. There was
only one choice. Go fish!

GEORGIA WAITED impatiently in the den for
Gus to finish showering and join her. She had
learned the hard way that instead of forcing discussions, she had to bide her time and gauge the
perfect opening. Gus worked long, hard hours
and made more than a comfortable living, for
which she was grateful, but sometimes he could
be maddeningly dense. Like now. How could he
proceed calmly through his day when Kylie had
been taken from them?

At last he appeared, pausing by the fridge.
"Would you like something?" he asked, holding
a glass aloft.

"Yes, mineral water, please," she said. *Don't
rush him.*

"One of the gals in your tennis group called
me today about a house project."

Small talk. So this was how it was going to be. "Oh?"

He poured water into both glasses. "Lora Neff. She wants to blow out the back of her kitchen and add a family room." He handed her a glass, then kicked back in his leather recliner. "Don't know if I have time in the schedule for her."

Georgia bit back a scream and raised her glass and took a drink.

He finally asked the question she'd been waiting for. "How was your day?"

Usually he faked attention to her answer, bored with recitals of bridge luncheons, golf rounds and shopping excursions. "I phoned Kylie this afternoon. Honestly, you'd think Trent would have called us before now."

"They just moved, hon. It takes time to settle in."

Why did Gus always have to be so reasonable? "I know, but I was dying to hear about her first couple of days at school."

"So what did she say?"

Her fingers chilled from the cold glass, Georgia set down her drink. "It's just as I'd feared." She paused for dramatic effect, gratified to see she had her husband's full attention. "She's unhappy."

Gus raised his eyebrows. "Could you be more specific?"

"She doesn't like the children in her class."

"She didn't like school here, either, so that's nothing new." He took a quick swig of water. "Surely she had some good things to say."

"Something about a dog and a cat." She sniffed. "Next thing you know, she'll probably have an allergic reaction."

Gus's face remained studiously blank. "What about where they're living? Her teacher?"

"Oh, Gus, can you imagine? They're living in a log cabin. Like Laura and Mary Ingalls, Kylie said. The very idea. She likes her teacher, though, so I guess Whitefish has at least one redeeming quality." Indignation swelled within her. "Couldn't you have offered Trent more money to stay here?"

Gus put his drink down on the table beside him. "I did." He pulled the recliner lever and returned the footrest to the floor, then stood and walked over to her. "Georgia, hon, it was something Trent had to do."

"What? Break our hearts?" When he laid a hand on her shoulder, she turned her head aside. *Did he care at all?*

"Follow his dream. Build a future for his daughter. You can't fault him for that."

"But I miss her so." She blinked furiously.

"It's not about you—or me," he said, his voice husky. "We need to do our best to support them in this new venture."

Georgia rose to her feet, leaving her untouched drink behind. "I swear, Gus, no matter how long we've been married, I will never understand you." Her voice rose. "I can't stand it!" Then she fled the room, her throat constricting and eyes welling with unshed tears.

LIBBY LOLLED in her desk chair and let out a relieved sigh. Another week over. Bart had gotten into a fight on the playground, Rory had yet to raise his hand to participate in discussions, and Kylie... Well, she was hard to figure. She had seemed pleased enough with their two reading sessions, but when the other kids were around, she clammed up, her body language defensive. When Trent had picked her up this afternoon, he'd told her she would be riding the school bus from now on, except for the mornings she came for extra help. Kylie had darted him a fearful look that rent Libby's heart. Yet riding the bus might be good. Kylie would be forced to interact with the other kids.

And Libby could avoid daily contact with Trent.

She was loading her tote bag for the

weekend, when she sensed someone at her class-room door.

"Libby, hi." Doug smiled at her, then hurried across the room, leaned over and planted a kiss on her cheek. "I just got in from the underwriters' workshop in Great Falls and couldn't wait to see you."

"Doug, what a surprise!" Flustered, she stood, smoothing the skirt of her dress. Her makeup had faded, her hair was frazzled and the dress was decidedly wrinkled.

"You look beautiful," he said.

She shot him an incredulous look. "More like Mary Poppins after a day with the Banks children."

He grasped her hands. "Don't do that."

"What?"

"Put yourself down. When a man tells you you're beautiful, believe it."

She looked into his eyes, which were soft with approval. To avoid the intensity of the moment, she withdrew her hands and gave a jaunty salute. "Yes, sir."

"I hope you're free this weekend. I have big plans for us."

Her weekend agenda included cleaning her kitchen, reviewing district performance standards and making phone calls to Bart's and Rory's parents. About as exciting as a visit from the exterminator. Yet she couldn't stifle a tic of irritation that Doug had assumed she would be available to do…whatever. "What do you have in mind?"

"For starters, do you feel like Mexican food tonight? Afterward we could take in the high-school basketball game or go to your place and watch a movie. Your choice. And tomorrow? I heard on the radio coming home that the snow at Big Mountain is great. I thought we might get in a few runs. When was the last time you went skiing?"

"Not since before Christmas, and skiing sounds like a lot more fun than what I had in mind." She figured she could get most of her work finished Sunday.

"Great. I'll pick you up for dinner at six." He bussed her cheek again, then left.

Mary stopped her on her way out of the building. "Could I see you a minute?"

"Certainly."

Libby followed her into her office and took a seat across from the principal's desk.

"Do you know a Jeremy Kantor?"

Frowning, Libby racked her brain. "Should I?"

"Not necessarily. He's a reporter for a national newsmagazine."

Libby experienced a sinking feeling. "Is this

about my stepfather?" She had taken great pains to distance herself from the senator, and his office had gone along with her request to keep her out of the limelight.

"He said he was collecting background information for a profile piece on Senator Belton and asked me to verify your employment. Since that's a matter of public record, I could hardly refuse."

"Is that all he wanted?"

"Apparently." Mary reached across the desk and seized Libby's hand. "You look pale. Are you all right?"

Libby shook her head to clear the ringing in her ears. "Yes. It's just that…my stepfather and I have never been close, and I resent his putting you in this position. Maybe it's nothing, but I don't have a good feeling about this." She would have to talk with Vernon. Ask him what was going on. He had phoned her at Christmas with his usual perfunctory holiday greetings, but they spoke only rarely—and never warmly. As a child, she used to imagine how different her life would have been had her airline-pilot father survived the crash that took his life when she was an infant. But as she grew older, she came to understand that such idle speculation was an exercise in futility. What was, was. Period. Yet would her father have been there for her when her world fell apart at age eighteen? The Honorable Vernon G. Belton certainly had not.

Mary studied her with concern. "Let me know how I can help. Or if Doug can."

"I appreciate the offer, but you needn't get involved. In the future, refer Mr. Kantor to me."

"You're sure?"

"Positive." Libby rose. "Thank you."

"Remember, Libby, you don't have to face anything alone. You have all of us for a family."

Unable to speak, Libby gave Mary a hug before dashing toward her car. No one could ask for a more loving mother-in-law than Mary.

Mother-in-law? Where had that come from? Yet in truth, she suspected that was where her relationship with Doug was heading. After all, she'd practically told him she loved him.

Practically. But not actually.

SATURDAY MORNING Trent stood in the tiny kitchen of the cabin, a box of pancake mix in one hand. Hotcakes would be just the thing to fortify him and Kylie for a day on the slopes. He'd been careful to buy huckleberry syrup, Kylie's favorite. He glanced out the window, where snow glistened in the sun like crystallized sugar.

"Daddy?" Wearing her footed pajamas,

Kylie trailed into the kitchen, rubbing sleep from her eyes.

"Good morning. Ready for our big day?" He measured the flour mixture, then added the milk and two eggs.

Kylie didn't answer. Instead, she picked up the crocheted afghan from the arm of the living-room sofa and curled up with it. She must still be sleepy. He hummed off-key while he stirred the batter, then heated oil in the cast-iron skillet. When he poured the batter into the skillet, it made a satisfying sizzle. After flipping the pancakes, he turned around. "Kylie, would you set our places at the table? Breakfast's almost ready."

She didn't move. "I'm not hungry."

In his gut, a curl of suspicion grew. "Why not?"

"I'm sick."

He set down the spatula and crossed to the sofa, where he knelt beside her. "What hurts?"

"My tummy."

He placed a palm on her forehead. "No fever."

"I don't care. I'm sick."

"But we're going to have such a fun day. You'll like skiing. Uncle Chad's a great teacher."

"I'm not going." She rubbed her hands over her stomach. "I might throw up."

That was not a pretty picture. Frustrated, Trent wondered how seriously he should take her complaints. He never knew when she was crying wolf. What might have upset her about skiing? "Don't you want to learn to ski?"

She shook her head violently.

"Why not?"

"I'll just look stupid. Besides, Mommy didn't ski."

She was right about that. Ashley had enjoyed summer sports like golf and tennis. He racked his brain for a suitable enticement. "Miss Cameron does."

Kylie straightened up and searched his eyes. "How do you know?"

Now was not the time to get into the subject of his and Libby's prior relationship. "Didn't you notice the ski rack on her car that night we went to her house?"

"Oh. I guess."

"You'll be missing out on the best fun if you stay home."

"Do you think she might be there today?"

Trent hadn't the slightest idea. The odds weren't great. "I don't know. We'll just have to go and find out, won't we?"

"Uncle Chad'll teach me?"

"He'll have you zipping down the beginner run in no time."

She laced her fingers through the yarn of the afghan. "Okay, I guess."

He heaved a sigh of relief and rose to his feet. "That's my girl."

"Daddy, what's that stinky smell?"

Trent wheeled around, his eyes drawn to the smoking skillet. Great! He could only hope blackened pancakes weren't an omen.

KYLIE REMAINED SILENT while her ski boots were fitted, but once she lumbered out into the snow, she grinned up at Trent and said, "I have monster feet, right?"

Chad made her giggle with his imitation of the abominable snowman before kneeling beside her and pointing out the techniques of some of the other skiers on the bunny hill. She listened attentively, then he showed her how to sidestep to the top of the gentle slope, where he pulled her against his chest, his skis outside hers. With a "Whee!" the two of them glided down the hill.

When they reached the bottom, Chad shot a pointed look at Trent. "Get lost, Daddy, will ya? You're slowing us down."

"Yeah, Daddy. Go away. Then when you come

back, I'll betcha you'll be surprised. I'm gonna ski."

"It's under control," Chad assured Trent.

Reluctantly, Trent headed toward the chairlift. He'd hoped to teach Kylie himself, but he was glad she seemed to be bonding with Chad and that Chad had charmed her out of her fear of failure.

The view from the lift was spectacular. The frosted peaks of Glacier Park dazzled against the cloudless blue sky and the lakes below sparkled like mirrors. Trent took a deep breath of the alpine-fresh air and relaxed against the seat back. He'd missed northwest Montana even more than he'd realized. With time, surely Kylie would come to love the place as much as he did.

So that they could live in Whitefish for his formative years, his mother had worked a variety of jobs—Glacier Park reservations agent, school-bus driver, desk clerk and finally waitress at the Kodiak Café. It was there she and Weezer became fast friends. Trent chuckled. If one of them wasn't making sure he toed the line, the other was. No wonder. His escapades had made them eternally vigilant.

That's what he wanted for Kylie—a community of people she could depend on.

With a shudder, the chairlift passed over a

support and Trent glided onto the ramp at the top of the run. Despite the sunny day and excellent snow conditions, there were few skiers on this particular section of the mountain. He pulled down his goggles, adjusting them for comfort, then planted his poles and shoved off, exhilaration fueling him with each *shush* of the skis. When he planted his poles at the end of the run, he couldn't suppress a broad grin of satisfaction.

He made an additional run, then skied back to the bottom, unwilling to impose on Chad. He unstrapped his skis, slung them over his shoulder and made his way to the bunny slope. To his amazement, Kylie was skiing all by herself, her brows knit in concentration. When she came to a stop, she looked up at Chad, and then laughed with satisfaction. "I did it, Uncle Chad, I did it!"

Chad exchanged a high five with her. "You sure did, kiddo. You're a natural."

Looking over Chad's shoulder, she spotted Trent. "Daddy, Daddy! I can ski!"

Trent approached and gave her a big hug. "I never doubted it."

"That'll show that stupid Bart Ames. When can we come again?"

"How about tomorrow?" Trent had always believed in striking while the iron was hot.

"Yay!" Her cheeks were pink with the cold and her eyes danced.

"Ready for some hot chocolate? That way Uncle Chad can have some time to ski himself."

"I love hot chocolate."

"Thanks, buddy." Trent extended a hand to Chad. "I owe you one."

"You don't owe me a thing. Kylie and I had a great time, right, Picabo?"

Kylie nodded, then confided to Trent, "He calls me that funny name—Peekaboo. That was a famous girl skier, you know."

Trent grinned. "So I've heard tell."

He helped her take off her skis and they walked toward the coffee shop hand in hand. They had gone only a short distance when Kylie stopped dead, shading her eyes and studying the base of an intermediate run that ended near the lodge. "Daddy, look over there. See that man kissing that lady in the red hat? I think it's Miss Cameron."

He didn't want to look, but as if drawn by a magnet, his eyes focused on the couple.

"Why is that man kissing her?"

In the cold mountain air, Trent suddenly went hot. "I don't know. Maybe it's not Miss Cameron."

"Yes, it is. See? She's turned around."

The man had an arm around Libby's waist. They were deep in conversation, laughing, talking. Oblivious.

Kylie jumped up and down, waving her mittened hand. "Hi, Miss Cameron!"

Now. Now was the time for a whiteout. Anything to avoid the proof right before his eyes. Libby and a man. Someone who obviously adored her.

Libby waved. "Hello, Kylie. Are you learning to ski?"

"I'm good!" Kylie responded, triumph evident in her voice.

"Wonderful!"

Trent gave a halfhearted wave, then watched as Libby and the man headed for the lift. "C'mon, Kylie. Let's go." Walking fast, he steered his daughter to the lodge.

No matter how sweet and creamy, the hot chocolate would be bitter on his tongue if he had to watch that guy kiss Libby again.

CHAPTER FIVE

DOUG'S BREATH stirred Libby's hair. "One of your students?"

Libby had only time to nod before the chairlift circled and hoisted her in the air, leaving the two figures—a man and a girl—shrinking beneath her. It wasn't so easy dismissing them from her mind, however. The joy in Kylie's greeting. The stunned hurt on Trent's face, as if he had some claim to her. It was enough she was required to interact with him professionally, but there would be no repeat of the pizza night.

"You okay?" Doug's arm settled around her shoulder.

"Yes. Why?"

"You're a million miles away. Have I worn you out with too much skiing?"

She sighed, aware of a bone-numbing weariness. "I am a little tired. How about this run being the last?"

"Suits me. I'll take you home so you can revive with a nice hot bath before tonight."

"Tonight? What's tonight?"

"I've made dinner reservations in Big Fork."

The skiing had been fun. Good exercise. Doug had been accommodating in every way. The weather ideal. Why should the prospect of dinner seem an obligation rather than a lovely romantic conclusion to their day? Summoning enthusiasm she didn't feel, she murmured, "Nice."

On her final run, Libby had difficulty concentrating on the snow-packed trail. How could a mere glimpse of Trent cast such a pall over her mood? She could not permit him to affect her this way. He was living in Whitefish. She would, of course, bump into him. But neither Trent Baker nor anyone else was going to threaten the tenuous peace she'd made with the past.

Beside her, Doug snowplowed to a stop. "Hey, beautiful, ready to head for home?"

"That bath sounds divine."

He kissed her, lightly at first, then more deeply. Instinctively she drew away, wanting to protest. "We'd better go," she said, mustering a tired smile.

Later as they walked across the parking lot toward his car, he picked up her hand and tucked it under his arm. "I had a great time."

"So did I."

"Would you do me a favor this evening?"

"Sure."

"Wear that red dress. You know, the one with those little straps."

Her stomach catapulted. "Umm… Okay."

They made small talk on the ride to her house. After he left, his farewell words lingered in her mind, prompting uncomfortable questions. "This was a special day, Libby. I want to make tonight even more special." Or was she reading too much into what had probably been intended as flattery?

She closed the door, stripped off her clothes, then hurried to draw a hot bath. Pulling her hair into a topknot, she sank into the welcome heat of the steaming water, which she'd perfumed with lavender bath oil. As she laid her head back against the cold porcelain, she let out a deep sigh. She had some decisions to make. If not tonight, then soon. Very soon.

The problem wasn't Doug at all. It was her.

"MAYBE THAT DUMB Bart won't make fun of me anymore." All the way home, Kylie had been exultant over her newfound skill.

"Language, please."

"What's wrong with dumb? That's what he is."

"Maybe, but how about calling him an igno-ramus instead?"

"What's that mean?"

Trent bit his lip. He'd started to say *dumb*. "Someone who's really stupid."

She tested the syllables. "Ig-no-ra-mus." Then he caught her grin in the rearview mirror. "I like that. And he's such an ig-no-ra-mus, he won't even know what it means." She giggled.

The word aptly applied to himself, Trent thought grimly. A red-hot flood of jealousy had inundated him when he'd watched that guy kiss Libby. For cripe's sake, he hadn't seen the woman in over a decade, yet he could no more control his body's reactions than fly! And most of those reactions involved physical sensations he'd thought had died with Ashley. Chad had tried to warn him. Weezer, with her keen eyes and intuitive heart, had questioned him closely. What if he did still have feelings for Libby?

What if?

Ignoramus. You do.

So now what?

After supper, Trent invited Weezer over to the guest cabin. They watched a bit of TV, and after Trent tucked Kylie in bed, Weezer told her a bedtime story. Scout lay in the doorway of Kylie's bedroom, as if guarding her. When Weezer returned to the living room, Trent poured her a cup of spiced cider, then one for himself. She sat on the sofa, legs crossed, and cupped the mug in her hands, studying the depths as if intent on divination. Trent relaxed in the lounge chair.

After a long silence, Weezer raised her head, her sharp eyes focused on him. "Well?"

"There's a man," Trent said simply, knowing he didn't have to explain the context.

Weezer said nothing, just waited for him to continue.

"We saw them at Big Mountain. He kissed her." Saying the words aloud pierced him almost as much as the incident itself. He set aside his cider, untasted. "Why didn't you tell me?"

Weezer's expression softened. "You didn't ask."

"Who is he?"

"Doug Travers. He and his family moved here shortly after you left. He's an insurance agent. His father is the hospital administrator and his mother is Libby's principal."

Trent groaned. "Of course. Mrs. Travers." It made perfect sense. Libby belonged with people like the Traverses. Solid citizens. What was he thinking? That he could just step in, take up where he left off? Maybe ruin Libby's life in the process? "How serious is it?"

Weezer shrugged. "They've been seeing each other off and on about six months." She leaned forward, as if to caution him. "He's a good man, Trent."

He should have been glad to hear it. Relieved to learn this Doug wasn't a Class A jerk. Somehow, though, that knowledge made things worse.

"But so are you, son."

His mind tried to put the pieces together to form a picture of Libby contentedly married to some guy with a desk job, nice parents and probably plenty of money. A happy made-for-magazine-ads family. No selfish husband who had run from his responsibilities. He cushioned his head with his hands and sat staring into the fire, aware only of his chaotic thoughts and Weezer's quiet breathing. Finally he said, "Is it too late?"

"I don't see any ring on her finger."

"What do you think I should do?"

"That's not for me to say. Your head and heart are locked in combat. You can wallow or you can act. It would appear the stakes are high."

He stood, walked to the window, then stared out at the snowy spires of pine and hemlock, incandescent in the bright moonlight. Before this Doug had entered the picture, he had entertained the idea of trying again with Libby. But now, after seeing them together, did he have any right to interfere? *You can wallow or you can act.* He faced Weezer. "I don't want to impose, but could you stay with Kylie awhile?"

Her all-knowing look bored into him. "I can."

He grabbed his parka off the peg by the door. "I don't know when I'll be back."

"Take as long as you need."

He crossed the room and laid a hand on her silver head. "Thank you."

"Be ruled by wisdom, son."

When he stepped out into the cold night air, he drew a deep breath, then looked up at the stars. *Ashley, if you're there, forgive me, but I don't want to be alone. Not anymore.* Libby could always reject him. But not before he had made one thing perfectly clear.

A part of him had always loved her. Loved her still.

HE SHOULD HAVE KNOWN. A new-model Suburban sat in Libby's driveway. The porch light cast a warm glow over the front yard, and from the house, one small lamp illuminated the living room. Trent ground his teeth. He couldn't control his runaway imagination. Was there soft music playing? A cozy fire in the hearth? A romantic scene set up?

He slid lower into the seat, ashamed of his thoughts, embarrassed that he sat in his parked truck behaving like the worst kind of voyeur. Who did he think he was? Sir Galahad riding to the rescue of his fair lady? In his gut he knew Libby would not welcome his attention. Why should she?

He'd been an unbelievably insensitive husband. Infantile. How on earth could he persuade her he'd changed?

He had no answers. Only the certainty that he needed to try.

Just then, the front door opened and Doug Travers emerged. Trent watched dry-mouthed as Doug turned, framed Libby's face in his hands and kissed her. The man's body shielded Libby. Only when he stepped away did Trent catch a glimpse of her in a sensational red dress that accentuated each and every curve of her body.

Stifling a groan, he watched helplessly as she placed a hand on Doug's cheek, then leaned forward to whisper something in his ear. At last the guy stepped away and started for his vehicle. Libby, outlined by the hall light, stood in the doorway watching him depart. Only when the Suburban backed into the street and drove off did she slowly close the door and turn off the porch light.

Overcome with self-disgust, Trent smacked the flat of his palm against the steering wheel. He'd been thinking only of himself. And Kylie. From all indications, Libby and Doug had a good thing going. After so many years of being single, she deserved the best. Who was he to cause complications?

Weezer had been right on target. His head and his heart were at war. *Be ruled by wisdom,* the wise old woman had advised.

Wisdom dictated he should start up his vehicle and drive away.

Instead, he pocketed his ignition key, climbed from the truck and walked doggedly toward her house.

In this case, no amount of wisdom could control the wild yearnings of his heart.

AFTER DOUG LEFT, Libby kicked off her high heels, removed her earrings and sank into the familiar depths of her rocking chair, studying the tongues of flame in the fireplace. Mona crept out from under the sofa, where she'd taken refuge, and hopped into Libby's lap. But even Mona's rhythmic purring couldn't calm Libby's jittery nerves. Maybe she was just tired, but Doug's pleasure in their day together and his excited plans for next weekend exhausted her. She wanted to share in his enthusiasm, to feel her heart race each time he kissed her, to contemplate with joy the future he increasingly hinted at. She appreciated the protective cloak in which he wrapped her, the thoughtful way he always made sure she was having a good time, but something was lacking. Something important.

She closed her eyes, remembering long ago nights.... Could she settle for a passionless marriage?

The knock at the door startled her. Flustered, she pushed Mona to the floor, then rose to her feet. Had Doug forgotten something? She calmed herself. That had to be it. No one else would be on her doorstep at this time of night.

She flipped on the porch light and put her eye to the peephole. Beneath her, the floor seemed to sway. Trent. Her heart started to race. Smoothing the fabric of her dress with trembling fingers, she stepped back and opened the door.

He stood, one hand braced on the jamb, his expression serious, his hair ruffled by the cold wind.

Barring the entry, she asked, "What are you doing here?"

"We need to talk."

She almost laughed. Since when did Trent Baker initiate serious conversation? A man of action, he'd always said talk made him nervous. The sudden unwelcome image caused her to stammer. "I...I can't imagine what about."

"May I come in?" His eyes found hers, the plea apparent.

"I think we've already covered everything that needs to be said."

"Please."

Whatever it was he wanted, she needed closure. Shrugging, she stepped aside. "Since you're here…"

"Thank you, Lib." He stepped across the threshold and into her living room.

She closed the door behind him, but paused for a moment in the entry, calming her runaway breathing. Lingering in the air was the outdoorsy, masculine smell of him. Despite herself, a lick of fire lapped at her belly.

He had no business reentering her world. Not now. Not when she was on the verge of falling in love with Doug.

Trent had ruined her life once. He would not do it again.

She walked into the living room and settled back in the rocker, stony eyes fixed on the man she had once loved. "Okay. So talk."

TRENT REMAINED STANDING. Now that he was here, doing his best not to ogle her body in the formfitting dress, he had no idea how to begin. "I couldn't stay away," he began lamely.

She cocked an eyebrow.

He was making a botch of this. He'd stayed

away twelve years, hadn't he? "What I mean is, I needed to see you tonight."

She made a show of glancing disapprovingly at the cuckoo clock. "What on earth could possibly be so urgent at this hour?"

"I want to know about Doug Travers."

"What about him?"

He ran a hand through his hair, then perched on the edge of the couch, leaning toward her, hands clamped on his knees. "How seriously are you involved?"

"What possible concern is that of yours?"

She had him there. Even to himself, he sounded like an idiot, charging in here and demanding access to her private life. "I'd hoped it could be."

"Trent, I am the teacher of your child. Beyond that, we have no relationship." Her eyes flickered, then she looked down. In that slight gesture, he found a kernel of hope.

Mona slunk from beneath the couch and rubbed against his leg. He leaned down and scratched her head. "You always did like cats," he said. He remembered the sleek black kitten they'd found outside a grocery store all those years ago. "Whatever happened to Beelzebub?"

"He lived to a ripe old age, then I had to have him put to sleep."

"Remember how he loved to curl up inside my ski boot?"

"Don't you think it's a little late for auld lang syne?"

He couldn't help himself. He reached out and grasped her hands in his. "Is it?"

In her eyes he read a history of sadness, much of it his fault. He waited.

After a heavy silence, she stood, dropping his hands and turning her back. Her spine stiff, she wrapped her arms around her shoulders as if to ward off a chill. "Please go," she whispered.

A log cracked above the thudding of his heart. More than anything, he wanted to put his arms around her, memorize the curves of her body, inhale the fragrance that was hers alone, suckle the tender skin beneath her ear. Convey somehow that he wanted to take care of her. Promise her he would never again run away from his commitments. From her. He raised one hand toward her, then let it drop to his side. "If that's what you want. But I'll be back."

She whirled around. "Why? Haven't you done enough to me?"

He brushed his knuckles along her cheek, fiery under his touch. "That was then. This is now."

"Nothing's different," she said.

"Only this." He stepped closer and pulled her

into his arms. Her eyes widened, but surprisingly she made no move to push him away. "I've made many mistakes in my life, Lib, but none greater than letting you go." He felt the pressure of her body against his chest, heard her startled gasp. "I came to ask you to give me another chance."

Before she could reject him, he lowered his lips and, as if coming home, plunged into the wild sweetness that was her mouth. With one hand he raked through her rich dark hair, which smelled of spring flowers, losing himself in a riot of sensations. He couldn't get enough of her. Unbelievably, her fingers twined in his hair and she stepped closer to him.

Before he could take encouragement from her response, she tore her lips from his and stepped back again, eyes blazing. "What do you think you're doing?"

He couldn't back down now. "Hopefully giving you something to think about." He picked up the jacket he'd thrown on the arm of the sofa. "I'll go now."

She straightened her dress, then walked to the door and flung it open. "Next time, wait to be invited," she said tersely.

He paused in the entry. "Lib, if Doug is the man for you, I'll do my best to accept that. But I'm not going to let you go without a fight." He stood in the doorway, the frigid air having the effect of a cold shower. "I want a chance with you. That's all. Just a chance."

"It's out of the question."

"Is it? I'm leaving, but not before I make one last observation. I don't think either of us could call our reactions to that kiss indifferent." He paused. "You set me on fire, Lib," he whispered. "Does Doug do that for you?"

"That would be none of your business."

He leaned forward and kissed her forehead with all the tenderness within him. "Think about it. Please. It's important."

Then he turned and walked rapidly toward his truck, second-guessing himself all the way. He'd either offended her beyond redemption, or planted seeds that just might bear fruit.

LOIS JETER CALLED Libby the next morning. "How was your weekend with Doug?"

Libby was thankful this wasn't in person. Protection from her friend's scrutiny. Lois would immediately zero in on her red eyes and the bags that no amount of makeup had masked. "Fine."

"That's it? *Fine?*"

Attempting to put lightness in her voice, Libby nodded. "At least for now."

"You're not off the hook. Ray has a meeting,

so you and I are going to the Kodiak for lunch. It's gut-spilling time, girlfriend."

When Libby started to object, Lois said she had to go and hung up the phone. Ordinarily she enjoyed spending time with Lois, but she was tired, having spent the better part of the night after Trent left trying to sort out her feelings, to rationalize her reaction to his kiss. Another chance? He had to be joking.

She was supposed to be in love with one man, yet she had turned to liquid the moment another had kissed her. *You set me on fire, Lib. Does Doug do that for you?*

She wasn't about to sacrifice her dreams of home and family over a great kiss. Besides, lasting relationships began with friendship, didn't they? No one could ask for a more caring friend than Doug.

But he doesn't set you on fire. A flush rose to her cheeks, and she glanced around, thankful she was alone.

Against history and reason, she was still attracted to Trent.

It was nearly noon before she and Lois slipped into a booth at the Kodiak Café. Weezer, busy at the register, waved at them. Lois eyed the crowd. "Looks as if half our school families are here."

Libby, her eyes mischievous, peered over the

top of her menu. "Ah, the joys of small towns. You can never get away."

"Tell me about it. I'm the preacher's wife, remember."

"Where are your girls today?"

"They went to a weekend student-government workshop in Bozeman."

Lois's teenage daughters were active in almost everything the high school had to offer. When she was with the Jeter family, Libby often experienced twinges of envy. Lucky girls. Lucky parents. "Well, well, so you and Ray had a weekend alone?"

Lois laughed. "Don't get any big ideas. Saturday nights at our house are reserved for last-minute sermon prep. I'm a whole lot more interested in your weekend."

Libby gave her the short version of her dates with Doug, then, when she saw the waitress approaching to take their order, made a quick scan of the menu. Both women selected the Cobb salad.

As soon as the waitress departed, Lois folded her hands on the table and leaned forward. "Lib, where's the joy?"

Buying time, Libby slowly unfolded her napkin. "What do you mean?"

"On paper, your weekend sounds idyllic. The

man is clearly crazy about you. But I don't hear any excitement in your voice."

"We were up late. I guess I'm tired."

Lois laid a hand on Libby's forearm. "Have you forgotten who you're dealing with, here? The pastor's wife. I hear a lot of confidential stuff, so over the years I've developed pretty good intuition, and it's telling me you have a problem."

Libby looked into Lois's concerned eyes and knew her friend was offering her a safe place to unburden herself. The temptation was overwhelming. "I do." She tuned out the din of conversation, the clinking of silverware. "Something's happened."

"Would you like to tell me about it?"

Before Libby could answer, she heard a lively voice behind her. "Look, Daddy, it's Miss Cameron." Kylie bounced up beside their booth. "Hi," she said, smiling up at Libby. "I can ski now," she announced triumphantly.

"That's wonderful."

Trent approached and put his hands on Kylie's shoulders. Libby turned to Lois. "You know Kylie Baker, of course, from school, but have you met her father? Trent, this is Lois Jeter, our gym teacher."

Trent extended his hand. "Glad to meet you."

Lois smiled. "Likewise."

Libby avoided looking up at him and, instead, turned her attention back to Kylie. "Will I see you in the morning for tutoring?"

"Yes." She stared down at her shoes before lifting her head again. "I'm still kinda scared."

"I know. But you'll soon be fine." Libby patted Kylie's shoulder encouragingly. Poor kid. To have fallen behind in reading as a result of her mother's death was one more blow the girl didn't need.

"C'mon, Kylie, we have to find a table."

"Okay, but first I gotta tell Miss Cameron something." She leaned forward and lowered her voice. "I saw you kissing that man. Is he your boyfriend?"

Out of the corner of her eye, Libby noticed Trent bite his lip. "That's kind of my secret, isn't it?"

Kylie nodded her head. "Yeah, but I hope so, 'cause you're pretty and you need a boyfriend." She looked up at her father, then back at Libby. "Well, bye, now. We gotta go eat 'cause we're going skiing after lunch."

Libby watched them until they sat down. Carefully she pleated the napkin in her lap, doing her best to conjure up Doug's face.

"Lib?" Lois snapped her fingers in the air. "Hel-lo."

"Sorry."

"No more games, honey. You're as transparent as glass. Who's Trent Baker really?"

Any lingering shred of appetite fled. Simply by standing there, Trent had accelerated her heart rate. "A man."

"But not just any man."

"No. He was my husband."

To her credit, Lois did not drop her jaw. Instead, she nodded as if her suspicions had been confirmed. "And you're not over him, are you?"

Libby gulped. It was the truth she'd lain awake all night trying to avoid. "Apparently not."

"So where does that leave Doug?"

"Oh, Lois, I wish I knew." Before she could stop herself, Libby confided in her friend. About her affection for Doug. About her need for a family and a man who could give her the children she so desperately wanted. And without going into detail, she touched on Trent's past disregard for her needs and his desire for a second chance. When she finished, she sat back, exhausted. Just then the waitress arrived with their salads. Libby picked up her fork and made a halfhearted stab at a tomato wedge. Then she added in a forlorn voice, "Lois, I don't know what to do."

"Give it time, honey. One day you'll know. I promise."

Libby hoped her friend was right, but she was also fully aware that reaching that point would involve painful decisions.

WEEZER INSPECTED the kitchen cleanup, then sat on a stool totaling the day's receipts. As she counted the money, she thought about Trent sitting at his table doing his best not to look at Libby, but failing miserably. Nor had Weezer overlooked Libby's obvious tension. Trent had confided nothing when he had returned to the cabin last night. But if she'd ever seen a lovesick calf, he was one.

She'd never known exactly what had precipitated his and Libby's breakup. Oh, sure, Trent had been a wild hare, but Libby had seemed to enjoy his adventurous streak, maybe even been attracted by it. The two of them had made a handsome couple—Trent with his confident smile and blond good looks; she with her joie de vivre and sparkling eyes. It was clear to everyone back then that they adored each other.

So it had been a complete shock when, out of the blue, Trent had left the area. The next thing anybody knew, they had divorced. Weezer had thought she knew the boy pretty well, but she'd been stunned. His mother, Lila, had been equally mystified, but Trent had made it clear their probing was not welcome.

As the years passed, Weezer figured Trent had moved on. She'd only met Ashley twice. A pretty thing, but vastly different from Libby. More citified. Less earthy. But if Trent was happy, that was all that mattered.

Stacking the one-dollar bills together, she slipped a band around them before beginning to roll coins. Trent had been back in Whitefish only a matter of days, and already the earth was rumbling beneath his feet.

And it was all because of Libby Cameron.

KYLIE WAS TEN MINUTES late for her Monday-morning session. Libby busied herself writing the day's assignments on the board, but that activity did nothing to corral the butterflies in her stomach. It had been hard enough to face Trent at the Kodiak, but in the quiet of this classroom? The more she tried to forget their kiss, the larger it loomed in her mind—the proverbial elephant in the living room.

And what about Doug? Maybe his mother had already told him about Trent's return to Whitefish, but it was cowardly to hope Mary had been the bearer of that news. Libby owed

Doug honesty. Since her marriage was a subject she avoided, they had never talked much about it. She had seen no reason to dredge up a past that filled her with sadness, and Doug had been patient with her. Libby sighed. Another of his admirable qualities.

"Do I hafta?"

Libby looked toward the door. That sounded like Kylie. Whining.

"Kylie, you like Miss Cameron. She's helping you."

"I'm still dumber than the other kids."

Libby moved quickly into the hall and knelt down to greet Kylie, who stubbornly refused to look up. "Kylie, honey, that's simply not true. Did somebody tell you that?"

The girl scuffed her shoe on the tile floor. "Uh-huh."

Libby held her gently by the arms. "Why do you suppose someone would say something like that?"

"'Cause they hate me?"

"No. Probably because they're jealous."

Kylie's head shot up and skeptical blue eyes met Libby's. "That's silly."

"Not at all. You're doing fine, much better than many new students when they first move here. And just think. Already you're learning how to ski, and if you keep working on the reading, pretty soon you won't need special help."

Tentative hope replaced doubt. "Really?"

"Really." Libby stood. "Now go on in and get your book ready."

After Kylie left, Libby moved down the hall out of earshot, then dared to look up at Trent. "What happened?"

He shrugged, lines creasing his forehead. "I don't know. I suppose it was wishful thinking that she'd be so easily cured of her school phobia. We had the stomachache, the complaining, the whole bit this morning."

"The move has been tough on her. You have to expect these ups and downs. But with time…"

"With time," he repeated, then stared at her in a way that let her know his next words were carefully chosen, the double meaning intended. "With time, all things are possible."

She returned his glance, determined to regain the lead in the discussion. "Just don't expect miracles."

"Ah, but I do. With Kylie…and with you."

She couldn't have looked away even if the fire alarm had suddenly pealed. There was no mistaking the fervor in his voice or in his eyes, or the ripple of panic that vibrated throughout her body. Chilled, she rubbed a hand over her upper arm. "Let's concern ourselves with Kylie right now."

"Fair enough. Do you have any idea how I can help?"

"You could practice her reading at home, of course."

"I try whenever I can."

She couldn't believe her second suggestion. It made all kinds of sense for Kylie—and none at all for her. "The class is taking a field trip next week. We need parents to chaperon. Would you be interested?"

"I'll check with Chad, but, yeah, I'd like that."

"Perhaps if you met some of her classmates, showed interest in her school activities…"

"Say no more. I'll make it happen. Just let me know when and where."

"Fine." She glanced toward the classroom. "I'd better scoot. And, Trent?"

"Yeah?"

"Don't worry. She'll come around."

Yet when she walked toward the reading table, she wasn't so sure. Kylie's head was down, cradled on her forearms. When Libby joined her and laid a hand on her shoulder, she didn't move. "Are you sad this morning?"

Libby barely made out the whispered "Yes."

"Could you tell me about it?"

Kylie didn't sit up, but turned, resting her head on her arms so she could see Libby. "Sometimes I just remember."

"What, sweetie?"

"Last winter. When Mommy was so sick." A lone tear trickled down the girl's face. "I wanted her to get better." She sniffled. "But she didn't."

"Sometimes, no matter how hard we wish, we can't have what we want." Before she could stop herself, Libby realized she had moved a hand protectively over her abdomen. "I think I know how you feel. My mother died when I was about your age."

Kylie reared up. "She did?"

Settling her arm around the girl's shoulders, Libby continued. "Like your mommy, she'd been sick awhile. I missed her so much. It's okay to miss your mother, you know."

"No-nobody here knows her."

"You need to talk about her, don't you?" Kylie lifted a fist to her cheek to dry away her tears, then nodded. "I understand. I'm sure your daddy misses her, too. Can you talk to him about your mother?"

"Not really."

"Why not, sweetie?"

"It makes him sad. And then he...he quits smiling."

"What about Weezer?"

"She's nice, but I don't know her so good yet."

"What would you say if you could talk to someone?"

"How Mommy had this soft hair, like a movie star. She let me brush it sometimes. And we liked to go shopping for girl clothes. She made good Rice Krispies treats and…"

No reading took place, not after the floodgates of Kylie's memories broke open. Not that Libby cared. In Kylie's recital was catharsis—both for the little girl and for herself. She remembered the sad, lost little child she'd been back in Oklahoma, huddled beneath the quilt, listening fearfully to the silence echoing in the huge house. Wondering what would happen to her. Who would love her.

Finally Kylie wound down, then slipped a warm hand into Libby's. "I told *you*, didn't I?" she said wonderingly.

"Yes, you did. And anytime you want to talk, I will always listen."

"That's 'cause you're not just a teacher, right? You're my friend."

Not wanting Kylie to see the tears gathering in her eyes, Libby pulled the girl to her, resting her chin on the blonde head and inhaling the sweet citrusy scent of her shampoo.

How had this happened? It was hard enough to keep her guard up with Trent. But with Kylie? It was simply impossible.

CHAPTER SIX

FOR THE REST of the morning Libby went through the motions of teaching, her thoughts preoccupied. The low-lying clouds outside matched her mood. How could her carefully constructed life have changed in such a short time? She felt relief when the boys and girls lined up and marched down the hall to the computer lab. Thirty minutes of blissful solitude.

Back in her room, she watered the plants in the science corner before sinking into her desk chair. At Christmas, her future had seemed both simple and assured. Doug's gradually intensifying courtship and her deepening affection for him would ultimately lead to marriage. Stability. Family.

Those dreams could still come true, but Doug deserved commitment, and that couldn't happen until she settled things with Trent. Maybe she should agree to see him again. To test her feelings.

Oh, right. Talk about the Queen of Rationalization.

She buried her fingers in her hair, frustrated by the dilemma she faced. She had to tell Doug about Trent.

But tell him what, exactly?

Picking up a red pencil, she began checking a set of arithmetic worksheets. Bart had missed over half the problems, and Rory had left several blank, preferring instead to fill the margins with cramped drawings of fighter planes. The bright spot was Kylie's perfect paper.

"Libby?"

Startled, she turned toward the door. The school secretary stood there, a perplexed look on her face. "You have a phone call in the office. A Senator Belton."

Libby's heart sank. A bad day had taken yet another downturn. She rose and headed for the office.

"Take it in here." The secretary nodded toward the vacant teachers' lounge.

Libby entered the room and closed the door. Then, dread mounting, she picked up the phone. "Hello. This is Libby Cameron."

"Miss Cameron," a clipped, businesslike voice said. "Please hold for the senator."

Her stepfather had never called her at school before. In fact, aside from their brief conversation over the holidays, she hadn't spoken to him since early autumn. What could be so urgent he would call during work hours? And why call the office, not her cell phone?

After several minutes, he came on the line. "Libby? Sorry to keep you waiting."

In the background Libby could hear the low hum of a news commentator on the senator's office television. "I can't be away from my class too long," she told him.

"I understand. I didn't want to leave a message on voice mail." He paused, and Libby could imagine him brushing aside some paperwork or gesticulating to one of his aides. "Has a reporter contacted you?"

"Not directly. Someone called the school to verify my employment."

"Let's hope it stops there."

"That what stops there?"

"Some eager young pup of a fellow, Jeremy Kantor, seems bent on becoming the next Bob Woodward. He's doing an in-depth piece about the personal lives of some of us on the Hill."

Libby's stomach plummeted. "Why would he have any interest in me?"

"Well, such as it is, you are my only family. And as we both know, he could ask some embarrassing questions."

"He can ask all he wants. There's nothing I could tell him of any interest." Libby swallowed the bile in her throat. "Or that would in any way compromise your position."

"Good girl. That's what I needed to hear." He cleared his throat. "Well, then, that's taken care of. Everything all right there?"

As if he cared. "I'm fine."

"You need to think about a trip to D.C."

"Why would I want to do that?"

"I could show you the sights. Introduce you around."

Now—*now* she was respectable. Too little, too late. "I'll think about it."

"Just a minute, Sarah. I'm coming." Libby rolled her eyes. Important legislative business, no doubt. "Sorry, Libby, gotta make a roll-call vote on the floor."

"No problem."

"Goodbye, then."

He was gone before she could whisper her own farewell. She hung up and moved rest-lessly about the room. A reporter bent on dig-ging up dirt. She hoped his investigation of her had ended with her employment history. Her involvement in the senator's life had come to an abrupt halt years ago. That was all she needed to say, if asked.

The door cracked open and the secretary studied her with concern. "Libby, is everything all right? Do you need someone to cover your class?"

Libby shook her head in an effort to dispel memories too painful to revisit. "No, I'm coming right now. Thanks."

For the rest of the day, she lost herself in the hustle bustle of second-graders, wishing she could somehow remain in the innocent, protected world of seven-year-olds.

TO KEEP THOUGHTS of Libby at bay, Trent kept busy inventorying gear and setting aside anything needing repair. Next week he and Chad would work on a quick remodeling of the office area, but for now their priority was getting the equipment serviced. "Looks like we need some new first-aid kits."

Chad glanced up from the counter where he was sorting their newly printed promotional brochures into piles. "That's one area where we can't scrimp. Order them."

Trent made a note on his legal pad, then picked up a kayak paddle to examine. "How're we coming on hiring guides?"

"I have a couple already lined up and interviews scheduled for Bozeman and Missoula in a couple of weeks."

"How soon can we expect bookings?"

"The former owners told me they'll start coming in around the first of April."

Trent made a mental calculation. He couldn't impose on Weezer much past that. Of course he was paying her rent, but many of her longtime, repeat guests would be expecting to rent the cabin during the season. That gave him a little over two months to get squared away with a house for him and Kylie. He hated even thinking about the child-care arrangements he would have to make. Kylie needed the security of a home, not a string of babysitters.

His train of thought had led him directly back to Libby, the one subject he was trying to avoid. In a way, he wished he'd never seen her home—and Kylie sitting contentedly in her rocker, a gray cat snuggled in her lap. No matter how hard he tried, he could no longer picture a future without Libby.

Yet he'd probably blown it Saturday night. He must have seemed deranged showing up on her doorstep so late, and then practically forcing that kiss on her.

But there was one encouraging sign. She had responded enthusiastically. At least until she drew away, perhaps shocked at her own reaction. He'd also taken heart that she couldn't look him in the eye when he'd asked whether Doug set her on fire. Nor had she been at ease with him when he'd seen her at the Kodiak Café yesterday. If she didn't care—at least a little—why would she seem disturbed by his presence?

Against all odds, he hoped her behavior was a case of "the lady doth protest too much." He would have to proceed carefully, though. No way did he want Kylie to get wind of his intentions. She was crazy about Lib and he didn't need to get her hopes up.

Chad slapped his arm with one of their brochures. "You gonna stare at that paddle all day?"

"Sorry. I have a lot on my mind."

"Kylie or Libby?"

Trent stowed the paddle and selected another. "Both."

"School going okay?"

"We have good days and bad days. I know most of it has to do with Kylie's missing Ashley and Billings. But she seems to be comfortable with Libby."

"That sounds like a good thing." Chad's tone was casual, yet Trent could hear the unasked question.

"I'm cautiously optimistic."

"Oh?"

Trent set the paddle on the counter. "I've got to get on with it. Either win her back or get her out of my system."

"But?"

"I don't want to interfere if she really loves Doug Travers."

"Let her figure that out, Baker. Doug's a big boy. So are you. Somebody wins. Somebody loses. It's that simple."

Simple? "Easy for you to say."

Chad laughed. "I've known you a long time, pal, and I have to say, you got it bad."

"Yeah, I do." With a crooked grin, Trent picked up one of the brochures and pointed to the heading. "'Adventure Specialists.'" He snorted. "Love is sure one adventure I'm no expert in."

"What man is?"

"You have a point. I guess all I can do is present my case and hope it's good enough."

Chad shrugged into his jacket, scooped up the packets of brochures, then headed for the door. Just before leaving, he turned back to Trent, a sympathetic expression on his face. "I have a feeling it will be. If I'm right, maybe I'll get my partner back."

In his words, Trent heard understanding and friendship, but also a plea. Preoccupation with Libby was diverting his focus from the business. Sooner rather than later, he needed to bring things to a head with her. And that meant talking openly about her miscarriage—and his role in driving her away.

WHY HAD SHE THOUGHT this was a good idea? Libby stood at the window that evening and watched Doug approach with a bag of take-out food under his arm. She could have waited until the weekend. But a sense of urgency had overcome her desire to delay, and she'd invited him over.

She greeted him. "Hi. I'm glad you didn't mind such short notice."

Doug leaned forward to kiss her lightly. "Mind? I was delighted. If I had my way, I'd see you every night of the week."

He handed her the food while he took off his coat and laid it over the back of the sofa. "I hope you're hungry."

Hungry? Even the delectable smells of Chinese food failed to stimulate her appetite. Her stomach was wound as tightly as any egg roll. "I suppose I could eat."

He followed her into the kitchen and played with Mona while she set out the plates, opened the containers and put serving spoons in each. "What exciting things happened today at school?"

One of the traits she liked about Doug was his genuine interest in her job. Yet she didn't know how to answer his question. Should she tell him how Kylie had opened up about her mother? About the senator's unsettling phone call? "The usual. The flu is going around, so I had three absentees. Then I had to send two little guys to the office after they got into a scuffle on the playground."

Doug grinned. "Ooh. They had to face the dreaded Mrs. Travers."

"Believe it or not, she can be formidable."

"Oh, I have no doubt about that. She was a no-nonsense mother."

"She's a wonderful principal, Doug. You should be very proud of her."

"I am." He dished up some moo goo gai pan. "She's pretty fond of you, you know."

His words immediately made Libby recall the quizzical look on Mary's face when she had learned Trent had been Libby's husband. Libby stared at the sweet-and-sour chicken she'd scooped onto her plate, wondering how she could manage even a single bite. How was she going to tell Doug? What could she say? "We have a great working relationship."

"She'd like it to be more than that," Doug said, setting his plate down on the counter and turning to face her. "So would I."

There was no mistaking his meaning. His warm eyes and gentle smile were intended to be reassuring. It was all she could do not to squirm like one of her students when caught in a lie. She cleared her throat. "What would you like to drink?"

Doug studied her as if checking to see if she had intended the change of subject. The smile slowly faded from his lips. "Water will be fine."

Libby set her plate on the table and busied herself with ice cubes, glasses, water and anything—anything—to avoid what had to be said.

When she returned to the table, Doug seated her, then slid into his own chair. He didn't touch his silverware, but rested his elbows on the table, his fingers clasped beneath his chin. "What is it, Lib?"

"What do you mean?"

"It's pretty clear I misread the agenda tonight. You define the term *uptight*. What gives?"

Libby shoved her plate aside, dread mounting. "I haven't been entirely forthcoming with you."

"Okay." He drew out the word, as if slowly processing the idea.

She couldn't dance around the subject all night. Taking a deep breath, she spit out what she had to say. "My ex-husband is back in Whitefish."

He shrugged. "And that's important because...?"

Rather than answer him directly, she asked, "Remember the little girl who saw us kissing Saturday at Big Mountain?"

"Your student?"

She nodded. "Kylie Baker. She's the daughter of my ex."

He frowned, puzzled. "So what's the problem?"

"I'm getting quite attached to her."

He dropped his hands to his side. "Well, that's no surprise. You love all your kids. It's one reason you're a super teacher."

How could she consider a life without Doug? Who else encouraged her in so many ways? "That's not all. Trent, um, my former husband, he..." She paused, choosing her words.

"He wants you back." Doug shook his head when she didn't disagree. "Great. That's just great."

The odor of the sweet-and-sour chicken nearly gagged her. "He hasn't said that exactly."

Doug spoke with deliberate irony. "What has he said 'exactly'?"

"I have the sense he wants to see whether I still have feelings for him."

"Do you?"

There it was. The big question. Libby ducked

her head. "I don't know," she said quietly. In the silence, the cuckoo clock chimed seven. She waited, holding her breath, until it stopped. "He hurt me badly once."

"And you're willing to let him do it again?" Doug rose from his seat and circled the table. "Not if I have anything to say about it." He pulled her to her feet and held her by the arms, searching her face.

Libby's eyes filled. She had never wanted to hurt Doug. "I'm confused. I—I need some time."

"How much?"

She shrugged. "I don't know."

"I'm not going to pretend I'm happy about the situation, Lib. But I care a great deal for you. I think we could make a good life together, so if you need to figure this out once and for all, I guess that's how it'll have to be."

She couldn't have asked for anything more from him. She almost wished he wasn't such a fair person, that he'd give her an ultimatum. Take him or leave him. And she so desperately wanted the life he offered that she would probably take him. "You're a good man, Doug Travers."

He pulled her closer, nestling her against his chest. "I don't want to be a good man. I want to be *the* man." Then, taking her face in his hands, he kissed her deeply, possessively, as if to seal her with his brand. His lips moved persuasively, and she tried, really tried, to respond with enthusiasm. When he finished kissing her, he ran his hands over her shoulders and down her arms. "You know, I'm not hungry after all. I think I'll be going."

She followed him into the living room and watched helplessly as he donned his coat. "Won't you take some of the food home?"

"There's only one thing I want to take home." The hurt in his eyes sliced through her. "You."

Cold air replaced warmth as he opened the door and left. Shame and regret lodged in every crevice of her body.

You set me on fire, Lib. Does Doug do that for you?

Sadly the answer was no.

But surely there was more to love than fireworks.

TRENT COULDN'T REMEMBER the last time he'd ridden on a school bus. One thing was for sure. The manufacturers hadn't done anything to make them more comfortable since then. Nor had the decibel level of excited schoolchildren decreased. At least these kids weren't teenagers screaming out the song about bottles of beer on the wall.

He sat in the back of the third bus of the convoy headed for Missoula and a tour of the Native American exhibit at the university. Kylie had been inordinately delighted when she learned that he was not only one of the chaperons, but the sole father making the trip. However, she had chosen to sit with a little redheaded girl named Lacey. He supposed that was fine—it meant she was adjusting, making friends.

Huddled beside him was a wiry little guy whose dark bangs fell into his eyes. The kid stared out the window and so far had said nothing. Brakes squealed and the bus shuddered to a stop at a railroad crossing, then with a guttural grinding of gears started up again. "Hey, fella, what's your name?" Trent asked.

The boy shrank away from him. "Rory," he said in a half whisper.

"Really? One of my favorite old-time cowboy actors was named Rory. Ever hear of him? Rory Calhoun?"

This time the boy ventured a quick glance at Trent. "No."

"No? You're missing out then. He was one cool dude. I'll bet you could rent some of his movies."

No answer.

"Do you like cowboys?"

The kid shrugged. "I guess."

"I used to do a bit of rodeoing when I was younger."

"Did you get hurt a lot?" At last. A spark of interest.

"Well, not a lot. But sometimes a hard fall knocks the stuffing out of a guy. But if you like to do something, you have to expect some knocks. Same thing with mountain climbing or river rafting. But the thrill of it makes the pain not seem so bad."

"My mom prob'ly wouldn't let me do something like that. 'Specially if I might get hurt. And I don't got a dad."

The boy's expression told the story. An overprotected kid crying out for a male influence in his life.

"If you could do something a little bit dangerous, what would it be?"

Rory frowned in concentration. "I'd be a paratrooper."

Trent laughed. "No lie? Jumping from a plane would take major guts."

"Lotsa soldiers do it." To Trent's amazement, the boy squared his shoulders. "I bet I could."

"You'd have to be in really good shape."

"How could I do that?"

Outside, the trees were whizzing by. Trent settled more comfortably into the seat, realizing he was enjoying his conversation with young

Rory. "You could start by getting yourself in condition." The seed of an idea occurred to him. "Do you do any hiking?"

He hung his head. "Naw. My mom thinks I'd get lost."

"She's right. You can't just set off in the woods or mountains. But I could take you out sometime after it warms up this spring."

Rory's head jerked up. "You could?"

"I'm a guide."

"And you'd take *me?*"

"Sure. Tell you what. When we get back to the school, you introduce me to your mom, and we'll talk about it."

"Wow." Rory's face was wreathed in a big grin.

Trent didn't know for sure, but he could swear the kid walked with more confidence the rest of the day.

WEARY BUT PLEASED the field trip had been a success, Libby strolled through her bus, checking for belongings left behind. The other teachers stood outside, crossing names off the roster as each student was picked up by a parent.

She paused by a window facing the parking lot. Trent stood deep in conversation with Rory Polk's mother, an older woman whose child-rearing ideas predated Dr. Spock. Libby permitted herself a little smile. Trent had been amazing. First, it had been no mean feat to capture Rory's interest, but by the end of the day, he'd gathered a troupe of boys around him like the Pied Piper. Who knew the man had such a way with children?

She grimaced. It had to be a recently acquired skill, and she wasn't sure she could trust it.

Until today, she hadn't seen him for a week. Nor had she spoken with Doug. It was as if each of them was waiting for her to make a move. Throughout the day, she had made sure that she and Trent were never alone. Yet, in spite of her intentions to the contrary, she frequently gazed at him. She saw the respectful way he listened to the boys, often kneeling beside them to explain the exhibits. She found herself watching his strong, expressive hands as he gestured. The same hands that had so maddeningly brought her to life again, just as they always had.

Somewhere a horn honked and she forced herself back to the present. Daydreams were useless and rarely reflected reality.

She stepped off the bus and looked around. Most of the students had already been picked up. Kylie was nowhere to be seen. Then Libby spotted her sitting in Trent's truck, head bowed, arms folded defensively across her chest, bottom lip protruding.

Odd. She looked angry. Yet she'd seemed to enjoy the field trip. In fact, Libby had been encouraged by her growing friendship with Lacey and her interaction with her classmates today.

What could have happened?

Before she had a chance to investigate, Trent left Mrs. Polk and approached her. "Thanks for a great day, Lib."

"No, thank *you*." She cocked her head and smiled up at him. "You seem to have made the trip for our little guys."

"I hope so," he said with a pleased grin. Then he sobered. "Some of them act starved for attention."

"Welcome to my world."

He glanced over his shoulder toward his truck. "I need to get on my way, but, Lib? When can I see you again?"

Oh no, more butterflies. "I suppose we do need to clear the air."

"At the very least." His eyes, set deep in his ruddy face, promised much more than conversation. "I'll call you." Then, laying one hand on her shoulder, he said, "Good night, Libby."

Libby watched him walk away, aware her body was thrumming with a need too deep for words. How long could she hold out for mere talk?

She steeled herself with a single thought. *My Baby Book.*

TRENT CLIMBED into the truck. The day had turned out much better than he'd anticipated. It had felt good to be able to help with the kids. From his brief visit with Rory's mother, he could see why the boy fantasized about adventure and escape. Trent had employed all his powers of persuasion to get her to agree that Rory could go on a hike with him in the spring.

It had been fun, too, watching Libby in her element. She was a natural—cheerful, organized, seemingly aware of ten things at once, and handling them all. Her students obviously adored her.

He didn't blame them. He did, too—more and more each time he was with her, even though she still wasn't giving him the time of day. At least she'd agreed they could talk. A small but significant victory.

He started up the truck and pulled away from the school. "Hey, sweetie. You're awfully quiet back there."

Kylie didn't answer. Only then did he notice the petulant set to her mouth, her rigid posture. "Did you have a good time?"

No answer except a small shrug.

What in the Sam Hill? He'd been pleased today to see her blend in with a group of little girls. Why, she'd even laughed out loud at lunch. What could've gone wrong? Had he done something?

"Did I embarrass you today, sweetie?"

"No."

"I liked your classmates. It was fun being with you."

"Don't come anymore."

A quick glance in the rearview mirror told him something important was going on in her head. "What do you mean?"

"The reason you came is 'cuz you like *her*."

She'd totally lost him. "Who?"

"Miss Cameron." She spat out the name.

"Honey, what are you talking about?"

Her voice rose in a crescendo. "You and her! You didn't tell me."

His gut coiled. "Tell you what?"

"You and Miss Cameron. You guys were married!"

Gripping the steering wheel in suddenly icy hands, Trent pulled into the deserted parking lot of a small office building. Hoping for the right words, he stopped the truck, then turned in his seat to face her blazing blue eyes. "Who told you that?"

A withering stare.

"I was planning to tell you, but I wanted you to get settled in school first."

Kylie kicked the seat back. "Mommy was your wife. Only Mommy."

"I loved your mother. Very much. Miss Cameron and I were married many years ago. Only for a short time."

"What did Mommy think?"

"She knew."

Another kick. "But you shoulda told me."

He reached back and laid a hand on her knee. "You're right. I should have."

Kylie swatted at his hand, her eyes welling with angry tears. "Miss Cameron. She coulda told me, too."

"This has nothing to do with her being your teacher."

"But I *liked* her."

"Don't you still?"

"No! I hate you both."

"Oh, sugar." He stared at her, dumbfounded that a seven-year-old child could make him deservedly feel like the lowest form of animal life. "I'm so sorry. I love you. I wouldn't hurt you for anything. I made a mistake."

She studied him, her expression obdurate.

"How did you learn about this?"

Then it came out. Two of the mothers had been

sitting behind her on the bus on the way home from Missoula, and one of them had known Libby in Polson, before he had moved away. She was gossiping with the other woman about the coincidence of Trent being on the field trip with Libby, his ex-wife. Kylie had overheard.

Trent had lived in small towns most of his life. He should have anticipated something like this. Should have protected Kylie from such a devastating revelation.

Libby could congratulate him all she wanted about how well he'd handled the boys today. But what possible difference could that make?

He'd failed his daughter.

CHAPTER SEVEN

NO BAROMETER was required to alert Libby a storm was on its way. The increased agitation of her students was a far more accurate indicator. The boys couldn't sit still. Never had so many needed pencils sharpened or banged their desk lids with such vigor. The girls, on the other hand, had an increased tendency to giggle or whine, depending upon the child. And the day was still young.

If that wasn't enough cause for concern, Kylie's seat remained vacant. Periodically, Libby checked the door, certain that at any moment she would appear. Yesterday on the field trip she had seemed fine, although twenty-four-hour bugs could strike suddenly.

Or had something happened to cause the sullen expression on Kylie's face when she'd sat in Trent's truck, waiting to go home? Had something revived her school phobia?

Libby intercepted Bart on his third trip to the trash can. Recess couldn't come soon enough.

She made it through the last reading group,

having to pause often to hush the rest of the class. Then she bundled up the students and sent them outdoors, grateful it was John's turn for playground duty. As soon as the last child trooped out the door, she went to the office. Maybe she was overreacting, but she needed reassurance that Kylie was all right.

"Have you heard from Kylie Baker's father this morning?" she asked the secretary.

"I'm glad you stopped by. I was just on my way to your room to give you a message from him." She handed Libby the phone memo.

Libby unfolded the note and read it twice, her anxiety mounting. *Kylie is upset and refuses to come to school. Call me as soon as you can. Trent.*

The number was scrawled beneath the message. Crumpling the note, she hurried into the teachers' lounge, grateful to find it empty. What could have happened? Her hand on her cell phone, she hesitated, summoning professional calm. Then she dialed.

When Trent picked up, he sounded agitated. "Lib? I'm glad it's you."

Her heart skipped a beat. "Is Kylie okay?"

"She's not ill, if that's what you mean. But she dug in her heels this morning and refused to go to school. She started crying and nearly made herself sick. I don't know what to do." His last words were both an appeal and lament.

"Something must've happened."

"It did."

Foreboding tightened her throat. "What?"

"She found out about us. Our marriage."

The implications of his words stopped Libby cold. She'd been afraid of something like this. "Oh."

"She's upset because she thinks we should have told her. *I* should've told her."

"But she's unhappy with me, too."

"That would be an understatement."

"Where is she now?"

"In her bedroom. She won't talk to me."

Libby's brain was teeming with remorse. Kylie had made such progress. This was a major setback, and she was partially to blame. She knew it was impulsive, but she had to do something. "Can you hold on a minute?"

"Sure."

Before she could second-guess herself, Libby went into the office to ask the secretary to locate a substitute teacher for the rest of the day. Then she returned to the phone.

"Given her history, we need to address the situation immediately. The secretary is calling a sub for me, and as soon as she arrives, I'll come over. Meanwhile, don't press Kylie. She's had a shock. Give her time to think things through."

"I would have told her about us, but I figured she couldn't handle too much more on top of the move."

"Don't beat yourself up. You were merely trying to protect her." She paused, knowing such platitudes were hardly consoling. "I'll be there as soon as I can."

Libby returned to her classroom and hurriedly drew up lesson plans for the remainder of the day, all the time wondering if she had lost her mind. Would she have left school for another child? Or just this one?

She had vowed not to get overly attached to Kylie, but it was too late. She cared with a passion that would be dangerous to examine.

WIND HOWLED DOWN the canyons, pushing whitecaps across Whitefish Lake. In the metallic-smelling air Libby could almost taste the imminent snow. She'd notified Mary of the situation, prepped the sub, said her goodbyes to the children and gotten away shortly before noon. What on earth could she say to Kylie? Could a child possibly understand their reasons for not telling her in the beginning?

As she drove up the lane to Weezer's guest cottage, she tried putting herself in the girl's position. Kylie had lost her mother, moved to a strange place, formed an attachment with her teacher and entrusted her entire future to the father she loved, only to discover he'd been married before to that same teacher in whom she had confided her fear and grief. Betrayal all the way around. Kids—usually honest, open and guileless—found such duplicity hard to understand or forgive.

After parking in front of the cabin, Libby sat for a few moments sorting through her emotions. It was hard enough under normal circumstances to see Trent, but now?

Obviously anticipating her arrival, Trent threw open the door, his expression begging her for something she had no confidence she could deliver. In his wavy hair were finger tracks, and instead of greeting her, he merely shrugged.

Libby stepped inside and took off her coat. "Still in her room?"

He nodded. "I waited for you."

"How did she find out?"

When Trent explained about the women on the bus, Libby bowed her head. They should have anticipated something like this. "What have you told her?"

"Nothing beyond the bare facts. Every time I try to talk to her, she covers her ears and starts singing at the top of her lungs."

"She's not going to want to hear what we have to say, but the longer we wait, the worse it will get."

He shook his head. "Maybe we shouldn't have moved from Billings."

Libby took hold of him by the shoulders. "Nonsense. You can't protect her from life. It happens. She'll come around."

"She has to," he muttered through clenched teeth.

"We've got to stay calm and answer all her questions. She doesn't need any more half truths."

"Okay, let's go."

The door to the bedroom was shut, and when Trent knocked, there was no answer. "Kylie, please open the door."

Nothing, then a muffled "Go away!"

"Miss Cameron is here. We want to talk to you."

"I don't care."

"Either you open this door, or we're going to."

Silence.

Trent threw Libby a helpless look, then pushed the door ajar.

The room was a mess. A heap of half-dressed Barbie dolls blocked the closet door, a wadded quilt rested at the foot of the bed, and books and toys littered the floor. Wrapped in a blanket, Kylie sat hunched against the headboard, holding a pillow over her ears. She refused to look at either of them.

Libby approached the bed and sat gingerly on the edge while Trent drew up a rocking chair, removing the stuffed animals before sitting down. "You're angry," Libby began. "I don't blame you."

"Nobody meant to hurt you, sweetie."

Without Kylie's apparent notice, the pillow slid to the floor, baring her ears.

"I'm sure your daddy intended to tell you," Libby said, prompting Trent.

Kylie folded her arms across her chest and huffed.

"I would have," Trent agreed, "but there was no reason to yet. Miss Cameron and I were married a long time ago. We were sad our marriage couldn't last, but sometimes those things happen. Then I met your mommy and fell in love with her—and with you when you were born." Trent paused, his throat muscles working. "I loved your mother very much. I still miss her. She knew I had been married before, but it didn't matter to her. I hope it won't matter to you. It has nothing to do with how much I love you and need you."

Kylie looked up at the ceiling, but not before casting a sidelong glance at her father.

Leaning forward, Libby rested a hand lightly on the girl's leg. "Can you tell us what you're feeling?"

"You lied to me." The words came out harshly, each one like the lash of a whip.

"I know it must seem that way," Libby began. "Would it have made a difference if you had known sooner?"

They waited while she considered the question, her fingers kneading the satin trim of her blanket.

"Kylie?" Trent's eyes had never left his daughter.

"I liked Miss Cameron," she finally said.

"So did I. I wouldn't have married her if I hadn't."

"How could you like her and like Mommy, too?"

Libby drew her hand from Kylie's leg and clenched her fingers, awaiting Trent's answer.

"There's lots of love to go around. I've been very lucky, haven't I, to find two such special women to love?"

"Ha! If you loved Miss Cameron, why aren't you still married to her?"

Trent threw Libby a tortured look. She cleared her throat. "Honey," she said, "you can love someone a lot, but then things change. The other person changes. You change. Sometimes it's better to move on. And just think, if your daddy hadn't met your mother and married her, he wouldn't have you—his precious little girl." Hearing her voice as if through a fog, Libby felt a deep regret for what might have been.

"Sweetie, you said you thought Miss Cameron was wonderful. You like having her for a teacher. What made you change your mind?"

Kylie bit her lip, her eyes moist. "I thought she liked me just for me. Not you."

Libby blinked back her own tears. "I *do* like you for you. You're a special little girl."

"Kylie, I'm really sorry I didn't tell you," Trent said. "Can you forgive me?"

A lone tear trickled down Kylie's cheek. "I guess."

Leaning forward, Libby asked, "Is anything else bothering you?"

The girl's answer was barely audible. "I don't have a mommy."

Trent looked stricken. "Oh, baby, I wish things were different."

Kylie looked at her father, then slowly turned to Libby, then back again to Trent, a wisp of a smile forming on her lips. "They could be, I betcha."

"I don't think—"

"You said you loved Miss Cameron," she continued, as if her father hadn't spoken. "You know, when you were married."

"I did."

"And things can change—you said so. And people, too." She nodded at Libby. "Like you and her."

"That's right, but—"

"So you two can get married again."

"Oh, honey—" Libby protested.

"You can, Daddy, you can. Then you'll be happy, and I can have a new mommy and we can have a real house and—"

Trent rose quickly from the rocking chair and cradled his daughter against his chest. "Kylie, sweetie, we can't fix everything just like that. I'd do anything to make things better, you know that, but—"

Kylie looked over Trent's shoulder at Libby. "Did you love my daddy then—you know, when you married him?"

Truth. No more lies. Libby sucked in air, then met the child's gaze. "Yes."

"See, Daddy?" Kylie drew back, holding her father at arm's length.

"What?"

"You can marry her." She nodded her head in Libby's direction.

"It's not that simple."

"It is too." Kylie stuck out her jaw. "You like her again, I can tell."

Libby held her breath, knowing they were about to cross a line.

"I do."

Kylie looked again at Libby. "Do you like my daddy?"

"Yes. But—"

"Okay, then." Kylie slipped from her father's grasp and jumped to the floor.

Reaching out, Libby caught her as she tried to move past her. "Honey, it's much more complicated."

"No, it isn't." Out went the jaw again. "I'm pretty sure Daddy loves you again." She whirled and faced her father. "Right, Daddy?"

Trent rose to his feet and turned his back, composing himself.

Kylie threw a triumphant look at Libby, then marched across the room and tugged on Trent's jeans. "Tell her, Daddy."

When Trent turned around, the room seemed to shrink and expand with the beat of Libby's heart.

"The truth? I love you, Lib. Will you give me another chance?" He laid a hand on Kylie's head, then met Libby's eyes. "Give us another chance?"

Rising to her feet, Libby stared at Trent for a

long moment, feeling manipulated, yet strangely giddy. How could he put her in this position in front of Kylie? Yet how dare his words thrill her the way they did? She walked across the room and knelt in front of the girl, gently running her hands up and down Kylie's arms.

"I care about you. I care about your daddy. But you know how it is with grown-ups. Things can't always be the way we want them to be. And some things take time. Lots of it. I hope you'll forgive us both for hurting you. And I hope I'll see you in class tomorrow. I miss you when you're not there. The other children miss you, too. One more thing. I promise from now on, I will never lie to you."

Kylie wrapped her arms around Libby's neck. Then, as if she hadn't heard Libby at all, she whispered, "I don't care what you say. Daddy loves you, and I don't really hate you. I…I love you. Please be my new mommy!"

With those words, Libby's wounded heart cracked open.

AFTER LIBBY LEFT, it was too late to take Kylie back to school, especially with a substitute teacher. Trent couldn't believe it when Kylie ate a big lunch, then carried her Barbies into the living room and played house, humming under her breath and making up pretend dialogue as if nothing had happened. Or as if everything were settled.

He wished he felt as confident about a future with Lib as his daughter apparently did. Libby had loved him once. She liked him now. But did she "like" him enough?

He rinsed the last of the lunch dishes and picked up a tea towel. The stakes were higher than ever. Before, he'd been the only one focused on wooing Libby back. Now Kylie was involved.

Seeing Libby work her magic on Kylie today made him even more certain he needed her. She was born to be a mother. Why hadn't he realized that before? Why had he never understood that loving Libby meant children? That a baby had not been a threat but an extension of who Lib was?

He set the dried glasses in the cupboard and picked up a plate and began wiping it. Back then, he hadn't been able to confess to anyone how much the idea of a baby terrified him. How utterly ill equipped he felt to be a father. How haunted he was by that hot summer night when he'd watched his own father storm out of the house forever.

Trent hadn't known at the time of Libby's pregnancy what he knew now. He hadn't experienced this strong need to stick by his child and protect her and provide for her. And, above all, love her without condition. The same feelings Libby must have felt for their unborn child.

Somehow, he had to convince her he was a new man, one worthy of her.

THE NEXT MORNING, Kylie showed up for her tutoring session, her disposition sunny, even carefree. Libby wondered at the change in the girl and feared she might have jumped to unrealistic conclusions. No matter how strong her feelings for Kylie, Libby couldn't let them blind her judgment about Trent.

What had happened to her safe, simple life? A job she loved, a home she enjoyed and Doug's affection and friendship?

Even as Libby corrected a word Kylie stumbled over, she mocked herself. Affection? Friendship? Where did mind-numbing passion fit in?

"Daddy might surprise you tonight."

"What?" Libby had been miles away from the Level Two primer.

"I heard him call a babysitter. Uncle Chad's daughter." Kylie smiled up at her with satisfaction.

"And that's okay with you?"

She nodded. "If Daddy's coming to see *you*."

Libby didn't favor this conversational turn. "Let's read another few pages."

Kylie cocked her head. "You look funny."

"I do?"

"Yeah, kinda goony. Like you like Daddy but you're pretending you don't."

So much for playing it cool.

"I told you I wouldn't lie, and I won't pretend, either."

Kylie opened the reader and spread her hands across the pages to flatten the book. "Good. Because I talked to Mommy in my prayers last night. And she says it's okay for you to love my daddy."

Libby was the adult here. She should be able to respond, but she couldn't. The lump in her throat was too big.

"So what's this word?" Kylie moved her finger beneath the letters as she began to spell it out.

"Family," Libby supplied, the unintentional irony causing her voice to waver.

IT WAS MIDAFTERNOON when Trent grabbed a minute to drop by the Kodiak. Weezer had been concerned when Kylie had refused to go to school. Last night he'd phoned to assure her things were better, but with Kylie within earshot, he hadn't been able to provide details. He hung his hat on the rack by the door.

At this time of day a sole customer sat at the counter wolfing down a burger and fries. Smiling in greeting, Weezer laid aside a food distributor's order form.

"Need a break? Let me buy you a cup of coffee."

She hooted. "I think I can afford us a pair of freebies. C'mon." She led him to a booth overlooking the street. "Jenny!" She beckoned to the waitress. "Two black coffees, please."

As soon as they were settled with their hot drinks, Weezer eyeballed him and said, "Out with it, son. What's going on?"

"Kylie found out Libby and I had been married."

"I see." Weezer waited for him to continue.

Briefly he explained about the field trip and Kylie's sense of betrayal.

"Small wonder," Weezer said. "How did you and Libby handle it when she came over yesterday?"

"How else? We told her the truth."

"And that was?"

Under her scrutiny, he felt like a small boy needing to confess.

"I explained I had loved Libby when we were married just as I had loved her mother."

"What did you tell her about now?"

"I told her I loved Libby." A peace he had not felt in months settled over him.

"What did Libby have to say about that?"

"That she liked me. Kylie, however, heard only what she wanted to hear." He toyed with the handle of his mug. "She, uh, told us to get married."

He could swear a smile was flirting with Weezer's lips. "And what do you think of that idea?"

He couldn't hold back his broad grin. "I think it's an ideal solution for everyone. The problem is getting Lib to agree."

"I don't think that's going to be particularly difficult."

"You don't?"

"I never knew you to run from a challenge. Heck, boy, you thrive on them."

"I've hired Chad's daughter to sit with Kylie this evening. Lib and I need to talk about the past. What happened…then."

"I reckon it's time, son."

"For Kylie's sake, I have to get this settled soon. It won't do for her to have false hopes."

"Sometimes children see more than we do. I'm betting on her intuition." Then Weezer's crinkly brown face broke into a satisfied grin.

As soon as he returned to the office, Trent called and left a message on Libby's home answering machine. He would feed Kylie, get her tucked in and arrive at Libby's shortly after eight-thirty. Surely she wouldn't refuse. She knew how important this meeting was.

As SOON AS she returned home, Libby stripped off her dress and threw on a pair of faded jeans and a worn MSU sweatshirt. The past few days had been emotionally draining, and despite Kylie's hint about Trent coming over, she had not heard from him. Just as well. She was looking forward to a quiet evening at home with Mona, a good book and soothing classical music. She needed time to gather herself and examine her feelings. It wasn't fair to leave Doug hanging, nor should she let Kylie nurture false hopes.

She fixed herself a cup of tea and a chicken-salad sandwich and sat at the table, eating and poring over the local newspaper. A small item at the bottom of an inside page caught her attention. Trent Baker had joined the area search and rescue team. That figured. When they were in college, he had been thrilled to be invited to train with the group and had often been first on the scene when an emergency call came through. In the beginning she'd been proud of him, but later she had felt neglected when, instead of coming home after meetings, he would go out with his team buddies. She set down her sandwich. Was that fair? Had it really been that way, or in her insecurity, had she put unrealistic expectations on a man who relished adventure and enjoyed male companionship?

She pushed a crumb around her plate with her forefinger. Her father had died, her stepfather had been detached and unaffectionate. Had she looked to her young husband to right all the wrongs—real and imagined—done to her by the men in her life? A pretty big load for a guy just out of college.

And what of Doug? Did she expect him to fulfill her fantasy of marriage and family? In a moment of searing honesty, she asked a big question: Could any man provide her with enough love to compensate for those years of loneliness or the ache in her heart unfulfilled by children of her own?

Her appetite gone, she carried the dishes to the sink, only then noticing the blinking light on her answering machine.

The first message immediately tapped into her guilt—Doug, reminding her he was giving her time and hinting at how difficult it was to be patient.

But the second one tapped into far more unsettling emotions—fear, yearning and a sense of inevitability. Trent was coming over.

TRENT HAD NO IDEA exactly how he would persuade Libby to give him a second chance. But with a certainty that had nothing to do with the naiveté of first love, he knew she was the woman with whom he wanted to spend the rest of his life. He'd struggled with his grief and loneliness for long enough. He would always be grateful he'd had Ashley in his life, but it was time to prove to Libby he was a wiser, better man now.

With Kylie's words of encouragement ringing in his ears, he approached Libby's door. Spits of sleetlike snow, driven by a bitter north wind, attacked the pavement. Would he find shelter from the storm in Libby's arms, or would the storm inside rival the one without?

She cared about Kylie. He knew that. But he needed her to care about him.

He stamped his feet on the stoop, then rang the bell. The minute she opened the door, he realized just how important these next few moments would be. "I hope I'm not inconveniencing you, but I figured we couldn't put this off any longer."

She looked up at him, her eyes clouded. "I agree." She motioned him toward the living room. "Can I get you something to drink?"

"No, thanks."

He took a seat at the end of the sofa close

to the rocking chair, knowing she would settle in it.

She sat down, gripping the arms of the rocker. "How did Kylie seem tonight?"

"Happy. She had a good day in school."

"I'm glad."

"There is a more important reason she's happy."

Libby looked down. "I know."

It was time to get it all out in the open. "She's convinced we're going to remarry."

Libby said nothing, just continued the gentle rocking motion. At last she glanced up. "How can we let her down with minimum damage?"

Trent's chest constricted. Was she saying there was no chance? He never took his eyes off her. "Do we have to 'let her down'?"

"There's too much history, Trent."

"I'd hoped we could talk about that."

"Why? Nothing can undo the past."

"Not if you keep us from going there."

She stood abruptly and moved toward the hearth, then stopped with her back to him, peering into the flames. After several moments she pivoted to face him. "You're not a bad man. And you've done a good job with Kylie. But..." Her voice trailed off and she studied the ceiling as if the words she sought were inscribed there.

He forced himself to remain seated, to pre-pare himself for the blow that was coming.

"Go on."

She wiped her palms on her jeans. "I can never forget that you didn't want our baby. That you didn't care when…" She couldn't finish, and he caught the quick sheen of tears before she wheeled back to face the fire.

He crossed the room in two steps and put his arms around her from behind, cradling her into his chest, burying his face in her hair. "Oh, Lib, nothing is further from the truth." She was unresponsive in his arms, but didn't disengage herself. "I hurt you, even more than I knew at the time. But we've never spoken about it. That's my fault. I was an immature jerk. But I want to talk about it now." He shifted her around to face him, then tilted her chin so that she couldn't avoid his eyes. "Please, Lib."

"I suppose we have to. *I* have to."

"Regardless of what happens in the future, we both need to understand what happened then—" he swallowed hard "—with the baby."

Libby pulled away, averting her face.

"But before we begin, I want you to know I love you now in a way I was incapable of loving you before. I was too self-centered, too insensi-tive…too scared."

"Scared? You were never scared. Of anything."

He picked up her hand. "That's where you're dead wrong. I was petrified."

She looked at him directly. "Of what?"

He led her to the sofa and sat close to her, his arm resting loosely around her shoulder. "Of everything. Most especially of being a lousy father."

"You could've learned. Look how well you do with Kylie."

"All I could think of when you told me you were pregnant was what a screwup I'd be. Just like my father. Like maybe a child would be too much for me, too. What if I had *his* genes? What if I walked out? And if I didn't, how would I ever be able to provide everything a kid would need? I didn't even have a steady job or the ghost of a career plan then. A baby would have to have diapers, clothes, a jungle gym. Then an older kid would need braces, dancing lessons, a car and college. I was overwhelmed, Lib. You were so obsessed with your pregnancy and decorating the nursery and the baby book and all, I—"

At the mention of the baby book, Libby whipped her head around. "Cry me a river."

He stared at her, stunned, her uncharacteristic sarcasm killing him.

She scooted away from him, then drew her legs up against her chest, her defensive pose putting more than physical distance between them. "I'm supposed to feel sorry for you? Excuse me for getting pregnant, but last I checked with the biology book, it takes two. But that was all just fun for you, right?"

He winced. "I loved you."

"Well, you had a peculiar way of showing it. What? I suppose you blamed me for getting pregnant?"

"Aw, Lib, you know better than that," he protested, swiping a hand through his hair.

"Do I? You'll never know how much I wanted our baby, Trent. Do you have any idea what it felt like when I started cramping, then bleeding? Hugging my arms around my stomach in the crazed, futile notion I could prevent what was happening? And where were you? Off on some camping trip with your buddies. Having fun. Fun!" She spat the word.

Trent hung his head. "You shouldn't have been alone."

Her eyes flashed. "No, I shouldn't. But no unpleasant messes for you. Women's business, right? And what kind of sympathy did I get when you finally did show up?"

He closed his eyes, anticipating the worst, yet understanding that until she spewed out her bitterness and pain, they would have no chance for a future.

"You said, 'We can always have another baby.'" Her face was taut with scorn. "You didn't get it, did you? Another baby was the furthest thing from my mind. I loved *that* baby. I wanted *that* baby. I was grieving *that* baby. But all you could do was talk about the next one, as if the precious life that had died within me was disposable. Or forgettable." She stared at him, her mouth set. "Let me tell you something, Trent. Hardly a day goes by that I don't mourn our lost child."

Silence filled the room and Trent knew he deserved every one of the ugly words she had flung at him. They were all true. He had been a total jerk. How could he not have understood how important their child had been to her? His stomach turned. What if Kylie, like that doomed little life, had never been born?

"Well, aren't you going to say something?" Her eyes glittered, but he could tell she was refusing to give in to the relief of tears.

"I deserve every last one of your judgments. I hurt you."

"And you moved on and I didn't."

"So we divorced. Two people at very different stages."

She relented. "That was then."

"Lib, I'm not that same man. I've learned a lot." His voice caught. "I'm asking you to give me a chance. Much as I would like to, I can never change the past, but I can promise you a very different future."

She bent her head to her knees, hugging her legs to her chest almost as if she sought to make herself invisible. What was she thinking? What was she feeling?

At last she raised her head. "I don't know if I can trust you."

He rested his hand on her knee. "You never will know if we don't try again. I think something powerful is going on between us." He picked up one of her hands and kissed her fingers. "I don't want to lose you again."

She withdrew her hand from his. "Please, Trent. Don't touch me."

At first her words struck him like a blow, but then he studied her eyes. Beyond the fear lay something else, burning intensely. "Lib, what is it?"

She rested her forehead on her knees again. He waited, not moving, scarcely daring to breathe.

"I'm afraid." He inclined his head to hear her whispered words. "I don't ever want to feel that way again."

"What way?" he asked, brushing his hand through her hair.

"Alone."

Mournful, the word reached a place deep within him.

"Tell me about it," he said, lifting her chin and rubbing his thumb over the ridge of her cheekbone. Then, when all resistance seemed to drain out of her, he pulled her across his lap, cradling her to his chest, reminding himself that gentleness and understanding were the keys. "Start at the beginning, darlin'. Take all the time you need."

She burrowed into his neck while he made gentle circling motions on her back. At last, with a shuddering sigh, she began. "It all started when my mother died."

Then came an outpouring of stories about a grief-stricken little girl who never felt she belonged. Not with her cold stepfather in a rambling house and not at school, where the stigma of not having a "real family" made it hard to make friends. Stories about her fantasy world in which a mother and father walked straight out of a greeting-card commercial, and rosy-cheeked babies romped and played. Then, haltingly, about meeting Trent—her Prince Charming.

He gave a bitter laugh. "Some Prince Charming, huh?"

She slipped off his lap and sat cross-legged, looking at him. "It wasn't your fault," she said quietly. "I expected too much."

"And I gave too little."

She picked up his hand and held it in her lap. "I don't know how we can overcome the past."

A question seized him. "Why didn't we ever talk about these things…back then?"

"I don't know." Libby inclined her head, deep in thought. "Fear of exposure, maybe. I've always resisted revisiting my old life in Oklahoma. I suppose, in my starry-eyed optimism, I thought I'd found everything I'd ever needed in you."

"I probably wasn't a very good listener."

She managed a wan smile. "I didn't give you much of a chance."

"Maybe that's where the answer lies, Lib."

"Answer to what?"

"How we overcome the past. By talking. Everyone has always accused me of being a risk-taker. And that's true in most things. But there's one thing I've never risked with you, and only with Ashley when it was too late—when she was dying."

"What's that?"

These were the single most difficult words he'd ever uttered. "My vulnerability."

She stared at him, eyes glistening, and raised

her hand as if she wanted to reach out to him. "Could you? Now?"

He'd clamped his knees to a bull's flanks, he'd leaped off a cliff, secured only by a belay, and he'd guided a kayak through roaring rapids. That was child's play compared with this. He picked up her hand and held it between his. "Yes."

Once he began to speak, the exhilaration and satisfaction of an eight-second ride, a successful rappel or a wild river run paled in comparison with the reward he saw on Libby's face.

Love.

CHAPTER EIGHT

WHY HAD SHE NEVER HEARD any of this before? Libby was seeing not the devil-may-care man's man of their marriage, but a little boy broken by abandonment, determined never again to let anyone get close enough to hurt him. As she listened to him explaining how desperately he had sought his father's approval, the pain in his words broke her heart.

"Nothing was ever good enough," he said. "I should've hated him. But I didn't." He rubbed a thumb across the back of her hand. "Not until after he walked out. At first, I thought he'd left because of something I had done wrong. That it was all my fault. If only I had said the right thing, done the right thing, he would've stayed. With time, I realized he wasn't coming back, and that he didn't care about Mom or me. Maybe never had. That's when I got angry. I decided to show him. I would be the best rider, hiker, kayaker, skier, you name it, that ever came along." He paused, lost in reflection. "I made up my mind no one would ever hurt me again." He gave a rueful shake of his head. "Ironic, huh? You don't live this life and escape hurting."

He closed his eyes, obviously thinking about Ashley and, Libby hoped, their lost baby. "No, Trent, you don't." For the first time it struck her that maybe they had unconsciously set conditions on their love. She'd done it to protect herself from her lonely, anguished childhood, and he to buttress himself against rejection and fear of failure.

When she uncrossed her legs and moved closer, settling into the curve of his arm, he opened his eyes. "That sounds self-serving and melodramatic, I suppose."

"Not at all. Looking back, I suppose we were both scarred and had something to prove—me to be the perfect parent and you to conquer the world."

"And we didn't communicate." After a pause, Trent continued, "We pledged Kylie the truth. Give me the truth, Lib."

"Don't do this to me," she pleaded, clutching the front of his wool shirt.

His lips were against her cheek, his breath warm, spicy. "Do what?"

Her answer came out as a squeak. "Tempt me."

He turned her face so she had nowhere to look except into his depthless eyes. "Like this?" His arms came around her and he caught her lips, gradually deepening the kiss until she was lost in a white-water vortex, powerless to surface. She had longed to kiss him again since that day he had first walked into her classroom.

It's been so long, a voice cried in her head.

He broke the kiss and gently cradled her in the crook of his arm and smiled at her so lovingly her breath caught. "I think you've given me the truth, darlin'."

A part of her wanted to hide her head in shame. Like dry tinder to a match, she'd exploded at his first touch. But he was right. There was an important truth here. "You still set me on fire."

He brushed a stray lock of hair off her forehead. "But there's more to it now, isn't there? Friendship, commitment, sharing. Can we try? Please?"

"I can't help being scared."

"Trust me, Lib. This time I won't let you down."

She tucked her head into the hollow of his neck, sensing the steady beating of his heart beneath her palm. "Okay," she finally said, all the pent-up breath leaving her body. "We'll try."

HEEDLESS OF the heavy snow falling, Trent sat behind the wheel of his truck waiting for the engine to warm up and the heater to kick in. He had a chance! Exultation alone warmed him more than the feeble drafts coming from the vent.

It had taken sheer willpower to tear himself away. But he had to prove to her that their attraction had moved to a new level, one beyond mere immature notions about what a relationship entailed.

They had finally talked. *He* had finally talked. Rather than threatening him, he'd discovered that unburdening himself had been liberating, and although it had twisted his gut to hear about the miscarriage, he had discovered that he wanted to absorb Libby's pain, not deflect it. Something that never would have happened all those years ago. That *didn't* happen.

They had lost so much. Misunderstood so much.

He put the truck in four-wheel drive and edged out into the road, the glare of his headlights piercing the thick blanket of falling snow.

Trust me, he'd said. As he drove through the white night, he promised himself he would never again disappoint her.

LIBBY COULDN'T SLEEP. She didn't know why she even tried, except that tomorrow was a school day. After staring at the luminous dial of her alarm clock for one excruciating minute after the next, she rose from the bed, put on her robe and sheepskin-lined slippers, grabbed an extra blanket and settled in the living-room window seat with Mona, watching huge snowflakes filter down through the haze of the streetlamp.

Important things had been said tonight. Trent had always been her knight—handsome, invincible, daring. Would it have made a difference in their marriage if he had been able to reveal the cracks in his armor then? Or had she needed a man confident to the point of cockiness? Had it been naive of her to expect him to embrace her pregnancy with the same enthusiasm she had? And, by extension, mourn as she had?

She pulled her knees up and rested her chin on them. What innocents they had been! He had understood no more than she about the kind of work it took to build a good marriage. No wonder. Neither of them had grown up with helpful role models. With her thumb, she rubbed her empty ring finger, feeling something beyond pain and loss. Now in that place where bitterness had festered for so long, forgiveness grew. For that needy young woman and vulnerable young man.

How blissful it would be to leave it at that. But Trent was asking more of her. He had shown her he understood that this time their relationship had to be much more.

She caught herself. *This time?* She had known in some subconscious part of her mind that she had made her decision about Trent even before tonight. A second chance, yes, but also a final chance.

When she stretched out her legs, Mona curled up in her lap, warming her to the core. There were so many unknowns. Had he really changed? Were his overtures more about securing a stepmother for Kylie than about his feelings for her? Was this enterprise with Chad yet one more in a string of dead-end jobs? Had she been blinded tonight? In the cold light of day, would she truly be able to move beyond the hurt he'd inflicted on her back then? Open herself to it again? What if they remarried and she got pregnant? Had he really reformed?

Yet even as she raised the questions, she realized she had to take the chance. She could either step forward in trust or retreat to the safety of the known and, in the process, risk missing out on the great love of her life.

She buried her face in Mona's soft fur. Because that's what Trent had always been—her great love. And could be again.

The wind picked up, rattling around the house and blowing drifts across her driveway.

She had tried so hard with Doug. Even now, giving up the security he and his family represented was almost impossible to contemplate. Warm, accepting Mary. Doug's dad, who had embraced her as a daughter from the very beginning. His sisters, who could in time become her best friends, and his witty brother. But Doug himself?

He deserved more. As desperately as she tried, she had not been able to love him in the way that she knew deep inside a woman should love a mate. And if she was honest, she had always known why.

She had never stopped loving Trent.

There was no other option but to break off her relationship with Doug. "Mona, Mona, what can I possibly say to him?"

Trust me, Trent had urged.

She now knew how an aerialist must feel performing for the first time without a net.

"WHADDYA THINK?" Chad stood back so that Trent could see the display board and banner they'd had made for the outdoor exposition to be held in March at the arena in Kalispell. Green lettering on a buff background gave the display a natural, outdoorsy look.

Trent grinned. "It captures us."

Chad eyed his handiwork. "It better. We have a lot at stake."

Trent set down the mountaineer's rope he'd been coiling. "Seriously, it's great. I know all this has to be done, but to tell you the truth, I can't wait for clients and heading out on the adventures we claim to specialize in."

"Libby not adventure enough for you?" Chad asked shrewdly.

"Where'd that come from?"

"The sappy look on your face ever since you arrived this morning. I don't suppose you're aware you've rearranged the same display twice?"

"That obvious, huh?"

"Like a neon sign, my friend." Chad began folding up the banner. "So what gives?"

Trent didn't want to say too much. After last night, he was optimistic, but the last thing he wanted to do was jinx the situation with Lib. He settled for understatement. "I may have my foot in the door."

"*May? Foot in the door?* That doesn't sound like the same guy who did the Grand Canyon rim-to-rim hike in one day."

"Believe it or not, I've mellowed. Subtlety. Patience."

"And a whole lot of charm?"

"That, too," Trent replied smugly.

Chad clapped him on the back. "Hang in there. I've got a good feeling about this."

Trent didn't say what he was thinking. *Me, too.* Instead he gave an ambivalent nod. Too much was riding on the next few weeks to get overconfident, and last night had been too special, too new to talk about.

Whistling under his breath, he worked on their fly-fishing display until he was interrupted by a phone call. When he heard the voice on the other end, he rubbed his temples, then collapsed into the desk chair.

"Yes, hello, Georgia. What can I do for you?"

Although she called periodically at home to check on her granddaughter, his former mother-in-law had never called his cell phone before. "Is everything all right?"

"It depends upon what you mean by 'all right.'"

The chill in her voice put Trent on full alert. He waited.

"We talked to Kylie last night."

Nothing unusual about that. Kylie had mentioned the call this morning, delighted her grandmother was sending her yet another Barbie doll. "She's doing better in school," he offered.

"She really likes her teacher, right? Uh, Miss Cameron, I believe?"

"They get along very well. The help she's giving Kylie in reading is really making a difference."

"Nice." Her tone was anything but approving.

Again he waited, and when nothing more was forthcoming, he said, "How's Gus?"

"Just as worried as I am."

"I beg your pardon?"

"In fact, we're planning to come there this weekend to check things out for ourselves."

He had reached the end of his tether. "Georgia, what are you talking about?"

"Your lady friend."

He jumped from his chair. "My *what?*"

"You heard me. Kylie went on for quite a while. She told me that you and her teacher had been married before. And she can tell you like each other. Let me recall exactly how Kylie put it. Oh, yes, you like each other 'like in the movies when people are in love,' and she hastened to assure us it will be only a short time before she has a new stepmother."

The bluebird of happiness had just crapped in his nest. "Georgia, she's gotten way ahead of herself—"

"Is it true?"

"Which part?"

"Do you have a relationship with this woman?"

Trent paced the length of the office. He'd known the Chisholms might be hurt by his deep feelings for Libby, but circumstances hadn't yet warranted a discussion with them. Until now. Luckily, bullet-biting was a talent he had perfected in his youth. "I hope to, yes."

He heard the clack of her long, manicured fingernails on the receiver. "Expect us tomorrow evening. And, Trent?"

"Yes?"

"Gus and I are not happy about this development. Kylie has just lost her mother. Your relationship with this woman is irresponsible and not in Kylie's best interests."

"I would never do anything to—"

"We will be staying at the Alpine Lodge. We'll expect you around eight. By yourself. I'm sure you'll come to your senses, and we can settle all this then. Goodbye."

He stood holding the phone, staring at it in disbelief. They were going to help him "settle all this"?

He could respect their position, but they had better reciprocate. They were not in charge of his life, or Kylie's. He was. And his daughter was happier than she'd been in months. He couldn't let anything jeopardize that—or the promise of a renewed relationship with the woman he loved.

LIBBY HAD NEARLY overslept and arrived at school breathless, just before the first bell. Some kindly deity was looking out for her, though. The children were well behaved, full of smiles and, best of all, cooperative. The geography lesson had gone well, and wonder of wonders, Rory had actually raised his hand to volunteer that map reading was required to excel at one of his video games, and Bart's breakfast must have been sugarless since even he sat attentively.

Then there was Kylie. Whenever Libby glanced in her direction, the girl flashed her the covert grin of a true conspirator. Kylie's implicit approval would make turning back that much more difficult.

But Libby wasn't turning back. However, she couldn't move on until she'd dealt with Doug. When she had seen Mary standing outside the office this morning directing traffic, her spirits had flagged. She didn't want to hurt Doug. Hurting him meant hurting Mary, as well. Libby was definitely not looking forward to the next few hours. She had called Doug over the lunch break and asked him to meet her after work. The hope and elation in his voice had nearly done her in.

For the umpteenth time she reminded herself he was a good man. But for reasons that last night had made abundantly clear, he was the wrong man.

THE DIM INTERIOR of the hotel restaurant should have been soothing, but the upcoming ordeal had set Libby's nerves quivering. Libby had deliberately chosen this site as neutral ground. Both her place and Doug's would have been too private, too full of memories. On the way here, she'd gone over and over what she would say, knowing full well that no amount of rehearsal would prepare her for the reality.

Doug, dressed in a sharply creased pair of tan slacks and a navy blue turtleneck sweater, rose from a secluded corner booth to greet her. "Hey, pretty lady, you're a sight for sore eyes." He kissed her cheek, took her coat and led her to the booth, which, given what she knew was to come, felt more like a cell.

They had just settled across from one another when the waitress approached. "What can I get you?"

Doug held out his hand, deferring to her.

She couldn't think. "I, uh, a glass of water, please."

"For you, sir?"

"A coffee."

As soon as she left, Doug reached across the table and clasped Libby's hands in his own. "I've missed you."

What could she say? "It's been a while."

"Too much of a while. Waiting is hard work." He squeezed her hand. "I'm hoping it was worth it. Was it?"

She wanted to glance away, to avoid his eyes, so full of expectancy. There was no way to do this easily. She drew a deep breath, the warmth of his hands on hers failing to thaw the ice locked in her chest. "I need to say some things, and I hope you'll listen until I've finished."

"I'll do my best."

Before she could begin, the waitress returned with their drinks, giving her an excuse to draw her hands into her own lap.

He waited patiently.

The script she'd so carefully prepared vanished, and she had no idea where to start. "You are a wonderful man—"

"Oops. That sounds like a line introducing a big 'but.'"

She shrugged helplessly. "I guess it does. I don't know how to put this gracefully."

He studied his coffee. "Just jump in."

"Remember at Christmas when you asked me if I could love you?"

He looked straight at her. "I remember. You

said you thought maybe you could. I took that as a yes."

"Oh, Doug, it was a maybe."

"So do you have an answer yet?"

She stared at her untouched glass of water. "I like everything about you. Your sense of humor, your thoughtfulness, the way you treat me as if I'm something special."

"You are," he murmured.

"Your family couldn't be more wonderful, and I've always wanted to be part of a loving family like yours."

"Another 'but'?"

"You deserve a woman who loves you totally and unconditionally. I've tried, Doug, really tried. I like you better than I like almost anyone, but—" her throat clogged with sudden tears "—I don't love you the way you deserve to be loved."

He didn't lift his eyes from the coffee cup he slowly rotated between his fingers. "It's him, isn't it?"

There was no use pretending she didn't understand. "Yes."

When he looked up, his expression was controlled, but bleak. "I wish he'd never come back."

"In the long run, I'm not sure that would have

changed anything. We would probably still be having this conversation."

"I'd hoped somehow—"

"I know. So had I."

"So what about you and your ex?"

"I'm not sure. We both made a lot of mistakes in the past. Hurt each other in damaging ways. But I can't deny that I still have feelings for him. Whether we can overcome what happened before, I don't know. All I know is I have to try."

"I won't kid you. I'm disappointed. From the beginning, I felt you were the woman for me. To know that feeling isn't reciprocated…well, it hurts. Big-time." He paused, then shoved his coffee toward the center of the table. "I want to tell you how much I desire your happiness, but it's hard thinking that some other guy will be responsible for that." He reached in his pocket, pulled out his billfold and slapped a twenty on the table. "I won't beg, Libby." He slid from the booth and stood. "There's no point in making this any more difficult than it already is."

Looking into his ravaged face, she started to stand.

He laid a hand on her shoulder, preventing her from rising. In a choked voice, he whispered, "Be happy, Libby." Then he turned his back and strode rapidly toward the door.

From a vent overhead, a blast of warm air enveloped Libby, augmenting the flush of shame and regret coloring her cheeks. A hundred things she could have said flooded her mind. None of them, however, would have softened the blow. He had loved her.

"Miss, is something wrong?"

She shook her head. This had been torturous. She cared about Doug, and nothing had prepared her for his anguish.

But it would never have been right between them.

Not once with Doug had she experienced the abandon she had felt in Trent's arms last night, when every cell in her body had cried out for more of him.

She stared at the two drinks on the table, symbolic of what would never be, and waited until the enormity of what she had done sank in.

For better or worse, she had chosen Trent. And despite how painful this scene with Doug had been, she felt she'd made the right decision. She could never settle for "maybe" love, not when she had known the real thing.

GEORGIA DREW her fur-trimmed leather coat more tightly around her and huddled against the passenger door, ignoring the wintry scenery.

The played-out mines on the hillsides around Butte served as grim reminders of her bleak childhood and the lost promise of Ashley's life. She could hardly remember the time when her most serious problem was whether she and Ashley would travel to Denver or Salt Lake City to shop for a prom dress.

Gus hadn't said a word in fifty miles. Instead, he had tuned the radio to some obscure local station and kept his eyes fixed on the highway. He had not been happy with her decision to visit Whitefish immediately, not only because he would have to leave his foreman in charge of the Loomis construction project, but because he had not felt the urgency to confront the situation with Trent and that woman.

Honestly, men could be so clueless. Didn't Gus understand that this relationship needed to be nipped in the bud? If it went forward, that would make it even less likely that Trent and Kylie would move back to Billings, a hope Georgia had secretly nurtured.

Trent had never spoken about his first wife, and Ashley had seemed totally unconcerned. Well, Georgia wished now that she and Gus had insisted on more details. This was all too precipitous. She couldn't bear thinking of Kylie with someone else, someone her granddaughter might eventually call "Mother."

She'd had a bad feeling all along about Trent's decision to move to Whitefish. And now she actually had the sense Gus expected her to be civil, not only to Trent but to this Cameron woman.

"You all right?" he said, leaning forward to turn off the inane radio station.

"What do you think?"

"Georgia," he sighed, "are you sure you want to go through with this?"

"How can you even ask?"

He waited until he had successfully overtaken and passed a semi. "We stand to lose a lot."

"What on earth do you mean?"

"If Trent is in love with this woman and Kylie is excited about the idea, what possible good can we accomplish by butting in?"

"Butting in? This is our only grandchild we're talking about."

He patted her knee. "Exactly my point."

She shivered. Despite the exasperation she felt with him, he had tapped into her secret fear—they could lose Kylie if they weren't careful.

Gus cleared his throat, then added, "I'm having second thoughts about this trip, Georgia, but I'll do my best to support you."

Turning away from him, she stared mindlessly

at the blurred signs whizzing by. No matter what it took, she would make sure Kylie knew she had grandparents who loved her and put her welfare first.

CHAPTER NINE

LIBBY WAS TEMPTED to call in sick the next morning. Her late evening with Trent, followed by the sleepless one last night, had done her in. Over and over she had replayed the scene with Doug, wondering if she could somehow have made it easier, less painful for him. She hadn't meant to be cruel. She'd wanted to say more. To explain. But in his hasty exit, she recognized his need to preserve his pride.

She dragged herself out of bed and into the shower. It was against her principles to say she was ill when she wasn't, so she wouldn't play hooky. Staying home, tempting as it was, would simply prolong the inevitable—a meeting with Mary. She owed the woman honesty, both as her principal and especially as Doug's mother.

In an attempt to make herself feel better, she dressed in one of her favorite outfits—black tailored slacks and a royal blue-and-black checked sweater. She swept her hair off her forehead with two black combs and put on her favorite lipstick. Studying herself in the mirror, she decided she didn't look too bad for someone who'd had a grand total of eight hours' sleep in the last two days.

When she spotted Kylie waiting at her classroom door, Libby mentally clapped a palm to her forehead. How could she have forgotten their tutoring session? *Easily,* she thought ruefully.

"You're late." The child had a penchant for stating the obvious.

"I'm sorry, honey. I had trouble getting myself out of bed this morning."

"I didn't. You know why?" She didn't wait for an answer. "Grandma Georgia and Grandpa Gus are coming this weekend. And you know what else? Grandma's bringing me a new Barbie."

Libby found herself momentarily at a loss for words. How would the visit from his in-laws affect Trent? Or her? "She must be very fond of you," Libby said, unlocking the classroom door. She reached her desk and set down her things.

"She is." Kylie trailed behind her and stopped at her side. "I love her lots. But she doesn't do stuff like ski. She prob'ly won't like it that I've been skiing all these times. She only goes to the beauty parlor and shopping. But she buys me lots of clothes." The girl's voice brightened. "I bet she'll take me shopping for my wedding dress."

"Your what?" Libby croaked.

Kylie bounced on her toes. "Yeah, I told her about you and Daddy. Getting married and everything."

Libby clamped a hand to her stomach. Big mistake not calling in sick. She took off her coat and hung it in the closet before leading Kylie to the reading table, where they both sat down. "Kylie, I have something very serious to say to you."

The girl's upbeat expression sobered. "Okay."

"You want me always to tell you the truth, right?"

"You promised."

"I know I did. And the truth is, your daddy and I haven't decided anything about a wedding. For now, we're going to spend more time together and see how things go. It would help us both if you would tell your grandparents you jumped to a conclusion about a wedding." Kylie crossed and uncrossed her fingers. "Do you know what it means to jump to a conclusion?"

"To do something before it's time?"

Libby nodded. "They miss your mother a lot. It might be hard to understand how your daddy could like someone else. It would be harder still to understand how he could remarry."

Undeterred, Kylie looked up with a smile.

"But they'll like you, too. I promise. We'll be a big happy family."

Her words tore at Libby's heartstrings, because in them she recognized the fantasy she herself had nurtured as a child—the myth of the big happy family.

She put her arm around the girl. "For now, why don't we begin our reading and leave all this grown-up stuff to your dad and me. Meantime, it would probably be a good idea for us not to talk to anyone else about this."

Kylie cocked her head. "Okay. But don't you and Daddy take too long. The sooner you get married, the longer you can be my new mommy."

Libby could scarcely concentrate on the girl's reading. Kylie had obviously made up her mind about what she thought would happen. Marriage. What in heaven's name had Libby and Trent set in motion? If things didn't work out between them, the emotional fallout for this child would be devastating. But neither could their relationship be built on the foundation of a child's welfare. First had to come genuine love and a lifelong commitment. The sparks sizzling on a physical level could sputter and die. A lasting relationship was a flame that required constant tending.

The headache began with tension gripping

her forehead like cold forceps, and it would only
get worse, Libby knew, as she anticipated her
after-school meeting with Mary.

"YOU WANTED to see me?" Mary, arms laden
with a stack of folders, entered the office where
Libby had been waiting.

"Yes, is this a good time?"

Mary set the folders down on the edge of her
desk, then settled into her chair. "I always have
time for you."

Libby knew the principal was fond of her, and
that knowledge made what she had to say even
more difficult. "I need to speak to you about
Doug."

Mary waited for her to go on.

"I care a great deal about him," she began
lamely. "Like you, I want the best for him. But I
wanted you to hear this from me. I've broken off
our relationship." Saying it aloud to this woman
she so admired was even more difficult than she
had anticipated.

"Doug called us this morning," Mary said
with a nod.

"I'd like to explain."

"You don't owe any of us an explanation.
Sometimes things simply don't pan out as we'd
like."

Why had she been so apprehensive about

Mary's reaction? Her depth of understanding was one of the traits Libby particularly admired. "You have all been so nice to me, including me in family events, treating me in such a welcoming way. Frankly, I fell a little bit in love with all of you."

Mary leaned forward, her hands clasped in front of her. "You didn't come from a big family, did you?"

The sting of tears betrayed her. "There was only my stepfather. I...I always wanted a big family."

"Was that part of Doug's attraction?"

"Yes—uh, no. I mean—" Libby squirmed like a student in the hot seat. "I am very fond of Doug. He's a wonderful man. In all honesty, though, I have to say I bought into the whole picture—Doug, you, the rest of the family. Breaking up with him was one of the hardest things I've ever done."

"Then why do it, dear?"

She hesitated, knowing there was no turning back. "I think I'm in love with another man."

"Your former husband?"

"Yes." Libby rubbed her hands nervously along the wooden arms of the chair.

"I see."

There was a moment's silence while Mary digested the truth. Then the older woman spoke.

"I've always admired you. You care a great deal about others. I have to admit that I'd hoped you would one day be my daughter-in-law, but only if you could love Doug with all your heart."

Libby nodded, mute.

"I wish you well, Libby, and I will miss seeing you at the house."

"I suppose we need to talk about how this affects our professional relationship."

"Not at all," Mary said, quick to assure her. "You are an excellent teacher, we're both adults, and I see no reason to create a problem where none exists. However—" she sat back "—there is Kylie to consider."

"Kylie?"

"Should she remain in your class?"

Libby panicked. She thought that issue had been settled. "Why not?"

"Can you be objective about her? How will it affect her if your relationship with her father doesn't work out? Or if it does? Are we asking too much of a seven-year-old?"

She shouldn't have been surprised, Libby realized. Mary was only giving voice to questions Libby herself had tried, unsuccessfully, to squelch. "I want only the best for Kylie."

"She's quite attached to you."

"I know, but with everything else changing in her life, I believe it would be counterproductive to move her to John's class. That being said, I realize I must treat her like any other student. I hope you'll let me keep her."

"I trust your judgment. However, I would caution you that she has already known too much pain and loss in her young life. She doesn't need any more."

Thinking of her own childhood, Libby nodded. "No one knows that better than I do."

"All right then." When Mary stood, Libby, too, rose to her feet.

"About Doug—"

Mary waved her off. "Nothing more needs to be said except that I appreciate your honesty and want to assure you this will not affect our relationship."

On her way back to her classroom, Libby reflected on Mary's words. Doug's mother was a generous woman, but in her heart, Libby knew the close bonds she'd had with the family had been severed.

The depth of Libby's hurt came as no surprise. The Traverses had represented her dream family. She hoped in choosing Trent she hadn't made a life-altering mistake.

TRENT SHOULD HAVE guessed. In a brief call to give Libby a heads-up about the arrival of the Chisholms, he discovered Kylie had beat him to the punch. He tried to reassure Libby, but he was far from confident himself about the upcoming discussion.

After dinner he bundled Kylie up to drop her at Weezer's on his way to the Alpine Lodge. "Why can't I see Grandma Georgia and Grandpa Gus tonight?"

"They're tired. Don't worry, they'll see you first thing in the morning."

"But why do they want to see you and not me?"

"Grown-up stuff."

"Like maybe about the wedding, huh?"

Trent stifled a groan. "Sweetie, you can't jump to conclusions like this."

"That's what Miss Cameron said."

Much as Trent didn't want to hear that Libby had her doubts about their future, he was grateful he didn't have to go into further detail. "She's right."

"I can't wait for Grandma and Grandpa to meet her. I 'spect they'll really love her, don't you?"

"We'll have to wait and see."

Weezer and Scout met them at the door. Weezer already had the card table set up for Chinese checkers, so Kylie happily waved goodbye and he was off for the meeting that had him as apprehensive as losing a trail map in the wilderness.

The Alpine Lodge, situated on a rise above the road, was illuminated by spotlights aimed at its inviting Tyrolean facade. Mountain "posh" was how Chad described it. The thick woven rugs overlaying the polished pine flooring and the expensive leather furniture in the lobby discreetly suggested both a sense of luxury and welcome, but all Trent could focus on was whether the reception he would get from the Chisholms would be remotely as warm.

After checking with the desk clerk, who phoned their room to announce him, he trudged up the wide wooden stairs leading to the second floor. He didn't want trouble. Yet he suspected that was exactly what he was walking into.

Gus answered his knock. "Come in, Trent."

Georgia, dressed in a white wool pantsuit with a lavender blouse, perched on the edge of an armchair, worrying her gold necklace with manicured fingertips. She acknowledged his presence with a cursory nod.

Her husband, however, embraced Trent warmly. "How you been doing, son?"

"No complaints."

Gus took him by the arm and led him to the love seat. "Drink?"

"Nothing for me," Trent said, sitting down.

Gus drew up a desk chair beside the love seat, the three of them forming a conversational triangle. Trent was uncomfortably aware of the symbolism—his back was against the wall.

"Who's with Kylie?" Georgia asked, her tone critical.

Did she think under these circumstances he'd leave her with Libby? "She's at my friend Weezer's."

"Weezer?" Georgia's lips curled. "What kind of name is that?"

Trent didn't go into detail. "Short for Louise. She's a woman I've known since I was a kid. We're renting her guest cabin temporarily."

"Does Kylie get along with her?" Gus asked.

"Yes."

A disconcerting silence fell, broken finally by Gus. "Georgia told you why we're here, I guess."

Trent nodded. His former mother-in-law's expression remained frozen.

"You can understand how shocked we were when Kylie told us you were getting married," Gus said.

"Let me clarify something. I have no wedding plans."

Georgia spoke up. "Then why would Kylie make such a statement?"

"She's a child. She thinks all she has to do is wish something for it to come true."

"Why would she wish such a thing?"

Trent considered his answer. How much could he tell them? Would they understand any of it? "She misses her mother. She sees my unhappiness. Maybe she wants to fix things for us."

"Fix things? By marrying your former wife?" Georgia turned glacial eyes on him. "Have you forgotten Ashley so soon? And do you want Kylie to forget her?"

"No, Georgia, I haven't forgotten Ashley. Quite the contrary. I think of her every day and will always be grateful she agreed to marry me. I know you didn't think I had much to offer her, at least not in a materialistic sense. But I loved her. I was happy with her. And with Kylie. There is no danger, either, that Kylie will forget Ashley. She talks about her all the time."

Gus's question was direct. "Then help us out here. Why pursue this woman?"

Trent rubbed his hands together before beginning. "I have a lifetime stretching out in front of me. I have a daughter I love more than anything. I want her happiness. Grieving is a long, sad business. There comes a point where you have to move on. That doesn't mean either of us will ever forget Ashley, it just means we can't live forever in a state of mourning. So, why Libby

Cameron? I could flip the question around and say, 'Why not her?'"

Needing desperately to move, Trent rose to his feet and walked to the small corner bar, where he paused, before turning to give them his answer. "Libby is a warm, caring person with a generous nature. Kylie was drawn to her as a teacher before she learned we had been married. For reasons I won't go into, I disappointed Libby big-time when we were married." He paused, forcing himself to ignore Georgia's audible sniff of censure. "We were both young, insecure in our own ways. But I loved her. I have a chance to love her again, and we've agreed to see where our relationship leads."

Georgia averted her gaze, but Gus now stood, his eyes full of pain. "You have no idea how difficult this is for us."

"No, sir, I can only imagine. All I can do is assure you that we will remember Ashley as long as we live."

"It's too soon," Georgia managed to say in a strangled voice.

Gently Trent asked, "When would be the right time?"

She looked up at him then, tears making her mascara run. All she could do was shrug.

Gus crossed to his wife and laid a hand on her shoulder. "We care about you, son. And we're nuts about Kylie. Your remarrying would change everything."

Trent drew a deep breath. "Nothing has happened yet. But if it does, I want you to be just as involved with Kylie and with Libby and me as you choose to be."

"That's asking a lot, son."

Trent nodded in agreement. "I'm aware of that. But you haven't met Libby. I'd like you to. She might change your mind."

"I don't like the idea of my granddaughter having a stepmother," Georgia said.

"You'd rather have her be with just me? She needs a family."

"She has one. Us."

Trent poked his hands in his pockets to conceal his doubled fists. "Won't you meet Libby? Please." When Georgia chose not to look at him, he turned to Gus. "This doesn't have to be unpleasant."

Gus removed his hand from his wife's shoulder. "This thing you have with, uh, Libby, it's important to you?"

"Very. And to Kylie."

"Georgia?" The woman continued staring at the wall. "Honey, Trent's not rushing into anything. What would be the harm of meeting Miss Cameron?"

"For Kylie's sake?" Trent added.

When the older woman finally turned to him, Trent read the resignation there. "If we must."

As concessions went, it was feeble, but Trent was ready to clutch at any straw. Kylie had so little family, the last thing he wanted was to alienate the Chisholms. Well, not quite the last thing. That would be to give up Libby.

"Okay, then. I'll set up a time when we can all get together. I'd like Kylie to be there so you can see how much she likes Libby."

Georgia remained seated, dwarfed by the protruding arms of the chair. Gus walked Trent out, then stepped into the hall, closing the door behind him. "Son, this is awkward."

"I'm sorry I've caused you and Georgia such concern."

Gus nodded toward the closed door. "It's more her than me. She had a rough enough time with Ashley's death. Now she's afraid she'll lose Kylie to this woman."

"I don't think that will happen. Libby knows the value of family. She would never want to come between Kylie and you two."

"You're determined?"

"Absolutely."

"All right then. I'll do my best to keep an open mind, but I can't promise anything about Georgia."

Trent extended his hand. "Fair enough."

They were not bad people, Trent thought as he drove slowly toward Weezer's. In fact, Gus was the closest thing he had ever had to a father figure in his life. He appreciated Gus's willingness to give Libby a chance, but by setting up this meeting, had he placed too great a burden on Libby too soon into their renewed relationship? Georgia would not be easily won over, nor was he prepared to tolerate any rudeness on her part. And who was right in the middle of it? Kylie.

A simple courtship was suddenly turning into a negotiated truce. Not exactly the most romantic development.

SATURDAY WAS a gorgeous day. When Lois called and invited Libby to join her for a workout, she quickly agreed. The past week's turmoil had tied her into knots.

At the gym Libby spent half an hour on the stationary bicycle, then another twenty minutes on the treadmill. Finally she slowed the speed to a walk, then wiped her forehead, content in the knowledge she'd challenged her body to the max. When she turned off the machine Lois motioned her over to the weights. "More?"

Lois grinned. "I'm a hard taskmaster."

"No kidding?" Libby bantered sarcastically.

"C'mon, Cameron, you're up to it."

So for fifteen more minutes they lifted weights until Libby's arms felt like overcooked spaghetti.

"You did great, girlfriend," Lois said as she mercifully removed the weights and stored them away. "You deserve a treat."

"At the very least."

After they cooled down and put on their coats, Lois linked her arm through Libby's and led her across the street to a small coffee bar. "Cappuccino's on me."

"Good. I want the giant size."

"Getting back at me for torturing you?"

"Something like that."

Other than at school, Libby realized she hadn't seen much of Lois lately. And not since that day for lunch had they done anything together, just the two of them.

Lois returned from the counter with steaming mugs. "Here," she said, setting one at Libby's place. "Consider this my peace offering."

Libby grinned. "Honesty compels me to tell you that I feel better now than I have in weeks. The exercise did me good."

"Great. You've looked strung out the last couple or three days."

"Trust a friend to tell you the bitter truth."

"Any particular reason?"

Libby knew she could avoid the question with

a teasing retort, but she needed an objective perspective on her situation, and who better than Lois? She nodded. "Several, starting with the fact that I broke things off with Doug."

"You did?" Her friend seemed genuinely surprised. "I knew with your ex back in town, things were bound to get complicated, but you're crazy about all the Traverses."

"That's just it. I like them all, but I can't seem to fall in love with Doug. I've tried."

"How did he take it?"

"How else? Like the gentleman he is. But I'm pretty sure I hurt him." Libby sipped the cappuccino through the froth of whipped cream.

"Oh, honey, that's better than finding out later that you've made a mistake."

"That's what I thought."

Except for New Age music playing on the store sound system and several distant, muffled conversations, quiet reigned. "I think I need to talk about Trent," Libby finally said, looking down into the depths of her mug.

"I'm listening."

That was all Lois said, but it was enough. In no coherent order, Libby recounted the times she and Trent had been together and the rekindling of her feelings for him. About his caring for Kylie so responsibly and lovingly. About the ways in which he seemed to have matured. But also about her fears that he might disappoint her again.

When she wound down, Lois spoke. "I'm not one to pry, but you've never told me exactly why you divorced Trent in the first place."

"Incompatibility?" Libby voiced it as a question, hoping that would be enough, yet knowing she needed to confess the rest.

"I'm not buying it," Lois said. "Not after seeing the sparkle in your eye whenever you mention the man's name."

Libby felt her face flush. "I can't seem to help myself. I want to believe he's changed."

"What does that mean?"

The moment had come to trust Lois completely. "When we were married, I had unrealistic notions of what a husband should be like. Trent was full of life and adventure. I loved that about him. It seemed very masculine. But I also wanted him with me. I pictured us as devoted parents with lots of babies. So I was ecstatic when I found out I was pregnant." She stopped, unwilling to go on.

"And Trent?"

"He was young. Fatherhood was pretty overwhelming for him. He couldn't get into the idea. That hurt me. All my life I had wanted children. Growing up, that's all I dreamed about. My father's plane crashed when I was an infant and Mother died when I was six. The only parent I had, if you could call him that, was the senator."

Apparently picking up on her bitterness, Lois held up a hand to interject a comment. "I've noticed you have difficulty even referring to him as a stepfather."

Libby hung her head. "He tolerated me, provided for me, but he didn't love me. I'm not even sure he liked me."

"Hmm. Trent had pretty big shoes to fill."

"What do you mean?"

"Perfect husband. Perfect father."

Nodding sadly, Libby looked at her friend. "With four words, you've gotten at the root of the problem. I expected Trent to make it all up to me, didn't I? To be the ideal loving husband, who would father the beautiful children that would make up our perfect family."

"So you were looking for Daddy."

Libby shook her head in wonder. "I guess I was. What an impossible expectation to lay on a twenty-two-year-old man."

"And he failed you?"

"Or so I thought at the time." Libby could no longer hold back. "We lost our baby. A miscarriage. I was convinced the world had come to an end, but Trent couldn't understand why I was so upset." She hesitated, unsure now if the memories she'd harbored for so long accurately reflected what had actually happened. "He said we could always have another baby."

"Couldn't you have?"

"I suppose. But that suggestion seemed so cold. So callous. As if he was dismissing the child that we'd lost."

"What makes you think he's changed now?"

Libby ran her finger around the rim of her cup, then sucked the residue of cream off her finger before answering. "Kylie."

Lois nodded. "She's a remarkable little girl."

"And Trent adores her."

"So maybe he's father material after all?"

"I'm hoping so."

"Have the two of you talked about the child you lost?"

"A little."

"Sounds as if some healing still needs to take place. Have you ever thought about a private memorial service for your child?"

Startled, Libby looked up. "A what?"

"For a long time people failed to realize the importance of memorializing children lost through miscarriage. Recently, though, studies have recognized that such unresolved grief can fester for years. A service is one way to acknowledge the loss and invite healing. You and Trent may want to consider that at some point."

Libby nodded slowly. "It makes sense. I have mourned our child ever since. I always will. A service…" She wondered whether it would make any difference. "I'll think about it."

"It might prepare the way to celebrate a new pregnancy."

"Whoa!" Libby managed a smile. "You're getting ahead of me there, but I would like children. A family."

"You would make a wonderful mother." Lois wiped the table with her napkin and picked up her mug, but before she stood to leave, she added one final comment. "And stepmother." Then she winked. "Race you back to the parking lot."

And, unbelievably, that's exactly what they did, not caring if they were making fools of themselves. The air swooshed by, Libby's feet flew over the ground, her breath came in short gasps but she didn't care. She was free.

OR SO SHE HAD THOUGHT until she arrived home and played the message on her answering machine. A cold, dispassionate voice belonging to Jeremy Kantor requested an interview with her on his upcoming trip west. Squeezing her eyes shut, she listened as the man tersely set forth his objective: insight into her past and present relationship with her stepfather.

How relentless would this reporter be? He had no right barging into her life, hounding her about matters best left unvisited. Even though Vernon had warned her, she had hoped to avoid being interviewed. She could always refuse, but that might raise more red flags than giving her carefully censored version of the truth. A truth she could not—would not—think about.

After this morning, she had hoped the stress of the past week was behind her. Now, with one simple phone call, her stomach was again in knots.

She went into the bedroom, stripped off her workout clothes, then stepped into the shower. For ten minutes, she simply stood there, letting streams of hot water play over her sore muscles. Reluctantly she finished and dried off, wrapped her wet hair in a towel and reached in her closet for her cozy fleece robe. Mona sprawled on the foot of her bed, head lifted, green eyes fixed on Libby as if she sensed the swirling emotions in her mistress. For one crazy moment Libby contemplated trading places with her pet. Then life would be no more complicated than sleeping, eating, preening and occasionally purring.

When the doorbell rang, Libby jumped. Retying the sash of her robe, she stepped into her slippers and made her way to the door, wondering what kid selling Boy Scout popcorn or tickets to a talent show would be standing on the other side. When she saw Trent instead, she was startled by the rush of blood to her face. She opened the door and stepped aside to avoid the blast of cool air. "Come in."

He stepped over the threshold, then stopped, noticing her state of undress. "I…is this a bad time?"

"I just stepped out of the shower." She closed the door. "Wait a minute. I'll go change."

"Sure, don't rush."

Despite his words, she hurried into the bedroom, threw on a pair of jeans and an old shirt and rejoined him in the living room, where he sat on the sofa, legs splayed, stroking Mona.

"It's seemed forever since Wednesday night," he said.

"I know." She curled up at the end of the sofa. "Thanks for giving me some time. I broke it off with Doug."

His fingers stilled on Mona's back. "How did that go?"

She shrugged, not wanting to revisit the scene. "All right."

"This decision we've made, it's affecting lots of people, isn't it?"

"Doug. Kylie."

"And Ashley's parents." He caught her hand. "I need to warn you. They're upset. Georgia in particular. Gus is taking a longer view, but they're both concerned and anxious. Georgia thinks Kylie will forget Ashley."

"We would never let that happen."

"That's what I told her."

"They're scared. I can understand that. Kylie is all they have left of Ashley. Were you able to reassure them?"

"I'm hoping you'll help with that."

"Me?"

"They've agreed to meet you. If you're up for it. Kylie will be there, too."

Jeremy Kantor was a mere blip on the screen of life, Libby thought. Ashley's parents were a formidable and unavoidable challenge. If she had any future with Trent and Kylie, it would have to include them. What kind of dynamic would a relationship with them present?

"Lib?"

She wanted to run and hide, like a little girl pulling the covers over her head to escape the bogeyman.

"Would you come to the cabin for dinner tonight? Meet them?"

She rested her forehead on her knees. Reluctant as she was, she realized that even the happy endings in fairy tales came only after the witches and dragons were confronted.

When she looked up at Trent, there was only one answer. "Yes."

CHAPTER TEN

"DADDY, how do you spell 'Georgia'?"

Trent looked up from the stove. Kylie was bent over the table, holding a red crayon. "I'm making those name thingies for the party."

"You could just say 'Grandma.'"

"Yes, but Miss Cameron can't call her that." Kylie giggled.

As he spooned the final layer of tomato sauce over the manicotti, Trent spelled the name. Kylie had such high hopes for tonight. After an inner debate, he'd settled on hosting this dinner. Kylie would be in her element, and the environment would be more conducive to conversation than the elegant Alpine Lodge or a noisy restaurant. He sprinkled grated Parmesan over the top of the casserole, then put it in the oven. The dish smelled good, but Trent didn't feel like eating a bite.

Weezer had contributed two loaves of fresh-baked bread and a word of advice—"Everything in its season, son."

By five minutes to six, the table was ready,

and Kylie's place cards stood at each setting. The tossed salad was chilling in the refrigerator and the aroma of marinara sauce and melted cheese filled the cabin. Trent had changed his tomato-spattered shirt for a forest-green turtleneck and stood anxiously peering out the window. Kylie danced nervously near the door. "I can't wait for Grandpa and Grandma to meet Miss Cameron. I know they're gonna like her, don't you?"

Trent settled for a noncommittal "Uh-huh."

Promptly at six, headlights appeared. "It's her, it's her," Kylie trilled. "That's Miss Cameron's car."

Trent's throat ached. He loved Libby and wanted so much for this to be right—for the Chisholms to see in her everything he did. But, he conceded, it would be difficult for them to look beyond the ghost of Ashley.

"You're right on time," he greeted her as he threw the door open.

"It's the schoolteacher in me," Libby confessed, looking beyond him questioningly.

"They're not here yet."

"Hi, Miss Cameron. Come see the name-tag things I made."

And before Trent could even link his fingers reassuringly through Libby's, Kylie had grabbed her by the arm and led her to the table.

Trent followed, standing behind Libby as she

oohed and aahed over Kylie's artwork. He set his hands on her shoulders, drawing resolve from the delicate fragrance of her cologne and the sheen of her dark hair. Then she turned and looked up at him, her eyes warm with caring. "We'll get through this okay," she whispered.

It amazed him how she intuited his feelings now in a way she never had before, as if years ago they'd set forth on the same path, which had diverged for a time, and now had come back together. "Somehow," he muttered.

"I hear a car, Daddy." Kylie ran onto the porch. "They're here."

"You ready?" Trent asked Libby before moving toward the door.

Her smile was tentative. "As ready as I'll ever be."

Kylie grabbed her grandmother by the hand and drew her into the room. Gus trailed behind.

After the removal of coats and a flurry of greetings, Georgia looked around the room. "Small," she said by way of comment.

Trent chided himself. Why hadn't he opted for the neutral ground of a restaurant? "We prefer to think 'cozy.'"

"Reminds me of an old hunting cabin my dad had," Gus added.

Trent placed a palm in the small of Libby's

back. "Georgia, Gus, I'd like you to meet Libby Cameron."

"She's my teacher," Kylie interjected proudly.

Gus stepped forward and took Libby's hand. "Miss Cameron," he said, the "glad to meet you" noticeably unspoken.

"A pleasure," Libby said, then turned to smile at Georgia. "Mrs. Chisholm, I've heard so many good things about you from Kylie. I'm looking forward to getting acquainted."

Georgia hesitated before responding. "Yes, well, I am quite close to my granddaughter."

Trent locked his fingers behind his back, desperate to appear calm. Fortunately, Kylie, oblivious to the tension, saved the day. "Grandma, come see my room. And my Barbies," she said, eyeing the gift bag in her grandmother's hand. "You come, too, Miss Cameron."

Libby cast a quick glance at Trent, who nodded his encouragement. "Excuse me, Mr. Chisholm," Libby murmured before following Kylie and Georgia.

After they left, Gus stood by the fireplace warming his hands, before glancing down the hall toward the bedroom. "This getting-acquainted business is going to take time."

"I know."

"Naturally, as grandparents, we're concerned first and foremost about Kylie's welfare."

"That's as it should be. If you give Lib a chance, I think she'll measure up."

"That's why I'm here. To see. But Georgia? I don't know. I hope she'll be open-minded, but I wouldn't bank on it. She's still mourning Ashley. I guess we both are. Probably always will."

"Understandable," Trent said. "But for Kylie and me, life has to go on."

Gus put his arm around Trent's shoulders. "We just hope that doesn't mean going on without us."

It was impossible not to notice the hint of fear in the older man's voice. "It doesn't. You will always be part of this family."

All Gus could do was nod, because, Trent suspected, he didn't trust his voice.

LIBBY STOOD in the doorway of Kylie's room, feeling invisible, her heart in her throat. Georgia sat on the edge of the bed and helped Kylie unwrap the latest Barbie—a princess arrayed in sparkles and satin. Lined up on the floor beside the dresser were at least a dozen other dolls.

Kylie turned to Libby and pointed to the array. "Sit down there. Pick one." Kylie knelt on the floor, then gestured to her grandmother to sit beside her. "Let's play Barbies."

Georgia frowned fleetingly, as if uncertain she wanted to join them, but gamely she sank down, tucking her legs behind her. Libby selected a nurse Barbie, while Georgia picked up the closest doll, a chef.

"I'm keeping this one," Kylie trumpeted, holding up the new Barbie. "She's beautiful. I'm naming her Ashley. Like Mommy."

Her grandmother flinched. "Do you remember your mommy?" the older woman asked.

"'Course I do. I've told Miss Cameron all about her, right?" Kylie looked at Libby.

"Indeed she has." Libby sought Georgia's eyes. "Your daughter must have been a remarkable and beautiful woman. I'm so sorry for your loss."

Georgia's demeanor stiffened, as if she was struggling for control. She merely nodded in acknowledgment.

Kylie held "Ashley" aloft. "See, she's the queen of you two. She wants nurse and chef to be friends, right, Ashley?" She gestured at the dolls Libby and Georgia held. "You hug each other, okay?"

For an instant, Libby thought the older woman was going to refuse, but finally she held out her chef for the nurse's hug. "Hello," Libby murmured. "Glad to meet you."

"How do you do," Georgia said.

"Good," Kylie announced. "Now, who's going to start? I want you two to tell Ashley everything you like about her." The little girl smiled. "She likes to hear why she's the best queen."

Libby looked at the painted face of the nurse doll, then walked her over to Ashley. Georgia sat, head down, holding her doll loosely between her fingers. "You are the best queen," Libby began, "because you have a good heart, and for that reason, everyone you meet loves you and will never, ever forget you."

Kylie turned expectantly to her grandmother.

When Georgia looked up, Libby saw the glaze of tears in her sad, gray eyes, and could only imagine the effort of will this "game" was exacting from her. Libby's heart melted. This was a woman desperately seeking to keep her mask in place, but one obviously in pain.

"Queen Ashley…" Georgia began, then stopped to clear her throat. "Queen Ashley, you are beautiful, both inside and out."

Kylie moved the Barbie's waist into a bow and then, with a beaming smile, added her own compliment. "Best of all, Queen Ashley, you are the nicest mommy I know."

Libby couldn't help herself. She reached out and squeezed Georgia's thin hand. "Your Ashley must have been an extraordinary woman," she said softly.

"She was," Georgia murmured, just before she rearranged her face into its customary impassive expression.

Nevertheless, in that moment, Libby experienced a glimmer of hope.

TRENT LEFT GUS enjoying the fire and stepped down the hall. "Would you ladies like a drink?"

Kylie looked up. "It's okay," she said to the women. "I'll play Barbies and you guys can do grown-up stuff."

The women went into the living room, where they sat at opposite ends of the sofa, while Trent went into the kitchen to check on dinner and pour refreshments for Georgia and Libby. When he returned to the living room, Gus commented on the weather, then Libby offered a brief account of Kylie's adjustment to school.

"Libby's been tutoring her in reading," Trent said.

Georgia looked surprised. "I didn't know she was having trouble."

"It's not unusual after a parent's death for children to regress temporarily," Libby told her. "She's already showing progress."

"I guess we should thank you, then," Gus said.

Libby smiled. "Not necessary. It's been a pleasure."

At another conversational impasse, they all, simultaneously, turned to their drinks.

Trent pulled a kitchen stool into their midst and perched on it. "Maybe it would relax us if we just admitted that this is an awkward situation for everyone."

The look in Libby's eye told him she was grateful for his candor.

"I've told you a little about my history with Libby and about my feelings for her. We've only just met again, so we plan to spend some time together, see where this goes. In no way, though, does that mean I would forget Ashley. She was too important a part of my life."

"Nor would I want you to," Libby said.

Gus was looking at him with interest, but Trent had no idea what Georgia was thinking. "Libby is a great person. Kylie is crazy about her. Exploring the relationship just makes sense for all of us."

"But Kylie...?" Georgia's voice faltered.

Libby took up the conversational thread. "What Kylie needs most is stability and harmony. I know the idea that Trent and I are involved has to be incredibly difficult for you. I am also aware how much he loved your daughter, and what a much better man he is for having known her. I honor that about him. And having lost my own mother at a young age, I can fully empathize with Kylie. I assure you she will never forget her mother. I've certainly never forgotten mine."

A silence followed Libby's words and Trent was helpless to fill it. At that moment, the oven buzzer went off, and with relief, he busied himself getting the dinner on the table. Libby offered to help and he gratefully handed her the salad bowl and a bottle of dressing. Kylie reappeared with Queen Ashley, and the Chisholms focused all their attention on their granddaughter. Trent couldn't remember, even on the most strenuous high-altitude hike, when he'd ever found it so difficult to breathe.

Dinner would have been a social disaster without Kylie's innocent banter. He'd give anything to see the world through his child's eyes. To her this was a gathering of people who cared about her, and from her limited perspective, the natural corollary was that they should all get along.

By the time Gus got around to asking more about Libby's background, the meal was nearly over. Georgia stared at her plate while Libby spoke, then finally raised her head. "Why did you marry Trent in the first place?"

The bread in Trent's mouth turned to sawdust. For him, the question brought back the memory of Georgia's outrage when Ashley said she was marrying him, with or without her mother's blessing.

Instead of belaboring the point, Libby gave a simple and, to Trent, thoroughly satisfactory answer. "Because I loved him."

Georgia smirked. "Apparently not for long. Why not?"

Casting a meaningful glance at Kylie, Gus intervened. "Let's save this conversation for another time." He turned to his granddaughter. "Now then, young lady, why don't you tell me about your school? Miss Cam—er, Libby tells me you're doing better and better."

While Georgia picked at her food and Trent hoped for a merciful conclusion to the meal, Kylie went into great detail concerning the wonders of second grade, marred only by "that ignoramus Bart."

She finished her description of the recent field trip with one last comment. "And guess what? Since we moved, I've learned to ski."

"Ski?" Georgia glared at Trent. "Why, she's way too young. Skiing is dangerous. But isn't that just like you, Trent." She shook her head in disgust. "It's one thing for you to try all these daredevil things, but I won't have my granddaughter subjected to your notions of what is fun." The "fun" came out as an accusation all its own. "Next thing I know, you'll have her hang gliding and riding motorcycles."

"Many children here ski quite young," Libby offered in his defense.

Georgia bristled. "Kylie is not just any child. I have lost a daughter, and I cannot countenance teaching Kylie to ski. Not until she's much older."

Kylie turned her head from one adult to the next. "I like to ski," she said decisively.

"That's beside the point," Georgia told her. "You're my granddaughter and I forbid it."

Trent had reached the breaking point. He laid down his napkin and rose to his feet. "It is not your place to forbid or permit it, Georgia. I am the parent here."

Her lips drawn in a tight line, Georgia averted her gaze from the others.

When Gus reached for his wife's hand, she pulled it away. "Sweetheart, Trent has the law on his side, and I'm sure he has no more interest in endangering Kylie than we do."

Georgia stood up. "He's never been responsible," she sputtered. "Always gallivanting up and down mountains—leaving his wife and daughter for river-rafting trips with his wild friends. He always cared more for his own amusement than for Ashley or Kylie."

Incensed, Trent stepped around the table. "That is absolutely not true, and I resent the implication."

Only dimly did Trent hear Gus try to intervene. "Sit down, people. Surely we can conduct ourselves like civilized adults."

"That's the problem," Georgia accused. "Since when has Trent ever been a 'civilized adult'?"

"Don't fight!" a small voice shrieked.

Stunned, Trent turned. Tears ran down Kylie's cheeks. "Oh, sweetie." He went to her chair and picked her up in his arms. Georgia had the grace to look ashamed. Out of the corner of his eye, Trent noticed Libby carefully folding her napkin and replacing it on the table.

"We aren't fighting, honey, just disagreeing," Gus said by way of addressing Kylie's anxiety.

"I feel as if I'm intruding." Libby rose to her feet. "Before I leave, however, I have one thing to say. I am very fond of Kylie. As a child, I essentially had no family, but Kylie does. All of you love her. She deserves your best. And that means setting aside your differences for her sake." She walked over to Trent and laid a hand on his arm, then kissed Kylie's wet cheek.

"Good night, sweetie. See you Monday morning bright and early. Okay?"

Kylie nodded. "'Kay."

Then she spoke to Trent. "I'll see myself out. You take care of your guests. Thank you for the dinner."

With her back to the Chisholms, only Trent observed the film of tears in her eyes. Watching her leave was the hardest thing he had done in a long while. He wanted to race after her and hold on to her for dear life. To thank her for adding this last touch of dignity to the evening.

"Daddy?"

Oblivious to his former in-laws, he stared into his daughter's reddened eyes. "What, honey?"

"I love Miss Cameron, don't you?"

On Georgia's face, shock registered. Gus hung his head.

"Yes, I do."

"And I can, too, ski again, right?"

His eyes locked with Georgia's for an instant before he turned back to Kylie and said as gently as he could, "Absolutely."

BEFORE STARTING her car, Libby sat for a few moments, replaying the evening. She had not anticipated a hearty welcome from the Chisholms, and there was no disputing the stressfulness of the situation. Despite all of that, she had seen cause for optimism after the Barbie game with Kylie and Georgia. But she had been stunned by Georgia's treatment of Trent over the skiing issue. Nothing excused that kind of behavior in front of Kylie. The child's plea lingered in Libby's memory, breaking her heart. *Don't fight.*

Libby started the car and pulled down the lane, aware of the treetops swaying in the wind, tossed about by forces they could not control. Just like poor little Kylie, caught up in the crossfire of adult needs and expectations.

Halfway home, Libby couldn't help wondering again if she'd made a huge mistake. The Traverses were easygoing, accepting. By contrast, the dynamics between the Chisholms and Trent were complicated. Was there even a chance to forge a family out of tonight's cast of characters? And had Trent truly changed? It was hard to ignore Georgia's accusations about Trent's outdoor excursions with friends, which had only triggered Libby's old insecurities and fears. She sighed. How important was her dream of the loving, inclusive family? Was it even attainable? Especially with him?

By the time she pulled in to her own driveway, she had calmed down enough to understand she had two choices. She could step out of the picture in an effort to restore peace to the Chisholms and Trent and Kylie—and perhaps to protect herself. Or…she could stick it out, fighting for the man she loved and for the family she hoped to create with him.

No doubt about it. The Chisholms were hurting, devastated by the loss of their only child. If she chose to stay with Trent, it would not be easy to win them over. Maybe even impossible.

But she could no longer delude herself. In her life she had taken the escape route before. Twice. Once in her awful eighteenth year—a time she did her best never to think about—and once with her divorce.

She wouldn't do that again. If she didn't face her challenges, she would risk losing life's most precious gift—love.

There was no choice to be made.

WHILE GEORGIA GOT Kylie ready for bed, Trent cleared the dishes from the table, then joined Gus in the living room. He saw no point in avoiding the obvious. "Looks like I've been pretty dense."

Gus looked up. "How do you mean?"

"I knew you both were upset when Kylie and I moved. Maybe I shouldn't have sprung Libby on you so soon."

"I won't kid you. It's strange seeing you with another woman. Georgia's having an especially rough time. She clings so to Ashley's memory,

it's hard for her to accept you with anyone else."
He sighed. "But I suppose we should've been
prepared. You're young. We can't expect you to
grieve forever. But we're very protective where
Kylie is concerned, and I have to admit to reservations. If you and Libby divorced once, there
must've been problems. What's to prevent them
from surfacing again?"

From Gus's perspective, it was a valid point.
"I was the wrong man for her then. We're different people now."

"How so?"

"For one thing, we communicate more
openly."

"And?"

"I have a direction for my life. Work that ex-
cites me."

"What about Kylie?"

"She is slowly adapting. Once we find a place
of our own, it will be even better. She's made a
few friends. School is not quite such an issue.
She and Libby have a real bond."

Gus eyed him shrewdly. "It's not enough for
you to take up again with your former wife
simply because she's good for Kylie."

"That's a plus, but there's a far more compelling reason."

"Like?"

What did he have to lose by telling the truth? "I love her," he said simply.

Gus kneaded his forehead with his first and second fingers. "In that case, you've given us no choice but to make the best of the situation. Give us time, son." His voice cracked. "We don't want to lose you and Kylie. *I* don't."

Trent released a pent-up sigh. "Thank you, Gus."

"Daddy!" Followed by Georgia, Kylie bounded into the room in her flannel nightgown. "Grandma told me a story 'bout Mommy when she was a little girl. How she was in this dance show and wore a bee-yoo-ti-ful…" She scrunched up her mouth. "Whaddya call it, Grandma?"

"A tutu."

"Yes, a tutu. Grandma still has it and thinks I'm almost big enough for it to fit. She's going to send it to me so I can be beautiful, too."

Trent looked from Gus to Georgia. "We will never forget Ashley. And that's a promise."

Georgia remained silent, as if processing his words, her eyes never leaving his. Then, after a hesitant nod, she turned to her husband. "I'm tired, Gus. We need to leave."

After her grandparents kissed Kylie goodnight and left the cabin, Trent tucked her in bed, smoothing the blanket around her shoulders and turning the bedside lamp to low.

"Daddy?"

"Yes?"

"Why don't Grandma and Grandpa like Miss Cameron?"

"It's not that they don't like her." He struggled to explain. "They're used to thinking of our family being you, me and Mommy. They want us to be happy, but it's hard for them to see us with another woman, even one as kind and wonderful as Libby. They'll have to get used to the idea. That may take some time."

"But they will, won't they?" The fear in her voice wrenched his heart.

He silently hoped he was telling the truth. "Yes, honey, they will."

"Good," she said, turning on her side and curling her fingers around the hem of the blanket she brought up to her chin. "'Night, Daddy."

He bent over and kissed her cheek. "Good night. I love you."

"Love you, too," she whispered.

He tiptoed from the room, certain he could give his daughter no greater gift than Libby, and knowing he needed to phone and reassure her there was no obstacle too great to overcome, so long as they loved one another.

LIBBY COULDN'T STOP smiling. Trent had come by after his search and rescue training meeting later that week. "Can't waste a babysitter," he'd said, engulfing her in a huge bear hug.

Now he sat on the floor, his back against the sofa, bits of red construction paper between his legs. She watched his frown of concentration as he carefully cut out paper hearts for her Valentine's Day bulletin board. Meanwhile, sitting cross-legged and facing him, she cut strips of white paper lace.

"You really think second-graders are into this love stuff?" he said with a grin.

Libby sailed a piece of construction paper in his direction. "Gotta train them young."

He reached out and touched her hand. "Oh, I don't know. I'm kind of enjoying being trained at this advanced age."

His smoldering eyes made it difficult to concentrate. "You were never particularly trainable."

He laid down his scissors, tossed a heart aside and crawled closer. "Try me," he said, nuzzling her cheek.

Waves of warmth raised the hairs on the back of her neck. She knelt and draped her arms around his shoulders. "See," she murmured. "That's just what I mean. No soft words, whispered endearments. Just the direct approach. Not good enough, mister."

"Okay. Here's a start." He took both her hands in his. "Sweetest of the sweet, will you take pity on this poor soul who loves you and say you'll be my valentine? Forever?"

She cocked her head. "Not bad for a first try."

He framed her face in his palms. "Lady of the beautiful eyes, I give you power over me. I am a lovesick pawn in your hands."

"I don't believe a word of it," she told him, trying not to laugh.

"Then how about this? I'm helpless with love."

"Mmm," she murmured. "This could be good."

Now he looked at her, his eyes so full of love, she shivered with anticipation. "No funny stuff, Lib. I love you. That says it all."

One spark. That's all it would take. She had to be responsible. Groping on the floor, she finally came up with a paper heart. "Here," she said, sitting up and holding it out to him. "Here is my heart. I *will* be your valentine."

He sat up straighter, a triumphant smile lighting his features. "See? I'm totally trainable."

"I might cut you a little slack," she said, smiling. "I'm not sure I want you 'totally' trainable."

She picked up a pair of scissors and handed them to him. "But you've proved your point, so it's back to work."

"Woman, you're driving me crazy."

"Definitely trainable," she concluded.

They worked without speaking for a few minutes, the only accompaniment a Wynton Marsalis CD.

Then out of the blue he said, "I'm taking Kylie skiing again this Saturday. Would you come with us?"

"Hmm. What would the Chisholms think? They really didn't want her to ski yet. Especially not with me, I'm sure."

"I can't be overly concerned with what they think. You were right. Kids around here learn to ski practically before they cut their teeth. I don't want Kylie to be the oddball. She's improved a lot in a short time. We'll take it slow and easy, but she'll be racing downhill before we know it."

"I don't want to do anything to further alienate Gus and Georgia."

"Listen to me, Lib. We can't live our lives forever anticipating their reactions. We can only do what we think is best for us and for Kylie. So—" he squeezed her hand "—will you come Saturday?"

He was right. They had to follow their instincts and hope for the best. "Okay."

"Great. Kylie has her heart set on it." He gathered up the scraps of leftover construction paper, stood and tossed the trash into the wastebasket, then pulled Libby to her feet. He laced his fingers through hers and laid his forehead against hers. "I have to get on home. But one last thing occurs to me."

"What?"

"Maybe Georgia and Gus are trainable, too."

Her breath caught with the knowledge that they both wanted the same thing—acceptance from the Chisholms. "Let's work on it," she said, lifting her face for the kiss she'd been craving all evening.

"Done," he said, just before putting his arms around her, pulling her close and lowering his lips to hers.

CHAPTER ELEVEN

LIBBY HAD JUST PULLED on her insulated under-wear Saturday morning, when the phone rang. She grabbed a turtleneck and struggled into it, then picked up. "Hello?"

"Lib, it's me." Trent sounded frazzled. "We've got a problem. I've been called to help with an emergency search and rescue operation. Wee-zer's at work. Could I drop Kylie off at your place?"

"Uh, sure. She'll be disappointed about the skiing."

"Yeah, unless…would you be willing to take her without me?"

In the background, Libby could hear Kylie's, "Please, Daddy, get her to say yes."

It was a big responsibility, but on the other hand, it would give her a chance to interact with Kylie outside of school. Besides, Libby didn't want to disappoint her. "If you're sure that's all right with you."

"Thanks, that'd be great. We'll be over as fast as we can get there."

Once she'd hung up the phone, she quickly donned the rest of her clothes. It was a beautiful day for skiing. And an awful day for someone needing a search and rescue operation. She uttered a silent prayer for the mission and for Trent's safety, because in his voice, she had recognized his resolve, as well as the familiar undercurrent of excitement.

LIBBY MARVELED as she watched Kylie negotiate the bunny slope. In the few short weeks Trent had been taking Kylie skiing, she had mastered the basics with the grace of a natural athlete. After several runs, Kylie skied up to her, a determined look on her face. "This is baby stuff." She pointed toward the chairlift. "Let's go up there."

"You're sure you're ready?"

She lifted her chin. "Positive. I already did it with Daddy lots of times."

"All right, then. Let's go." Libby knew how important confidence was for a beginning skier, and the particular intermediate slope she had in mind was relatively benign and well within Kylie's ability.

Sitting beside Kylie on the lift, Libby curled an arm around the girl's shoulders, feeling both protective and joyful. This was what it would be like to have a daughter. To take pride in each new accomplishment. To share special times together.

"This is kinda like flying, isn't it?" The girl's eyes sparkled. "I love skiing, don't you?"

"I sure do. Did you know your daddy and I used to work at a ski resort?"

Her eyes widened. "You *did?* Was that a long time ago?"

"Just out of college we worked in Park City, Utah, before we got married and moved to this area."

"So you're a really good skier then. Kinda like Picabo and Lindsey."

Libby had no idea how Kylie knew about Picabo Street and Lindsey Vonn. She laughed. "No way. I'm good, but nowhere near that good." Libby took note of the upcoming stop. "Get ready to jump off."

"Okay." Somewhat clumsily, Kylie managed to ski off the lift.

Kylie studied the terrain below. "It looks scarier from up here. Kinda like when you stand on the high-diving board."

Libby detected a note of hesitation. "Are you sure you want to do this?"

"Of course!" Without another word, Kylie planted her poles and started cautiously down the slope, slowly picking up speed as she felt more secure.

It wasn't the most exciting run Libby had ever had, but it was, hands down, the most gratifying.

TRENT BRACED HIMSELF against the bulkhead as the helicopter swooped lower toward their landing site, the cleared area of an old logging camp. Chad Larraby and Chuck Patterson sat on either side of him—all three of them studying the terrain map Trent held in his hands. Three other team members sat across from them. The last sighting of the small aircraft had been about two miles north of the logging-camp staging area. Although there was still hope the pilot of the private plane had managed a soft landing in a snowfield, there had, so far, been no radio contact except for the homing beacon. When the chopper landed, the men leaped out, then unloaded their equipment, which included first-aid supplies, sleds, snowshoes and mountaineering gear.

Moving away from the rotor backwash, Chad held the radio up to his ear. "Roger that."

Behind him, Trent stood strapping on his pack. "What's up?"

Chad shook his head. "It doesn't look good. Spokane flight control says there were three passengers aboard, including a teenager. Lemme see the map again."

Trent unfolded it and Chad pointed out new coordinates. "We're about a mile and three-quarters away, but it's almost all uphill." He motioned to the other four team members. "There's another crew coming in off the railroad bed, but we should arrive first on the scene. Strap on those shoes and hit the trail. Watch for avalanche threat."

In the thin, cold air, Trent could feel his heart pounding. He would need all his strength, skill and mountaineering experience. He didn't know what they would find when they reached the downed plane, but he prayed their fast response would make a difference.

Chuck clapped him on the back. "It's good to have you with us, Baker."

As he studied the position of the sun in the sky, Trent mentally calculated how much daylight they would have to work with, then grinned at his old friend. "I'm glad to help."

"Move out!" Chad called.

Kylie and Libby had a good day for skiing, Trent thought as he followed the trail Chad was blazing. He pictured Kylie's delighted smile when she mastered a new skill. Nothing in a long while had pleased him so much as her enthusiasm for a sport he loved and could envision the three of them sharing.

Those thoughts came to an abrupt halt half

an hour later when they reached an ice field, requiring them to rope themselves together. Out came the ice axes and crampons—and a grim determination to overcome the obstacles lying ahead. One misstep, one freakish accident of nature and the condition of the plane's occupants would become moot.

Briefly Trent longed for the safety of the bunny slope. Then adrenaline kicked in, and he set one foot in front of the other, slowly, carefully traversing the potentially deadly expanse of white.

KYLIE SET DOWN her half-eaten hamburger. "Can't we ski some more after lunch?"

A spoonful of soup halfway to her mouth, Libby studied her young charge. "I would think you'd be pooped."

"Not yet," Kylie said matter-of-factly. "Just a few more times, please?" The imploring look on her face made the request hard to deny.

Libby glanced out the window. "The clouds are coming and the temperature's dropping."

Kylie studied her with the shrewd eyes of a veteran haggler. "Okay, just two more times."

Libby couldn't help remembering the outings with Daddy Belton when she'd wanted one more ride at the county fair or a second hot dog at an Oklahoma University football game. With experience, though, she'd learned not to ask. The answer had always been no.

Brushing aside memories of the man she'd dismissed from her life at age eighteen, she swallowed the last of the chicken noodle soup. "You drive a hard bargain, kiddo."

"Goody!" Kylie practically bounced in her chair.

"After that, it's home to my house for hot chocolate and a movie."

"Miss Cameron?" Kylie wrung her paper napkin. "Do you think my daddy's okay?"

From her wistful expression, Libby knew the girl was fearful. It wouldn't do for her to dwell on Trent's safety. Libby sighed. That was good advice for herself, as well. "He's experienced and careful, sweetie. The team is trained not to take unnecessary risks." She could tell Kylie was unconvinced. Better to distract her. "If you're finished eating, let's hit the slopes."

After Libby paid the cashier, Kylie shyly tucked her hand into Libby's. "I'm glad you let me ski today, even without Daddy. It's my favorite thing to do and I'm getting really good. Thank you." Then, after they picked their skis out of the rack and headed for the lift, Kylie added one last thought. "I think you'll be a really great new mommy."

Those approving words warmed Libby's heart

as she guided Kylie down the intermediate slope later, carefully avoiding the small, strategically placed jumps, which provided youngsters the illusion of moguls. A steady stream of boys whooped it up as they made their jumps. The morning sun had caused some surface melting. Now with clouds overhead, the watery patches were refreezing. The areas just beyond the jumps, well worn with ski tracks, would be especially icy, so Libby avoided them. At the bottom, she framed Kylie's cheeks between her gloved palms. "Are you tired? We don't have to do this last run, you know."

Kylie's eyes narrowed and her chin jutted forth. "You promised."

"I know. But you can always change your mind."

"No way," the girl said, already starting for the lift. Libby shook her head. Trent wasn't the only Baker with the stubborn gene.

At the top, Libby heard children's voices calling excitedly, "Miss Cameron, Miss Cameron. Kylie."

When she drew closer, she spotted several boys from second grade. Bart Ames, his cheeks rosy with cold, approached them. "It's my birthday. We're havin' a blast."

"Well, happy birthday."

"Yeah," Kylie said halfheartedly.

A bearded man separated himself from some of the other boys. "Miss Cameron? Jeff Ames. Good to see you."

She turned to greet Bart's father. But before she could utter a word, she saw Kylie plant her ski poles and shove off down the hill, not following the usual path, but heading straight for the first jump, only a few yards from the edge of a dense grove of trees.

Libby sped after her, crouched over her skis. She hoped she could reach Kylie before she attempted the jump. Time stood still, each foot of snow seeming to take endless seconds to cover. Libby executed a quick turn to avoid hitting the skier in front of her, then hunkered lower over her skis, her poles held behind her. She was gaining on Kylie. Another twenty feet and she could catch her.

But Kylie, too, had increased her speed, the small but potentially difficult jump rising to meet her.

At the last minute, Kylie glanced over her shoulder as if making sure others would witness her feat of daring. Then she sailed onto the jump, head low, legs spread.

Libby watched helplessly as the little girl, spread-eagled against the sky, fought for control, then landed safely and swooped to the base of the run. As Libby skied after her, Kylie's triumphant shout rang in her ears. "I did it!"

Although she didn't want to take anything away from Kylie's sense of accomplishment, after congratulating her, Libby admonished her for taking chances and suggested they head for home. Bart and his father, trailed by the other boys, caught up with them at the edge of the parking lot, which had been cleared except for occasional patches of packed snow. "Miss Cameron, do you have a minute?" Jeff Ames pulled her aside. Behind her, Libby was aware Bart and Kylie were discussing something heatedly. She couldn't quite hear what they were saying because Bart's father was asking her about his son's behavior in her class. She glanced over her shoulder, satisfied that Bart was moving off, leaving Kylie alone.

Just then the boy's voice rose in a taunt. "You're a stupid girl. Just 'cuz you can jump, you're not so hot."

"Am, too."

"Bet I can run faster'n you."

"No you can't, you big ignoramus!" And heedless of the traffic, Kylie dashed across the lot toward the far end, chased by a rapidly gaining Bart.

"Kylie, come back!" Libby started after her, her words lost in the wind.

Bart closed in on Kylie and in a frantic lunge, Kylie stretched toward the fence bordering the lot. In that moment, a horrified Libby watched as the girl lost her footing and fell.

Legs churning, Libby raced toward Kylie, her breath coming in frantic gasps.

But it was too late. Kylie landed sideways on a patch of treacherous ice and slid toward the base of a metal light pole. With a cushioned "thunk," her head came to rest against the pole, her body sprawled awkwardly on the thin layer of snow.

A violent wind roared in Libby's ears. As if from a great distance, she heard a howl, which she finally recognized as her own tortured scream. "No-o!"

Somehow she made it to Kylie's crumpled body, aware only of a deathly silence. The girl's blue-veined lids were closed over her eyes, and a trickle of blood oozed from beneath her ski cap, turning the snow beneath her head a cruel pink. Oblivious to the cold, Libby sank down beside Kylie, leaning her ear to the girl's mouth. Frantically she stripped off her gloves, then laid two fingers on Kylie's slim neck, searching for a pulse.

"Let me," a woman behind her said, drawing her away. "I'm a nurse."

A young man huddled beside Libby, holding

her by the shoulders. "We've sent for the ski patrol. Help will be here soon."

Then Libby heard Bart's disembodied voice behind her. "I didn't mean to, honest, I didn't mean to."

The nurse, a woman with kindly eyes, turned back to Libby. "She's breathing. I'm putting a compress on her wound. Meanwhile, we can't risk moving her. Are you her mother?"

The world around her revolved in a kaleidoscope of colors, and Libby felt tears fill her eyes. She shook her head, then croaked a ragged no. A mother? She barely controlled a bitter, hysterical laugh. A mother would never have let this happen. Trent wouldn't have let this happen. "Trent."

The kindly young man leaned closer. "What?"

Libby's mouth was cottony. "The girl's father. He needs to be notified."

"The ski patrol will take care of that. Tell me, are you all right?"

She would never be all right again. Remembered accusations deafened her. She had called Trent irresponsible. What if Kylie was seriously injured? What if…

She couldn't lose another child, not Trent's child. Not this precious girl she loved with all her heart. Libby suddenly whirled away from the man and vomited into a snowbank.

Dizzy and shaky, she wiped her mouth, then looked back at Kylie. So beautiful. So peaceful. So still.

Behind her, she sensed onlookers stepping aside. Then, to her relief, two members of the ski patrol replaced the nurse and began taking Kylie's vital signs.

At the insistent tap on her shoulder, Libby turned around. Bart stood there, clutching his father's hand. "Miss Cameron, I'm sorry. It was just a dumb ole race. Is Kylie all right?"

"It was an accident," the boy's father said quietly.

Bart wiped his nose with his gloved hand. "I didn't mean to hurt her."

When she saw the boy's tear-streaked face, her first instinct was to scream at him, but then she looked into his fear-riddled eyes. "Maybe not. But this is a good lesson about not teasing people, isn't it?" Fearing she could no longer be civil, she attempted to stand, tottering against a bystander, who hooked an arm through hers. "Miss, let us help you to a bench."

"Not yet. I have to know how she is."

One of the paramedics glanced over his shoulder. "Looks like a concussion with head lacerations and a possible broken arm."

"But she's not conscious," Libby said, her voice thready.

"Not yet. We're taking care of her, and an ambulance is on the way. I suggest you meet her at the hospital emergency room."

"Her father…we need to contact him."

"Where is he?" the other member of the ski patrol asked.

Swallowing the fear in her throat, Libby said, "With the search and rescue team on a mission."

The man exchanged a guarded look with his partner, as if he'd heard about today's rescue attempt. "We'll do our best to reach him by radio. What's his name?"

"Trent Baker."

The paramedic stabilizing Kylie's head and neck said, "I know him. Good man."

Libby closed her eyes. A *good man*. But good enough to forgive her for this unspeakable carelessness?

No way.

JEFF AMES and the bystander who'd helped her now escorted Libby across the parking lot to her car. They offered to drive her to the hospital, but she shook her head. "I'll be okay," she assured them, even as she fumbled for the keys. She needed a few moments to herself—to replay the awful scene and to pray that somehow, someway, everything would turn out all right. Yet even as the ambulance wheeled from the parking lot, she had a sick feeling in her stomach. Kylie had not yet regained consciousness.

While her car warmed up, she used her cell phone to call Weezer, who said she'd be waiting for her at the hospital. They had to get hold of Trent somehow. And the Chisholms. As the enormity of that thought struck her, Libby feared she might be sick again.

Somehow, as if driving a fun car in some surreal carnival ride, she made it to the hospital with absolutely no recollection of the route or other traffic. She ran to the emergency-room entrance and flung open the door. Weezer, already seated in the waiting room, rose to greet her.

"How is she?" Libby asked.

Her face creased with worry, Weezer shook her head. "No word yet."

"Trent?"

"The paramedics notified the emergency dispatcher. They're trying to reach him." Weezer took her by the hand and led her to a seat. "But it's going to be a while before he can get here. He'll have to be evacuated by helicopter."

Libby grabbed her stomach and rocked to and fro, feeling as if she might hyperventilate.

A nurse knelt in front of her, offering her a cup of coffee, and for the second time in one day, someone asked if she was Kylie's mother. "No, I'm her teacher…and her friend."

"Here, take this." The nurse thrust a paper cup into her hand. "You've had quite a shock."

After one sip, Libby set the coffee aside. The bitterness nearly choked her. "Please, how is Kylie?"

"The doctor will be out shortly." The woman stood. "We've had no luck reaching the father yet. Are there other relatives we should notify?"

Libby looked at Weezer, her stomach sour with dread. "Do you know how to reach Kylie's grandparents?"

"Trent gave me that information to have in case of an emergency." Weezer dug in her purse and handed the nurse an index card with the names and number.

"Thank you." She bustled off toward the treatment rooms.

With Weezer's hands gently and lovingly kneading her back, Libby's tears came at last, not in a violent spate, but in an unrelenting stream. "Ooh, little one," Weezer crooned. "I know, I know." The long, rounded vowels intoned by the older woman had a soothing cadence all their own. "It's too much, too much to carry."

Letting her head fall into Weezer's lap, Libby listened to the comforting words, accompanied by the healing pressure of Weezer's hand rubbing circles up and down her back. "You're blaming yourself. You mustn't. It was an accident. All the what-ifs in the world can't change what happened. Now, all we can do is pray and love."

Pray and love? Libby had been praying from the moment she watched Kylie slide into the base of the lamppost. As for love, her heart was cracking under the pressure of all she was feeling. Libby sat up, then leaned her head against the wall, expelling a long-pent-up sigh. "Oh, Weezer, she's got to be all right."

The old woman squeezed her hand and simply said, "She will be."

IT WAS NEARLY TWO when the team reached the site of the crash. One broken wing of the plane tilted at the sky and the nose was buried in a snowdrift, but miraculously the fuselage was more or less in one piece. Damaged tree limbs and long skid marks told the story. The plane had apparently skimmed the treetops before gliding into a snow-covered upland meadow. The man strapped in the front passenger seat was dead, but the pilot, though unconscious, was still alive. Huddled in the backseat was a high-school-age boy, white with shock, his lips blue in the cold, a deep gash in his shoulder.

The team immediately began treating the two survivors. Chad raised the second group of rescuers on the radio and gave them an update. He had already called for a medevac chopper to be dispatched from Kalispell.

"What a deal," Chuck muttered as they helped steady the plane and extricate the passengers.

"I hope we got here in time to do some good," Trent replied under his breath. Arriving first at the scene, he had taken one quick glance in the cockpit before yielding to the paramedics. He hoped he never again had to view such carnage.

Within twenty minutes, the helicopter hovered overhead, unable to land. Carefully, first the adult survivor and then the boy were strapped into stretchers and hoisted into the chopper. When they were safely aboard, the pilot gave a two-finger salute and lifted off.

While the teams waited for the return of the chopper to remove the body, they worked to secure the plane for the FAA investigation team. By midafternoon, they were ready to hike back to the base site, where other helicopters could land to pick them up. Trent didn't relish making the trek back across the ice field, weary as they all were.

Finally the medevac chopper returned, and they loaded the body in a reverent silence broken only by the *wacka-wacka* of the rotors. Then, subdued, they started down the mountain. Halfway across the ice field, rubbery legs made Trent realize he was more out of shape than he'd thought. By the time they reached the camp, he shrugged out of his pack, removed his snowshoes and sank onto a rock, overcome with weariness. He sat that way for several minutes before he felt a hand on his shoulder. Looking up into Chad's agonized face, he trembled with a powerful premonition. "What is it?"

"I just got word from the dispatcher. It's Kylie."

Trent heard nothing but the volcanic roar in his head. Scalding tears stung his eyes. Faltering, he stood up. "What?"

"There's been an accident. She's in the hospital. We're trying to patch you through to the base."

A silent scream ripped through Trent's gut. "Will she be all right?" He turned back and grabbed Chad's parka, his eyes raw.

Chad hung on to him with one hand and pulled out the radio with the other. "I don't know. I wish I did. I'm calling now." He stepped away from Trent, then clicked to open the line. "Team One to base. Over."

Over. It couldn't be. "It's not over. I won't accept 'over.' Not for my little girl." Then he crumpled to the ground, where he remained until Chad knelt beside him and offered him the handset.

WEEZER SAT QUIETLY, eyes closed. They'd been waiting nearly two hours, with still no word. Patients and families had come and gone. The irritating inanities of the television program no one was watching spun on endlessly. A new shift of nurses, dressed in their colorful scrubs, had arrived. Once, Weezer had walked down the hall and called the emergency dispatcher. The news hadn't been encouraging. The men would not be lifted off the mountain until dusk, if weather conditions were favorable. And judging from the rising wind and overcast sky, that was a big if.

In broken tones, Libby had managed to tell her about the accident. Under other circumstances Weezer might have smiled, the daughter so like the father in her response to a dare.

Sensing a new presence, Weezer opened her eyes. Another nurse was approaching. "Ms. McCann, Miss Cameron, would you come with me? The doctor will talk with you now."

They scrambled to follow. She led them to a small room just beyond the swinging doors. Within a few moments, a woman with short salt-and-pepper hair and glasses entered and introduced herself as Dr. Coker. "I've talked with the girl's father and he has given me permission to fill you in on Kylie's condition." She shrugged sympathetically. "Patient-privacy concerns, you know."

"Will she be all right?" Libby asked.

"We hope so. We've set her broken arm—fortunately it was a clean break—and stitched the gash in her head and treated her lacerations. Our main concern right now is her concussion. She hasn't regained consciousness. That is not unexpected, but we're doing a CT scan to check for bleeding between the brain and skull."

Beside her, Libby staggered, then sank into a chair. "Oh, no."

"We're guardedly optimistic. Children can take a blow like that far better than an adult. Let's wait to see what the scan shows. Meanwhile, she could wake up anytime. She'll have a horrendous headache and we'll have to keep her under observation for several days, but she should recover just fine."

Libby lifted tortured eyes. "But if the scan shows something worse?"

The doctor laid a hand on Libby's shoulder. "Then we would have to consider other measures, but let's not cross that bridge yet."

"Can we see her?" Weezer asked.

"As soon as she gets back from the lab, I'll have a nurse come get you. In fact, it would be a good idea for someone to be with her all the time in case she wakes up." She smiled encouragingly. "Seeing familiar faces will be comforting for her. Meanwhile, we'll keep you posted on her condition."

They thanked the doctor then returned to the waiting room, where the receptionist handed Weezer a message. She scanned it silently, then handed it to Libby, who read it before looking up, her eyes swimming with tears once more. "I can't begin to imagine what I can possibly say to the Chisholms."

Weezer drew Libby to her and whispered gently, "Whatever is in your heart, little one."

When they were seated, Weezer read the note again. The Chisholms would arrive in the morning. These five people could either come together as family, or be forever alienated from one another.

CURSING HIMSELF for his negligence in leaving Kylie with Libby, Trent leaped from his truck and ran across the parking lot, ignoring the visitors departing from the hospital and the flashing lights of an ambulance pulling up to the emergency-room entrance. He stopped just inside the door, scanning the waiting room. No Weezer, no

Libby. Nobody he knew. He ran a hand over his stubbly beard then turned to the vacant reception desk, wanting nothing more than to pound on it and scream out Kylie's name. He'd been excused from the debriefing and given a seat on the first chopper out, but even so, it had been an hour and a half since he'd heard the news. The longest hour and a half of his life.

"Sir?" A matronly woman in a plum-colored scrub suit with a hospital ID badge approached the desk. "Can I help you?"

"I'm Kylie Baker's father. Where is she? How is she?" He knew he was ranting, but he needed information. Now.

"Follow me, please. She's resting quietly. Her vital signs are good." The woman swung open the doors dividing the waiting area from the treatment rooms. "She just got back from the CT lab."

"CT? CAT scan?" His stomach imploded.

The nurse stopped, then faced him. "She's had a concussion. The scan is to determine if there's been any brain injury."

"Brain injury?" For a moment he thought he might pass out.

"She's in a coma, Mr. Baker. But that is not unusual in these cases. Hopefully, she'll awaken soon. The CT is just another diagnostic tool."

Coma. Brain injury. Concussion. The words dinned in his ears. "I need to see her doctor."

"I'll tell her you're in your daughter's room. She will come give you an update soon." The nurse led him down the well-lighted hallway, then paused outside a door. "Here we are. Don't be too concerned about her appearance. She has some lacerations and bruising. Also, her broken arm has been set."

Broken arm? Was there no end to the bad news? He took a deep breath, steeling himself for Kylie's sake, then stepped inside. The lights were dim, making it difficult at first to see the small, still form lying beneath the blanket, one side of her head shaved and dressed with a bandage, her left arm swaddled in a bulky cast. He stifled an involuntary sob. "Kylie? Honey?" He approached the bed and stood, clasping her tiny hand in his. Bending, he brushed her cheek with his lips. "Kylie, Daddy's here."

When he felt a gentle hand on his arm, he became aware for the first time of another presence in the room. "Trent, I'm so sorry."

Slowly he faced Libby, his emotions in violent conflict. *Sorry* had to be the lamest word in any language. Her ravaged expression, the deep shadows beneath her eyes, the haunted look in them terrified him. He knew he should say something. Tell her it was all right? It wasn't.

Accept the blame, rightfully his, for sending Kylie to the mountain with someone else? Shake Libby until her teeth rattled? Pound his head against the wall?

Instead, he turned back to the bed, his gaze never leaving his daughter's face. He tried to speak and couldn't. Clearing his throat, he mustered the awful question. "How did it happen?"

Libby's terse words cascaded around him with deadening finality. The visual image they created was all too vivid. He barely heard her repeated apology. "I'm sorry."

Logically he knew it was an accident. Nobody's fault. But logic was cold comfort when worry and anger had turned his brain to mincemeat, leaving only mind-numbing fear. He glanced over his shoulder at Libby, who waited, head bowed, for his judgment.

"We'll talk later" was all the comfort he could offer.

She nodded, her eyes awash in pain. "May I stay with her?" she asked in a tremulous voice.

He didn't know how he felt about her in that moment. All he knew was he couldn't bear to be alone. "It's up to you."

"I'll stay then," she said quietly.

He pulled a chair close to Kylie's bedside and

sank into it, his head resting on the edge of the bed. He was exhausted from the day's events. But the weariness overtaking him had nothing to do with physical exertion. It was rooted in his soul.

CHAPTER TWELVE

LIBBY SAT in the shadows, keeping watch with Trent but averting her gaze to avoid the accusation she knew she would read in his eyes if he looked up. All that mattered right now was for Kylie to come out of the coma unscathed. So she remained, motionless.

His voice, abrupt in the silence, startled her. "I thought Weezer would be here."

"She was. She only left to go feed Scout and Mona."

"Oh." He rubbed his palm over Kylie's good arm, back and forth in gentle massage.

"A nurse called the Chisholms. They'll be here tomorrow." He gave a faint nod of acknowledgment.

Trent was still dressed in his hiking clothes and sturdy boots, and his tan chamois shirt strained across his back when he leaned over the bed. His bloodshot eyes and unshaven face tore at Libby's heart. He was a man on the brink of despair. And all because of her. She should have been watching Kylie. If only she could roll back the tape, turn away from Jeff Ames and stop Kylie before she accepted Bart's challenge.

She shuddered, icy fear racking her. Kylie's words thundered in her memory. *I think you'll be a really great new mommy.* Her stomach in spasm, Libby bent over and covered her face with her hands. She wasn't supposed to be a mommy. Not Kylie's and not—she smothered a sob—anybody's.

"Mr. Baker?" Dr. Coker stood in the door.

Ashen, Trent jumped to his feet. "Yes?"

"I'm Mel Coker, Kylie's doctor." She shook Trent's hand, then rounded the bed, studying the chart she held. "We have cause, at the moment, to expect a favorable prognosis. The arm was a clean break and should heal well. Her pulse, respiration, blood pressure all look fine. She had to have several stitches in her head, but aside from some ugly bruising, that will heal quickly. It's the concussion we're still concerned about."

Libby waited, her heart thudding.

Trent shook his head. "She's got to be all right."

"The CT scan looks good. There doesn't seem to be any blood between the brain and the skull. She had a nasty bump, but we're hopeful she'll wake up within the next twenty-four hours. You can expect her to have a headache, perhaps blurred vision for a time. We'll keep her under observation for possible seizures."

"Seizures?" Trent's pale face turned gray.

"They are sometimes a temporary side effect of a concussion. It's just a precaution." She tucked the chart under her arm. "Any other questions?"

Trent seemed dazed. Finally he shook his head. "No. Thank you, Doctor."

"Try to get some rest yourself," she suggested, pausing in the doorway. "If you're exhausted, you'll be no good for your daughter."

He nodded, then turned back to Kylie. Libby could barely make out his next words. "Hear that, sweetie? It's going to be okay. Just come back to us, wherever you are. We need you."

Then his voice broke and he laid his forehead on the bed, his shoulders shaking with silent sobs.

Libby longed to go to him, to comfort him, but it was no longer her place. Quietly she tiptoed from the room.

TRENT DIDN'T KNOW how long he'd been at Kylie's bedside fighting sleep, watching for any hint of movement—the flutter of an eyelash, the quirk of a finger. When the door opened, he looked up. Weezer stood there, her wrinkled face a road map of compassion. "Any change?" she asked.

He shook his head. "Not yet."

She came closer and put her strong hands on his shoulders. "It's after nine. You need a break."

"No."

"Son, she's going to be all right."

With the calm words and the pressure of her fingers, he felt a peace come over him, as if this wise Native American woman actually had prophetic, healing powers. He waited, letting her message infuse his body with hope.

She squeezed his shoulders. "But you won't be if you don't get something to eat. My treat."

"But—"

"Libby will stay with her." She pulled him to his feet. "Come on now, son."

He took a long, last look at Kylie, then permitted himself to be led away. Libby, small and forlorn, waited in the hall. Unable to summon words, he nodded briefly at her, then followed Weezer to the cafeteria, where the only choices at this hour were prepackaged foods. They made their selections, then carried their trays to a table. Weezer nursed her coffee while she waited for him to eat. The chicken sandwich might have been tasty, but he couldn't tell. Neither it nor the banana was anything other than fuel to get him through this awful night.

"You can't blame yourself." Weezer studied him with knowing eyes. "No parent can be everywhere all the time. You wanted Kylie to love what you love, to try new things. To dare." She patted his arm. "It was an accident. The Ames boy's parents called the hospital. Their son is a wreck."

Trent stopped chewing. "I hope you'll understand if I can't work up much sympathy for him."

"Maybe not yet. I hope someday." She blew on her coffee, then took a sip. "Just as I know you'll forgive Libby."

His head snapped up. "I can't talk about her right now."

"She's devastated, Trent."

He threw his banana down on the tray in disgust. "Is that supposed to make me feel better? Bring Kylie back?"

"You're angry."

"Yes."

"Be careful where you direct that anger. It's gotten you in trouble before. You love Libby. What you do in the next few hours may well determine the course of your life."

Libby, his Libby. Weezer was right. He *was* angry. Up on the mountain he'd shaken his fist at whatever force was in charge of disease and accidents. It was all well and good for others to spout platitudes about how accidents just happen—and not always to the other guy. But, this time his Kylie was the victim. He should've been there. Maybe he could've prevented it.

As if she'd read his mind, Weezer went on. "You can't blame Libby, Trent. It could just as easily have happened if you'd been there."

"We'll never know," he said forlornly.

Weezer sat back and stared straight at him. "Son, you can torture yourself and punish Libby the rest of your days, and it won't change a thing. It will only serve to make you bitter."

He pushed his tray toward the edge of the table, then bowed his head, succumbing to the truth. He couldn't face life without Kylie. Nor without Libby. No matter what. He heaved a tortured sigh. An accident. That's what it was. Nobody's fault.

Weezer continued quietly drinking her coffee, leaving him alone with his thoughts. After several minutes, he squared his shoulders. "Thank you. I'm ready to go back now." Before he stood, he managed a faint grin. "Are you sure you're not a shaman?"

LIBBY SLIPPED into Trent's chair by Kylie's side. She picked up one tiny limp hand in hers, marveling at how quickly she had come to regard this child as her own. Not just because Kylie represented the child she and Trent had never had, or because she had fallen in love with Trent all over again. She had to admit, though, that for a time, subconsciously, she had perhaps been using Kylie as a means to compensate for her own losses. But Kylie was much more than a replacement, much more than a token of what Libby had thought was "owed" her.

No, that wasn't it. At the heart of the matter was an indisputable fact. She loved Kylie for the precious, unique child she was. No matter what happened from this moment on, Libby promised herself she would never make comparisons with what might have been.

And if Trent couldn't forgive her, she would somehow have to find the strength to accept that judgment.

I think you'll be a really great new mommy. Libby closed her eyes. *Please, give me this one chance.*

A nurse entered the room and quietly checked Kylie, then made notations on the chart. When Libby raised her eyebrows, she smiled encouragingly. "So far so good. You know, it might help if you talked to her. On some level she may be able to hear you."

"Thanks."

After the nurse left the room, Libby sat on the edge of the bed, her back to the door, clasping Kylie's good hand between her own. What could she say? Maybe the words didn't really matter. All she could do was share what was in her heart. Drawing a deep breath, she began.

"Sweetie, I'm so sorry this had to happen to you. If I could've prevented the accident, I would have. I hope you'll still love skiing like your daddy does. He doesn't give up easily, and I'll bet you don't, either."

Trent had never been satisfied with anything less than his best. She had nursed his bruises, rubbed analgesic balm on his aching muscles, but she'd never been able to keep him down.

"I'm sorry, too, that you lost your mommy. I remember what that's like. It's as if everything that is vibrant in the whole world suddenly fades to gray." She swallowed with difficulty. "You're lucky, though. You have a wonderful daddy who loves you.

"My stepfather, though…" She closed her eyes at the memory. "He didn't hate me. It was worse. I think he just didn't care one way or the other. So long as I kept out of his way, we got along. For a time. Until…" She censored herself. "More than anything I wanted a loving family. A mommy and daddy who were crazy about each other and adored their children. Who laughed. You're luckier than many kids, Kylie. You have a wonderful daddy and grandparents who care so very much about you. So, please, wake up, and come back to them. To me."

She picked up the girl's hand and kissed it, her tears spilling over.

"I love you, sweetie. I...I couldn't bear to lose you." Her voice sank just above a whisper. "Not like my other babies."

"Babies?"

The word, barked into the quiet room, nearly stopped her heart. For a second she sat, paralyzed, incapable of turning around. Nothing registered except the sudden sickening memory of the strange doctor leaning over her, his glassy eyes fixed on hers, his unfeeling words destroying the most basic part of her.

"Libby?" Trent's tone was more urgent.

As if in a trance, she forced herself to face him. He stood at the foot of the bed, his expression one of shock. "What do you mean 'babies' plural?"

Each syllable struck her with the force of a blow, and without pausing to think, she covered her mouth and fled past him out of the room.

DUMBSTRUCK, Trent stood halfway between the bed and the door, torn between his need to rush after Libby and his need to stay with Kylie. What had Libby meant? Had she miscarried twins? He paced to the window, then turned back. No, he would have known. He glanced at the door, then at Kylie, his eyes fixed on each rise and fall of her chest. He couldn't leave her.

Yet he had to go after Libby. The look on her face as she ran past him haunted him. Anguish, yes, but beyond that, panic.

He rubbed his sandpapery face. What was it she hadn't told him? Whatever it was, it was significant. Only recently they'd vowed to tell the truth to Kylie. But what truth had Libby withheld from him? And for how long?

He sat down in the recliner in the corner, his fingers steepled beneath his chin, lost in thought. Right now he had to focus his attention on Kylie, on getting her well.

But at some point he would confront Libby. He loved her, but obviously she still couldn't trust him with her secrets. If he'd learned one lesson from bitter experience, it was that a relationship without trust was doomed. His arms dropped to his sides and he leaned his head back. He couldn't remember a time when he'd been so physically exhausted or mentally heartsick.

Everything he'd hoped for—a fresh beginning in Whitefish, security for his daughter, a renewed relationship with Libby—now seemed threatened. But he'd sacrifice all his hopes and dreams for one sign from Kylie that she was coming back to him.

Everything about the hospital—the smells, the hushed efficiency of the staff, the long, uncomfortable hours in a bedside chair, even the bitter-tasting coffee—was a vivid and wrenching reminder of those excruciating hours with Ashley, when hope faded with each new blood test.

He was drained way past the point of tears. He let his head droop, his eyes close.

And that was how Weezer found him an hour later, his soft snores a rhythmic counterpoint to Kylie's gentle exhalations.

LIBBY STARED BLANKLY at the wall of the nearly deserted waiting room, her body beyond numb. She shouldn't be here. Yet she was powerless to leave before she had word about Kylie. She had run from Trent straight to the restroom, where she had bathed her face and neck in cold water until she could stop crying. Wiping her face with the coarse paper towels, she'd stared in the mirror, shocked by her own splotched, alien reflection. What kind of woman kept secrets from the man she loved?

Approaching footsteps. Anxiously Libby looked up from her seat. An orderly walked briskly toward the elevators. She exhaled. No word on Kylie.

Weezer had tried to comfort her when she'd returned to the waiting room, no doubt assuming Libby was upset about Kylie. But Libby had shrugged her off, pleading exhaustion and worry. Although the quiet presence of the older woman had been comforting, Libby was relieved when Weezer finally stood up and said she'd check on Trent and Kylie.

The pastels of the landscape hanging on the wall did nothing to soothe Libby, whose thoughts, despite her efforts to banish them, kept returning to that balmy May day in Oklahoma when she had told Daddy Belton her news, then to the moment she declared her independence from him and to that stormy winter night months later, the loneliest of her entire life. She rubbed her eyes, willing her mind to stay in the present. Anywhere but in that past she'd spent years banishing from conscious memory.

Sadness overwhelmed her, not just for that cruel time, but for what would happen between Trent and her once he knew. What she had done was worse than a lie. She had expected him, out of some kind of supreme sensitivity, to understand what she had never explained. And, beyond that, to make it all right.

Unbelievable.

She stood and paced past the TV, in front of the reception desk, then back. Arrested by the painting, she stopped. A rushing mountain stream, a grove of aspen quaking in the soft mountain breeze and a doe, head up, alert, poised to bolt at the first snap of a twig. She raised a hand, wanting to touch the deer, to whisper she understood. She wanted to bolt, too. Danger was at hand. Not a natural predator, though, but the death of her dream.

WEEZER STOOD by the window, her eyes fixed on the horizon, now showing the faintest streaks of light. The dark night was past; dawn was breaking. Just as the world stirred, so, she hoped, would Kylie.

The child would bounce back, of that she had few doubts. She wasn't sure she could say the same for Trent or Libby. Something had happened between the two of them. She hadn't for a moment accepted worry about Kylie as the sole reason Libby had returned to the waiting room hollow-eyed and desperate. Up to that point, she'd managed her anxiety and self-inflicted guilt with grace. No, something had happened.

As for Trent, he hadn't spoken the entire time she'd been here in the room. He looked much the same, stricken and out of his mind with worry. But there was also a grim set to his lips that hadn't been there before.

Growing up on the reservation, Weezer had learned the rudiments of tracking. But the majority of her life had been spent seeking clues in body language and expressions, rather than damp paw prints beside a stream.

Whatever had happened between these two, it was torturing them both.

Over the distant mountains, a robust sun rose. Weezer bowed her head in contemplation, and at first didn't hear Trent's sudden gasp. Then his words penetrated. "Sweetie, open your eyes again. It's Daddy."

Trent stood over Kylie. Weezer stepped closer, but observed no change in the girl's expression.

"Please, honey, open your eyes."

The movement was at first nearly imperceptible, then more pronounced. Kylie's eyelids fluttered.

This time Trent spoke more forcefully. "Open your eyes, Kylie."

Weezer clutched her folded hands to her chest.

The child's eyelids twitched again, but remained closed. Then they both noticed the fingers of her good hand bend feebly in an effort to clutch the sheet.

Trent looked up at Weezer. "Oh, please."

"I'll get the nurse," she said, "and Libby." As she left the room, she heard a noise like a stifled sneeze and realized it was Trent, gulping back his tears of relief.

She had barely reached the door when she heard another sound—a quavering whisper full of love. "Daddy?"

LIBBY LOOKED UP as Weezer entered the waiting room, a broad smile on her face. "Come."

Holding her breath against hope, Libby moved quickly toward the older woman. "Kylie?"

"She's conscious."

Like a deflating balloon, Libby released her breath.

Weezer put an arm around Libby's waist. "Come see for yourself."

"Is she all right?"

"They've called the doctor. We won't know anything for sure for a while. But she certainly recognized her daddy."

Only a desperate need to see Kylie propelled Libby toward the room. She didn't know how she could face Trent, but she had to.

Weezer ushered her into the room. A shaft of sunlight made a stripe across the white bedspread where Trent sat, holding Kylie's hand.

"She's resting," he said, his eyes glazed with emotion.

Libby approached Kylie. "Honey, it's Miss Cameron. Can you hear me?"

Kylie's eyelids slowly opened. A sweet smile formed on her lips. "Hi," she said in a weak voice before her eyes closed again.

Libby steadied herself against the bed. Never had a greeting filled her with such gratitude. "Bless her heart."

Weezer approached and beamed down at Kylie. "It's been quite a night, but all will be well with time." Then she glanced from Trent to Libby. "You two are exhausted. Why don't you let me stay with her. Go home, get some rest. Come back later."

"No," Trent said. "I want to talk with the doctor. And I need to wait until the Chisholms get here."

Libby's stomach did a somersault. She'd nearly forgotten about them. She gave a faint shrug. If Trent couldn't forgive her, it hardly mattered what the Chisholms thought.

"Go on, Libby." Trent's words would have been a comfort had they been offered with solicitude, but a drill sergeant could not have made the directive more clear.

"Okay," she said, then bent and laid a kiss on Kylie's cheek. "Could I come back later?"

She noticed Weezer do a quiet double take at the question, then glance quickly at Trent.

"Kylie will expect you," was all he said.

Resigned to his censure, she started to leave the room, when she heard him add something else. "And so will I."

She clutched on to those words as she headed for the parking lot. Call it wishful thinking, but maybe, just maybe, there was still hope.

But only if she told the truth.

And that meant living through the pain she'd locked away for years.

As THEY PULLED INTO the outskirts of Kalispell, Georgia dabbed at her eyes. "An accident. And all because of going skiing. I still can't believe it. We told Trent how we felt about endangering Kylie like that."

Gus concentrated on his driving. "Speak for yourself. You told him how *you* felt about it. Besides, it wasn't a skiing accident. She fell in the parking lot. She's a kid, Georgia. These things happen. You don't want her to be protected like a hothouse flower, do you?"

At this moment, a "hothouse flower" sounded far better than a girl lying seriously injured in a hospital bed. "It's just so like him."

"What?"

"To go off on his own like that. To entrust her care to someone else."

"The someone else was Libby Cameron, a highly responsible adult. And you make it sound like he frivolously went off on his own. According to the news report, he was helping rescue two people from certain death."

Georgia stared straight ahead, oblivious to the never-ending stream of franchise businesses lining the highway, willing the hospital to materialize. Fear lodged in her chest like a knife. If only Gus weren't so reasonable. Just once couldn't he raise his voice and yell at Trent and that woman the way she herself longed to? "Say what you want, but if anything happens to our Kylie—"

"What? You'll blame Trent?"

She shrugged. "Yes. It will be on his head."

"Just like Ashley?"

She snapped around to face him. "What's that supposed to mean?"

His jaw worked, but he kept his eyes trained on the road ahead. "You never accepted Trent. I'm wondering whether, somehow, you've blamed him for Ashley's death?"

Georgia tightened her bony fingers around the rigid clasp of her purse. "Are you out of your mind?" She let out a feeble laugh that sounded more like a snort. "As if Trent could control leukemia."

"I meant that somehow, in your mind, you figure everything would have been all right if she'd married a different man."

It was irrational, Georgia knew, biting her lip, but she had never stopped asking the futile questions. What if Ashley had married that nice Browning Lafferty and moved to Denver? What if there had been some vile toxic substance in the walls of that dreadful condo where Trent and Ashley had lived? And now, would Kylie be lying in a hospital bed if Trent hadn't moved with her to Whitefish? Had never interested her in skiing?

She closed her eyes, anger and insight warring within her. Although she didn't like what her husband was suggesting, a dreadful truth lay at the root of his question. She wasn't that awful a person, was she? *Had* she made Trent the scapegoat for everything bad that had happened?

Gus drove on in silence. Up ahead, Georgia saw the blue-and-white sign directing them toward the hospital. Her heart seized up in her chest.

After a few blocks, Gus spoke again. "Trent doesn't need our anger or our judgment. He's undoubtedly been through hell."

Images of her beautiful, laughing Ashley flitted through Georgia's mind, then froze on one frame in particular. The absolute radiance on her daughter's face the day she told her mother she was pregnant with the child of "the only man I will ever love."

A tear trickled down Georgia's cheek and her mouth tasted salty. Only then did Gus look at her, his eyes full of an intuitive kind of understanding. "What they need, sweetheart, is our love."

"I know," she murmured, wondering why all these bad things had happened.

Then, as if the matter was settled, he patted her leg. "You have a lot of it to give, and here is as good a place as any to start."

With that, he wheeled into the hospital parking lot. And for reasons she couldn't explain, especially since she hadn't yet seen her granddaughter, Georgia felt calmer, lighter than she had in years.

LIBBY HUDDLED in her bed, the shades drawn against the harsh sunlight, Mona curled at her side. A bracing shower had done little to relieve her body of its aches and pains, and there was no balm for her soul, except for the fact that Kylie was better. Shivering, she clutched the blankets around her and adjusted her pillow for the fifth or sixth time. She couldn't get comfortable. Couldn't shut down her mind.

She rolled over on her back, folding her hands across the flat of her stomach, her only comfort the warmth of Mona's body. She knew now she'd deluded herself that she had put her anger at the senator and her own overriding guilt behind her. Could she actually have thought she'd paid for her sins? That a lifetime devoted to loving and teaching children served as suitable atonement?

And what about Trent? She curled into a fetal position. She had been so high and mighty, so sure she was right, that she could judge him and find him lacking. If the situation weren't so tragic, it would be laughable.

Had she been living in never-never land? Where everything came up roses and people actually did fly over the rainbow?

The illusion of the happy family.

She thought of the baby book buried in the cedar chest. Of the thwarted dreams of the naive eighteen-year-old she had been. Of her stepfather and his arrogant assumption he knew what was best for her.

And of the only thing that had saved her—

Trent. The man she had cast off because of her own misguided self-righteousness.

Even if he didn't blame her for the accident, she needed his forgiveness for so many other things. It was asking a lot from a man she'd once dismissed as selfish and pleasure-loving. The father she'd observed at Kylie's bedside tonight proved he was so much more.

She reached for a tissue and let herself weep into the pillow, a much-needed physical release that did nothing to soothe her soul.

Finally, cried out and exhausted, she felt her eyes close and her breathing slow as she welcomed the escape of sleep.

At first, when the phone jangled in her ear, she started up, sure it was the school dismissal bell. Where were the children? Why weren't they lining up? She rubbed her eyes and fell back against the pillow. The bell rang again. Where…? What…?

Then, reluctantly, she realized she was in her room, that only three hours had passed since she'd climbed into bed, and that someone was calling her. With a stutter of her heart, she grabbed the phone as Mona hopped to the floor. It could be the hospital. Something might have happened. "Hello?" she said, placing the receiver against her ear.

"Miss Cameron?" The voice sounded vaguely familiar, but she couldn't place it.

"Speaking." If it was a telemarketer, he was going to get an earful he wouldn't soon forget.

"Jeremy Kantor here. We spoke earlier about a possible interview."

Libby closed her eyes, dumbfounded. Not now. Not when everything was crumbling around her. "I remember," she croaked.

"I'm in Oklahoma City concluding my research here. If it works with your schedule, I'd like to talk with you Tuesday or Wednesday."

"This week?"

"Yes. I plan to fly to Missoula and rent a car. We could work out a mutually convenient time."

Her instinct was to postpone the meeting. And yet, since she didn't plan to tell him anything of significance, she might as well remove this one thorn from her side. There were plenty of others festering there. "Tuesday," she said dully, "after school at my house. Do you have that address?"

"Yes, I do. Will four-thirty work for you?"

"I'll be here."

She slipped the receiver back in its cradle, then collapsed against the pillow. It was lucky for the Honorable Vernon G. Belton that the interview wasn't happening right now, when it would be tempting to tell the whole truth.

But she'd long ago promised she wouldn't. Besides, she mocked herself, she was only too practiced at dissembling.

CHAPTER THIRTEEN

IT WAS NEARLY DUSK when Trent roused from a deep sleep. The cabin was dark and empty without Kylie. Groggily, he sat up and swung his legs over the edge of the bed. The events of the past twenty-four hours swirled in his brain, each one a drama in its own right, but nothing compared with the overwhelming relief he'd experienced when Dr. Coker gave him the news that Kylie would, most likely, recover completely. It was with reluctance that he'd left the hospital—and then only because Georgia and Gus were staying with Kylie.

As he lurched to his feet, he shook his head in bewilderment. He'd expected Georgia to give him an earful for allowing Libby to take Kylie skiing. He'd prepared nothing in his defense, knowing he deserved the full brunt of her anger and blame. Instead, to his amazement, she had entered the room, gone immediately to Kylie, who greeted her with the single word *Grandma*. When she turned to him it was with kindness, not indictment. "I'm so sorry, Trent. You must have been beside yourself with worry."

Her unexpected generosity had put him at a loss for words.

Then Gus had laid a hand on his shoulder. "Son, it's going to be all right."

"We're here to help for as long as you need us," Georgia added, and Trent remembered being overwhelmed by a sense of relief, despite his confusion about Georgia's uncharacteristic kindness.

When he and Weezer left the hospital together, she had stopped him in the parking lot. "Trent, has something happened with Libby?"

The glare off the snow hurt his eyes. He reached in his pocket and put on his dark glasses. By way of answer, he merely nodded.

"You're tired now. Get some rest. But don't wait too long to see her. You need each other now more than ever."

Weezer's words continued to challenge him as he made his way toward the shower. He knew she was right. Yet he dreaded what he might find out when he talked with Libby. Beyond the miscarriage he knew about, had he fallen short in other ways? Or had their marriage been based on half truths? Was it even possible to start over?

Under the shower's pelting spray, he did come

to one realization. If Libby had kept something from him, she must have had her reasons. From the look on her face when she bolted from the hospital room, whatever lay behind that one word *babies* was eating her up. If he loved her, and he did, he would listen with his heart.

Something he had not done the day she had miscarried their child.

AFTER JEREMY KANTOR'S call, Libby knew it was useless to go back to bed. Instead, she phoned Mary to tell her about Kylie's accident. Although Mary urged her to stay home from school the next day, Libby knew she couldn't accept the offer. Her sole escape from painful memories and the anguish of the present lay in the nonstop activity of her second-graders.

She showered, washed her hair, dressed in navy slacks and a red pullover, then set out for the hospital, knowing she couldn't function until she had seen Kylie again and reassured herself about her condition. She couldn't even bring herself to think about Trent.

It was a brilliant winter day. Hemlock and spruce trees stood in stark contrast to the azure sky and bleached white of the snow-blanketed mountains. Outside the hospital, Libby drew in deep, cleansing breaths of the pure Montana air, bracing herself for whatever awaited her inside. Trent? The Chisholms? Bad news?

When she peered around Kylie's half-open door, she saw Gus Chisholm sitting in the corner recliner with his head back and eyes closed. Georgia was standing over her granddaughter, singing a soft, off-key version of "Hush, Little Baby."

Tears started to Libby's eyes. The look on Georgia's face conveyed pure love, and the song she crooned was one Libby's mother had often sung to her.

"'...and you'll still be the sweetest baby in town.'" When the last note died, Georgia turned slowly toward the door. "Hello, Libby," she said quietly.

Libby ventured closer. "How is she?"

To Libby's amazement, Georgia reached across the bed and took hold of her hand. Nodding encouragement, she smiled. "She's going to be fine."

"I'm so glad," Libby breathed, helpless to prevent her tears. Wiping her cheek with her free hand, she looked into the older woman's eyes. "I'm so very sorry."

Georgia withdrew her fingers from Libby's grasp and pulled the sheet up closer around Kylie's shoulders. "I held you responsible at first," she said, her attention fixed on her granddaughter.

Libby struggled to gain control of her emotions. "I don't blame you."

"Yet when I heard what happened, I doubt whether even Trent could have stopped her."

A low voice came from the corner. "It was an accident," Gus said.

Georgia nodded. "After Ashley died, I had a desperate need to control my life by trying to protect Kylie—to protect myself from being hurt again. I now know that's an impossibility." She paused to regain control, then smiled tremulously. "Kylie's been asking for you."

"She has?"

"Yes. You are obviously very important to her." Georgia hesitated, as if drawing courage for what she needed to say next. "And if you're important to her, you're important to us."

Libby's ears rang, and a wave of dizziness engulfed her. They were *forgiving* her? All she could say by way of response was what was in her heart. "I love Kylie."

Behind her, Gus rose to his feet. "Young lady, I think I speak for both of us when I say we're more than willing to let you be part of our granddaughter's life."

Before, that might have been possible. Once, those words would have filled her with joy.

Now? It was up to Trent. "Thank you" was all she could manage by way of response.

She approached the bed and laid her hand gently on Kylie's cheek. "Take care, honey. Do what the doctor says. All of us at school will miss you." Her voice choked. "I will miss you." Then she turned and, nodding to the Chisholms, left the room, anxiety, regret and sadness compounding her exhaustion.

No VISITORS WERE in the room when Trent arrived at the hospital, but Kylie was awake and asking all kinds of questions. She couldn't remember the accident itself, only that Bart Ames had dared her to race. "I almost beat him, Daddy. I'll do it next time."

The "next time" filled Trent with relief, as well as a measure of dread. "But it'll be a while before you're racing boys and skiing again."

"I know. My arm." She rubbed her cast with her free hand. "But after that?" She looked up, eyes full of hope. "I did the ski jump, you know."

"Okay, when you're well, we'll try skiing again."

"Sounds like she's a chip off the old block."

Trent turned around. Gus stood in the doorway, a big grin on his face. "There must be a streak of daring in your family."

"Some call it stubbornness."

"That, too."

"Hi, Grandpa."

Trent stood aside to let Gus approach Kylie.

"Hi there, honey. How're you feeling?"

"My head hurts. And my arm a little."

Gus picked up her hand. "That's natural."

"Where's Grandma?"

"She stepped down the hall for a minute."

"I want to see her."

"Here I am, sweetheart." Georgia entered the room, setting two cups of coffee on the bed table.

"Did you bring me a Barbie?"

Georgia's laugh tumbled out. "You're shameless. Not today. But tomorrow, I promise."

"Sounds as if she's getting back to normal," Trent said with a grin.

Gus leaned against the closet door, his arms folded across his chest. "Your Libby was here earlier."

He couldn't be sure, but Trent thought he heard approval in Gus's words. "I'm sorry I missed her."

"Weezer McCann told us Libby was here all night with Kylie."

"She was."

"Daddy?"

Trent turned back to Kylie. "What, sweetie?"

"I love Miss Cameron."

Trent didn't know what to say. All bets were off for the moment, at least until he saw Libby.

Stepping forward, Gus put his arm around his wife. "I think our granddaughter just said a mouthful, don't you, sweetheart?"

Georgia's face, usually so perfectly composed, betrayed an internal struggle. "Trent, you know I had a difficult time accepting you as a son-in-law, but in the long run, you made Ashley happy. Kylie adores you." She cleared her throat. "You deserve happiness. I won't stand in your way."

Her words were so unexpected, Trent was afraid he might be misinterpreting the signals. The Chisholms seemed to be offering tacit approval. Before he could frame an answer, Gus went on. "Nothing is more important to us than Kylie's happiness." He gazed directly at Trent, as if communicating more than the mere words. "Whatever may be involved."

Overcome with emotion, Trent nodded, then found his voice. "I appreciate that."

Georgia drew away from her husband. "All right, then. That's settled." She picked up the two cups. "Now, who wants coffee?"

"Not me," Kylie said, and they all laughed.

LACEY DIDN'T MINCE WORDS Monday morning. "Miz Cameron, are you sick? You look terrible."

And to think one of the reasons Libby loved teaching was the refreshing honesty of her students. "No, honey, just tired." Weary as she was, she'd still had trouble falling asleep last night, especially after Trent's phone call. They had talked only briefly, tension underlying every word. After an especially awkward pause, Libby had said, "I know we need to clear the air."

"I have some serious questions," he'd said.

Libby had sighed, acknowledging her responsibility to give him some serious answers. Finally they had agreed he would come over tonight after hospital visiting hours. When she'd offered to postpone their meeting, he'd declined. "I don't think this can wait."

The students, sensing her edginess and worried themselves about Kylie, were subdued. Bart was especially cooperative, as if good behavior could somehow atone for his role in the accident. Several times during the morning, Lois and Mary popped in to check on her. At noon, Libby called the hospital and learned from Georgia that Kylie was doing so well she might be discharged within the next twenty-four hours. But throughout the day, Libby was aware she was only half-present with the children. The other half of her kept tiptoeing into the past, then retreating—the need to unburden herself overpowering, yet terrifying.

If she could have, she would have slowed the hands of the wall clock, delaying her meeting with Trent as long as possible. That way she could cling to the illusion that she and Trent and Kylie could form a family. Regardless of the outcome of their conversation, she knew one thing with certainty. She would never stop loving him.

FINALLY, late in the afternoon, Trent was able to stop by the office. It seemed a lifetime ago that he and Chad had sat side by side in the rescue chopper. When his partner saw him, he crossed the room and wrapped Trent in a bear hug. "Man, you've been through the ringer. How's Kylie?"

Trent gave him the update, then added, "I've never been so scared in my life."

"It's a helpless feeling, isn't it? We're used to being able to fix things."

Trent hoisted himself up on the counter, legs dangling. "I couldn't fix Ashley. To have lost Kylie, well…" His voice trailed off.

"From what you say, the news sounds encouraging."

"We're not totally out of the woods yet, but it

could've been so much worse. I stopped by to, you know, apologize for not being able to come to work. It may be a few days."

"Baker, give me some credit. Nothing is more important than family. We'll pull it all together here." Chad tossed a clipboard at Trent. "There's some more good news. Take a look. Two bookings for July. Partner, I think we're in business."

"That's great. Maybe this day's ending better than it began."

Chad studied him, eyes narrowed in suspicion. "You don't sound convinced. What's up?"

"Lib."

"Man, you don't blame her, do you?"

Trent shook his head. "No. But…" Again he didn't have the words. "Something's come up," he finished lamely.

"Well, whatever it is, get it straightened out. The sooner the better. You don't need any more stress."

"Tell me about it."

"What I'm gonna tell you is that the woman's good for you. So whatever it takes—compromise or apology—don't screw this up."

Easing off the counter, Trent clapped an arm around Chad's shoulder. "Thanks for being my friend."

"That's easy. Now go on home or back to the

hospital or wherever. But whatever this thing is
with Libby, settle it."

When Trent left the office, he headed back
to the hospital, preoccupied with Chad's advice.
Settle it. His stomach tightened. Tonight would
tell the tale.

AT DINNER, Libby could hardly eat a bite. Sensing something was wrong, Mona stayed close
beside her, rubbing against her legs, then jumping up on the table when she started to grade
papers. But it was useless trying to work. Her
thoughts kept turning to the loneliness of her
senior year in high school when Daddy was
more often than not out campaigning in his
first senate race. To Libby, their home had never
seemed so remote, imposing or silent.

Spring had come early to Oklahoma that
year—the redbuds a riot of color, daffodils and
tulips brightening the lawns. Ever after Libby
would associate the fragrance of lilacs with that
one ethereally beautiful moonlit night when
every strand of hair, every pore of her skin,
every hormone stirred with possibility.

Long ago she had destroyed every photograph
of herself in her prom dress.

Determined, she turned back to the worksheets in front of her. Just as she finished mark-
ing Rory's, noting a degree of improvement in

his work, the knock came on the door. In that instant she froze, knowing that the next hour could well determine her entire future. All her efforts to rehearse her explanation had been in vain. No matter how she tried, she couldn't find the words to bridge the gulf formed by her secretiveness.

When Trent knocked a second time, she slowly roused herself and headed for the front of the house. Opening the door, she realized nothing could have prepared her for the jolt of yearning coursing through her when she saw him standing there so tall and strong, his jaw resolute, his eyes full of questions. "Come in," she said, not trusting her voice to say more.

He rubbed a hand up and down her arm. "Hi, there."

The cold air filling the entry hall brought her to her senses and she closed the door.

She started for the living room. "How's Kylie tonight? She seemed better when I stopped in after school."

"Tired, but eager to get home."

Trent sat on the sofa and Libby sank to the floor, her back against the armchair. Mona crept quietly across the room and settled into her lap, her warm body and soft purr comforting.

With strident urgency, the cuckoo clock struck, and for once, Libby had an impulse to pull it off the wall and silence it permanently. The way she had silenced herself.

"Lib?"

She slowly raised her head and looked at Trent, who leaned forward, his hands clasped between his knees. "I'm here to listen. But before you tell me, I want you to know one thing. There is nothing you can say or do to make me stop loving you."

A huge lump formed in her throat. "Don't be too sure."

"I want you to start at the beginning."

Where was that? When her mother had married Vernon Belton, a man Libby was reasonably certain she hadn't loved? The day her mother died? Or the winter when, desperate for companionship and love, she had begun to date Brett Perry?

No, the secret she'd kept all these years had been born out of her stepfather's insistence that no pregnancy was going to interfere with his political ambitions. With irony, Libby noted her Freudian slip. The secret *born*. If only.

She glanced up again, her lip trembling. Quietly, Trent slid to the floor, sitting opposite her, his long legs stretched beside hers. Only when he laid a calming hand on her ankle did she dare speak.

"I—I couldn't tell you before. Couldn't tell anyone." Then she fell silent.

"Couldn't tell me what?"

Desperate to avoid the question in his eyes, she looked around the room, but knew the moment could no longer be avoided. "About my other baby."

She heard him release a long sigh. "I thought so. What happened?"

"The spring of my senior year in high school, I fell for a boy in my class. We thought we were so in love…so we got married, secretly. Not long after I found out I was pregnant."

She paused, remembering how desperately she had wanted to be included with the in crowd, to have someone love her. She and Brett had run off and tied the knot just before the prom. And when she discovered she was pregnant, she had pictured her future—a loving husband and then a tiny, perfect infant.

"What happened?"

She sent him an arch look. "Two days after learning we were going to have a baby, he walked out. Suddenly Brett wanted nothing to do with me and certainly not with a 'stupid kid,' as he so aptly put it. He had big plans. University, then law school. He couldn't be saddled with a child—or with me."

"Sorry," Trent muttered.

"Oh, it gets better." She realized she was unleashing a flood of bitterness, but nothing could stop the flow of words. "Neither could my ambitious stepfather be handicapped by what he saw as a stain on the family honor. What if the media got wind of my predicament? He more or less bought off Brett and his family, arranged for the marriage to be 'undone,' then gave me an ultimatum. Have the baby in secret and give it up for adoption or forget about money for college."

Trent's mouth dropped open and his cheeks turned crimson. "Lib—"

"Please. Let me finish. All I'd ever wanted in my life was to be a wife and mother. To have children who would know they were loved and accepted. Brett's actions were cowardly and base, but I got over that. All I wanted was my baby. And I vowed to do anything I could to keep my child. Even if that meant going up against Daddy—" she choked out the name "—Belton. Quiet, docile little Libby put up a fight."

"But you didn't have any leverage."

She smirked, remembering. "Oh, I was desperate, but not stupid. I threatened to expose everything to the local newspapers. That sort of thing wouldn't have gone over very well in our conservative congressional district."

He started to move toward her, but she held up her hand. "There's more." She couldn't let him comfort her. Not now. She had to purge herself of memories she had entombed for years. "I agreed to go someplace far away and have the baby. He assumed I would give it up for adoption." She remembered the scene in his home office when the life of her unborn baby was reduced to a business agreement. "He told me I could never mention my 'shame' to another person, or attempt to find my child so long as my stepfather held public office." She shrugged. "I moved to Oregon three days later."

Mona stretched, then crept over and settled on Trent's legs, but he seemed oblivious to her.

"The baby...?"

Until now, Libby hadn't realized she was crying. She swiped at an errant tear, then shook her head. "He didn't make it."

"What do you mean?"

As if in a classic black-and-white movie, the doctor's grim face loomed over her again, the delivery room behind him ominous with the unrelieved gleam of white and stainless steel. The doctor's clipped "Sorry" still haunted her nightmares. "Your son is dead."

Lost in her thoughts, she hadn't realized Trent had moved beside her until he gathered her in his arms. "He was stillborn at six and a half months."

"Oh, no." Trent's wail nearly deafened her.

"I was there in Oregon all by myself."

He cradled her, rocking back and forth, his head bent to hers. How long they sat that way, drawing from each other's pain, she didn't know. Her heart ached with her losses and her tears seemed endless. But slowly she came to realize they were not her tears alone. Trent's were mingled with them. At last, with a mournful sigh, he drew back, framing her face in his hands. "Why didn't you tell me?"

"I—I couldn't." She cast her mind back, trying to remember why she hadn't. "Out there in Oregon, I made a choice. I would have as little as possible to do with my stepfather from that point on, but I would most certainly let him pay for my education. That's how I ended up at Montana State. I vowed I would start my life from that point, never looking back, never acknowledging the neglect and loneliness and heartache of the past. I would be just like any other carefree coed. It was the only way I survived those first awful months afterward. I've spent years keeping that secret, even from myself. Otherwise, I would have fallen to pieces."

"So when you got pregnant with our baby…?"

"It was as if I'd been given a whole new chance, a whole new life. I had a husband who loved me and a child on the way. My dream of family was coming true at last. You can't imagine how happy I was."

"And I was too insensitive to get it."

She laid her head in the crook of his shoulder. "We were young, Trent. So very young. Besides, how could you have known?"

Emotionally and physically spent, she comforted herself with listening to the steady beat of his heart, relieved there was nothing more to tell, but knowing that for a lifetime she would mourn her lost babies.

WHEN LIBBY EXCUSED herself to go to the bathroom, Trent stood up, working the kinks out of his legs. But he couldn't work the kinks out of his mind. What a shallow, unfeeling jerk he had been. And what did it say of him then that she hadn't been able to confide in him? What kind of marriage had they really had?

He paced from the fireplace to the window, fury building inside him. Senator Belton was a real piece of work! Selfish, egotistical—there weren't enough adjectives in the book. His behavior was inexcusable. Trent thought of Kylie. What if someone treated her so callously?

The wonder of it was that Libby had come out

of her experiences still able to love his daughter unconditionally and all those other children lucky enough to have her for a teacher.

He wanted to be the man she loved so completely, and he would spend a lifetime proving to her that although he had been the wrong man for her all those years ago, he was the right one now.

When she entered the room, her face was devoid of makeup and freshly scrubbed. Despite the redness of her eyes, she managed a soft smile and walked into his waiting arms. "I should have told you, Trent. Don't blame yourself for what happened back then." She snuggled closer. "And I want you to know one other thing. I love Kylie. Not because she represents the children I couldn't have, but because she's so special." She paused, then looked up at him with such love it nearly blew him away. "And because she's part of you, the man I will always love."

He felt the same rush he experienced after scaling a fourteen-thousand-foot peak. "I love you, too." He kissed her lightly. "I'm not that same old guy, you know."

"I know," she said. "Nor am I that same frightened girl." She ran her hand through his hair. "I promised Kylie. Now it's your turn. Trent, honey, I will always tell you the truth."

He clutched her to him. "Marry me, Lib. Again."

Before she threw her arms around him, she chuckled, then uttered the most welcome words he'd ever heard: "How soon?"

CHAPTER FOURTEEN

GEORGIA SAT QUIETLY in the corner working a cross-stitch piece while Kylie slept. Gus and Trent were in the hospital cafeteria eating breakfast. From the hallway she could hear the clatter of meal carts and the distant hum of a floor waxer. The heater kicked on, sending a blast of warm air against the cold window.

After a good night, Kylie had awakened ravenous. Yesterday she had complained of a headache and had slept a great deal, but this morning she'd been talkative until, finally tiring, she'd dozed off. She was determined to ski again, she had told her grandmother, and Georgia had decided not to fight her. Kylie was, after all, Trent's daughter, and perhaps it had been his very zest for adventure that had attracted Ashley to him in the first place. She could hardly fight nature or nurture. Besides, she'd come to understand that accidents could happen anywhere—skiing or simply crossing a street.

Her thoughts turned to the disturbing question with which Gus had confronted her Sunday.

He had been pretty rough on her, accusing her of making Trent a scapegoat for all the disappointments and tragedies in her life. In a way, maybe that was what she had done with her father, as well—blamed him for all the deprivations she'd experienced as a child. Had she done the same thing with Trent—let anger and resentment, even her selfishness, compound her grief? Could she move beyond her own sense of loss? Glancing at Kylie's still form on the bed, she reproached herself. Life in a hothouse wasn't really living. Her beloved daughter had died far too young, and now this accident had brought home, in a way nothing else could have, how much she could still lose and how precious were the years remaining to her. Those years needed to be *lived*.

Trent and Kylie had a long future ahead of them. Georgia stirred in her seat and, for a moment, let her hands fall idle in her lap. She wanted them to be happy, fulfilled. Ashley would have wanted that for them, too.

If she were honest with herself, she had no reason to object to Libby Cameron, other than the fact she and Trent had been married before, yet Georgia had never seen the slightest evidence that he had carried a torch for her into his marriage with Ashley. No. He had been devoted to Ashley, and his grief at her death had been genuine and heartbreaking. Last night in their bed at the lodge, Gus had reminded her that people change and grow. "Even us," he'd said, chucking her under the chin before he drew her into his arms, where she fell asleep, secure in his love.

"Grandma?" Kylie's voice sounded sleepy.

Georgia set her needlework aside and moved to the bed. "I'm right here."

"I had a dream." She yawned. "Mommy was in it. She was so beautiful."

"I can just imagine."

"Know who else was in my dream?"

"Tell me."

"Miss Cameron."

"What were they doing?"

"Mommy had a crown. You know, like the Barbie princess. And she was putting it on Miss Cameron's head. She looked pretty, too."

Georgia sat on the edge of the bed and raised Kylie's fingers to her lips. "It sounds like a wonderful dream."

"It was." Kylie closed her eyes, a smile hovering on her lips.

Georgia's heart rose in her throat. If Kylie needed a new mother, it was not her place to stand in the way.

"You know what? Miss Cameron doesn't have a mommy." Kylie's eyes opened again and she studied her grandmother soberly. "She was little just like me when her mommy died."

"How do you know that?"

"She talks to me. We're friends." Kylie cocked her head. "She could be your friend, too, if you want."

Even if Georgia spent the rest of her life lavishing all the Barbie dolls in the world on Kylie, it wouldn't be enough. What she needed to give her granddaughter was a loving stepmother.

"What're you gals doing?" Gus stepped into the room, trailed by Trent.

"Talking, of course," Kylie said.

Georgia turned to her husband. "Could you give me the car keys?"

He looked startled. "Are you going somewhere?"

"Yes. To Kylie's school, if Trent will give me directions."

"Sure," Trent said. "But can I save you the trip?"

"No. This is something I have to do. I'm going to see Libby."

Trent turned to Gus, as if looking for answers, but the older man merely shrugged. "She'll probably be in class."

"That's all right," Georgia said, picking up her coat and purse. "I'll wait."

After drawing a map on the hospital scratch

pad, Trent tore the page off and handed it to her with a word of explanation.

Georgia glanced at Kylie. "Bye, honey, I'll be back in a little while." Then she breezed past them, a mischievous grin tugging at her lips. She hadn't set foot in an elementary-school classroom in years.

Hurrying down the hall, she felt immense satisfaction. For the first time in many months, her heart soared on the wings of promise.

LIBBY SAT at her desk, lulled by the sound of the movie the class was watching. The life cycle of honey bees had failed to keep her interest. She'd floated through the day in a daze, relief that Trent could forgive her almost palpable. She couldn't have asked for a man to be more understanding. Maybe she hadn't given him a chance all those years ago, or maybe life had taught them both the lesson of trust. Whatever the case, he had made her feel loved and protected.

In fact, she might be totally at ease, were it not for this afternoon's meeting with Jeremy Kantor, the one dark cloud in an otherwise beautiful day.

"…honeybees are very good housekeepers. Their hives…"

Libby felt a small hand on her shoulder. She opened her eyes, embarrassed that maybe she had dozed off. Lacey patted her. "Miz Cameron, look. There's a lady at the door."

When Libby wheeled around in her chair, expecting to see the secretary or maybe Mary or Lois, her eyes widened in surprise. Georgia Chisholm?

She rose and greeted her quietly. "Georgia? Is something wrong with Kylie?"

"No, indeed." Georgia held her coat over her arm. She nodded toward an empty chair by the reading table. "I came to visit. Do you mind?"

"Certainly not, but—"

"Do you have a recess or lunch break soon?"

"The children will be going out for recess in a few minutes."

"Good. I'd like to talk with you. What I have to say won't take long."

"Very well." Libby escorted her to the empty chair.

Libby settled at her desk once again, attempting to appear interested in the film. Parents and relatives were encouraged to visit the classrooms, but she was ill prepared for Georgia Chisholm, dressed immaculately in a designer sweater and trim slacks. Kylie's grandmother looked out of place in the child-size chair, her attention seemingly fixated on the life cycle of bees. Libby studied her, seeking any clue to her purpose for being here.

Nothing she'd imagined could have prepared her for the first words out of Georgia's mouth once she'd sent the children out for recess. "I want to apologize," Georgia announced.

"What for?" Libby asked, joining her at the reading table.

The older woman straightened the neck of her sweater, then leaned forward. "For being a bitter old lady."

Something important was happening here, Libby realized. But before she could say anything, Georgia went on.

"Tell me about your growing up."

Libby didn't know what she'd expected, but not this. The dilemma was in knowing how much to reveal, but as she looked into Georgia's empathetic eyes, she realized it would be safe to admit to the pain of those excruciating years. She talked for several minutes about her father and mother's deaths, about feeling like a misfit in school and about her stepfather's indifference to her in the face of his political ambitions.

"You loved your mother a great deal," Georgia said when she finished.

Libby lifted her head and stared out the window at the faraway peaks, missing her mother, even after all these years, with an acute longing. She turned back to Georgia. "Yes," she said.

"Kylie told me she had talked with you about Ashley."

"Kylie and I have much in common."

"I imagine you have a strong desire for a family."

Once again the conversation had taken an unexpected turn. What did she have to lose by baring her soul? "You are very perceptive. All my life I've dreamed of being part of a happy, loving family." She sighed. "Maybe it's nothing more than a pipe dream. But I long to be a mother, to have children. To spend my life with the man I love…" She trailed off, the pressure in her chest making it difficult to continue.

Georgia laid a hand on hers. "Is Trent that man, Libby?"

In the older woman's gaze was a compelling urgency. "Yes," she said.

"Good." Georgia sat back, as if relieved. Absently, she picked up a primer from the stack on the table, running her hands over the cover before setting it down again. "In my bitterness and grief, I have been guilty of being judgmental. Of Trent…and of you."

"I would never try to take Ashley's place."

"I know that now. But in a way, strange as it may seem, I want you to."

From the hall, Libby heard the giggles of children. "I don't understand."

"You have no mother. I have no daughter. Kylie needs a family." Georgia blinked rapidly. "She needs a mother. I see now what I couldn't see before. She wants you." Georgia held up a hand when Libby tried to say something. "Wait. Let me finish." She collected her thoughts, then said, "*I* want you."

Libby's cheeks flushed with a tide of emotions—all of them welcome. "A family?" Her eyes filled.

"A family. You, Trent, Kylie, Gus and me. Sometimes we aren't blessed with the families we wish for, just the ones we're given. And we have a choice." Again she laid a hand on Libby's. "Mine is to build something wonderful out of what *is,* and not merely for Kylie's sake. For all of us."

Libby slipped out of her chair and knelt beside Georgia. "Are you sure?" she said breathlessly.

"Positive." The older woman put an arm around Libby's shoulder in a way that made her feel cherished. "Welcome home, Libby."

"Are you sick?" Bart Ames's unmistakable voice interrupted the moment.

"Yeah, Miz Cameron," another child added, "is that lady a nurse?"

Libby gave Georgia a knowing smile, then got to her feet and faced the curious second-graders. "She's not a nurse, boys and girls, she's my new mother."

"Huh?" Bart looked totally flummoxed.

"Yes, children," Georgia said, standing beside Libby. "Sometimes families aren't born, they're made."

"Whatever." Bart made an adults-are-so-weird face, then led the charge into the room.

"I'll see you later," Georgia said, then slipped from the room, leaving Libby so overcome with emotion it was all she could do to restore order to the classroom.

AT FOUR-FIFTEEN, Libby arrived home. This should have been a day of joyous celebration. Georgia had accepted her, Kylie would be released from the hospital in the morning, Trent loved her despite the past, and she had learned an important lesson about self-revelation and trust.

But in fifteen minutes, Jeremy Kantor would appear on her doorstep, probing, digging, cross-examining. And she still had no idea how she would handle him. Or whether she had reached a point where she could forgive Daddy.

When the doorbell rang, she stood in the middle of the living room, panic edging its way into her thoughts. She squared her shoulders. This issue had to be faced. If not Jeremy Kantor, then it would be another reporter.

As if watching herself from a distance, she moved toward the door. *Okay,* she assured herself, *you can do this.*

But it wasn't the magazine reporter. It was Trent.

She was thrown off guard. "Trent?"

He grinned lazily. "You don't sound very glad to see me. Let's try this again." He closed the door and rang the bell again. She loved his playfulness, but his timing was awful.

She opened the door. "Trent...*darling?*"

"That's better," he said, crossing the threshold and giving her a hug. "I left work early and I'm headed for the hospital, but I wanted to see my best girl."

"You just surprised me, that's all."

"Were you expecting someone else?"

"As a matter of fact—" The bell pealed yet again.

Trent threw her a quizzical look, but remained where he was as she went to answer the door. Standing on the porch was an intense, dark-haired young man with longish hair and wire-rimmed glasses. "Mr. Kantor?"

"You must be Libby Cameron."

"Yes." She stood aside. "Please come in."

Libby introduced Trent, then added for his benefit, "Mr. Kantor is a reporter, here to get information for an article on Senator Belton."

Trent's mouth thinned. "I see."

"Please sit down." Libby gestured to the living room. "Both of you." She took her place in the sanctuary of her rocker. Mona crawled out from under the sofa and sniffed suspiciously at Jeremy Kantor's tasseled loafers. Reaching down, Libby scooped the cat into her lap, relieved to have something to occupy her hands.

"I appreciate your agreeing to see me. I have a few questions that shouldn't take too much of your time." The reporter pulled out a small tape recorder and set it on the table. "Do you mind if I record our interview?"

"Now, just a minute," Trent said.

Libby overrode him. "It's all right." And it was, because in that moment she knew what had to happen, knew with certainty that this moment had been a long time in coming. But now it was here, and she would say what had to be said. She turned to Trent and smiled. "It'll be fine."

"Well, let's get started then." Kantor flicked on the recorder. "Can you tell me about your mother's marriage to Senator Belton and something about your childhood in Muskogee?"

Libby obliged him without going into too

many of the details of her miserable loneliness after her mother died.

"How would you characterize your relationship back then with your stepfather?"

This time Libby couched her words carefully. "I had no physical needs that went unaddressed. He was generous in that regard. However, Vernon Belton was, and is, first and foremost a political animal, not a family man. I don't imagine being left with the responsibility of fathering a stepdaughter was part of his plan."

"So you weren't close?"

She sidestepped the question. "He was very busy."

"Did you ever feel neglected?"

"Not purposefully."

The reporter's eyes narrowed shrewdly. "But emotionally? You must've had lonely times. Am I correct it was only you, the senator and a housekeeper in the home?"

She answered his last question first. "Yes. But as for being lonely? I don't assign any blame for that." And, she realized, she didn't. "That was simply the way it was." Why hadn't she seen any of this before? That maybe Vernon Belton had simply done the best he could, given who he was.

"But is it fair to say you were never close?"

Out of the corner of her eye, she noticed Trent edging forward. "That would be fair."

Kantor pulled a notepad from his jacket pocket and thumbed through it, studied a page, then looked up. "According to one of my informants, once you left Muskogee after high school, you seldom returned. Is that accurate?"

"Yes."

"And you have never visited the senator in Washington?"

"Correct."

Trent glanced nervously at Libby, then turned to the reporter. "What are you driving at?"

Ignoring Trent, Kantor looked directly at Libby. "Miss Cameron, I notice you don't use the senator's name."

She stared right back at him. "I chose not to."

"But he'd adopted you, so you must've made that decision after you left home?"

"Yes."

"Why? Did something happen to cause an estrangement?"

What did she owe the Honorable Vernon G. Belton? Libby wondered. What did she owe herself?

"Yes."

Trent leaped up and took a step toward her, as if to protect her.

"No, Trent." She waved him back to his seat. "I know what I'm doing."

Kantor's eyes had taken on an almost feral gleam. "Once you moved west, it was as if you turned your back on your past."

"I did. You want the story? Here it is." To her amazement, once the words flowed, she grew increasingly calm. "Not all people are cut out to be parents. Vernon Belton was such a man. I have the utmost respect for his record of dedicated public service. The fact he couldn't be the father I needed or wanted, while regrettable, wasn't something either of us could do anything about.

"When I was a teenager, some of the things I lacked emotionally weren't his to provide, like acceptance by my peer group, boyfriends, that sort of thing." She paused to consider her next words, the crux of the matter. "I assume you'd like to know more about our estrangement. In fact, that's probably why you're here."

She sent a silent plea to Trent. *Don't stop me now.* She appreciated his need to protect her; in fact, it made her feel loved. But this was something she had to do.

"When I graduated from high school, my stepfather wanted to continue directing my life." She smiled ironically. "After all, he was used to doing that for his constituents, and he was good at it."

"And you rebelled?"

Libby could have kissed the reporter for putting the words into her mouth—and for believing them. "Could you blame me?" She laughed softly. "I needed to get away. Far away." *That wasn't even a white lie. It was the truth.* "We agreed that was best. He would provide funds for my education, I would follow my dreams. He would be free of responsibility for me. I could be myself, without the pressure of being a politician's daughter."

"But surely you harbor resentment about a childhood that sounds far from ideal?"

"*Ideal?* Mr. Kantor, surely you're not so naive as to believe there's such a thing as an ideal family?" She could hardly refrain from applauding her own epiphany. "My childhood was what it was, and it has shaped who I am. We don't get to choose our families—" amazingly she found herself echoing Georgia's wisdom "—but we have the opportunity to make our own. Unfortunately, the senator and I failed in that endeavor. I hope he can forgive me, because I have only very recently come to realize, I can forgive him."

"So are you saying you hope to heal the rift between you?"

Libby picked up Mona and snuggled her against her cheek. "I plan to try. But that's between him and me and not for public consumption."

Kantor reached out to turn off the recorder, but Libby stopped him. "I have one more thing to say."

"Shoot."

"The senator has been a conscientious public servant, responsible for some important legislation. Politics requires a person's lifeblood. Perhaps he was simply giving where he could. I hope from what I've said that you'll be left with a favorable opinion of both of us. Beyond that, I have no comment."

Kantor rose, followed by Trent. "Thank you, Miss Cameron. You've been most forthcoming."

"I'll see you to the door."

When she returned to the living room, Trent was standing by the fireplace, looking so at home it made her heart soar. "Did you really mean all of that?" he asked, his tone incredulous.

She walked closer. "I meant every word. Life is too short to carry around bitterness and resentment, particularly about things you can't change."

"Come here, woman." He held out his arms,

and when she walked into his embrace, she felt freer than she could ever remember.

She snuggled against his chest, wanting nothing more than to purr with contentment. "Have you spoken with Georgia?"

He chuckled. "That's one reason I'm here. That woman told me if I didn't give you a ring pronto, she'd change her mind about me."

Libby felt him reach in his pocket and he withdrew a small box, the velvet finish worn and faded.

"This ring is not like the first one I gave you, and it will need a new setting." He studied the box, then looked up. "Libby, I promise. This time we'll be a family."

She couldn't stop smiling.

"Open it," he said, thrusting the box at her.

Inside, nestled in the cream-colored satin, was an exquisite emerald-cut diamond ring in an old-fashioned silver setting. She looked up, puzzled. "Where? How?"

"Georgia gave it to me. It belonged to her mother. She had a neighbor send it overnight. She wants you to have it. So do I."

"Trent?" The question hung on her lips, but the proof of her answer lay in her hands. Tears of joy coursed down her cheeks, and she put her arms around him, pulling him close. "I'm so happy. We *are* a family at last, aren't we?"

WEEZER HAD ARRIVED EARLY and taken a seat near the front of the church. She looked around, soothed by the muted sunlight streaming through the stained-glass windows. Above her soared an overarching wooden ceiling, and around her, rows of empty pews amplified the silence. The sanctuary smelled faintly of furniture polish, flowers and candle wax.

Soon the family would gather. Another rite of passage, this one long overdue. She closed her eyes in a prayer of thanksgiving that the winter of their souls would soon be past, replaced by healing. When Trent had told her about the miscarriage and his immature reaction all those years ago, his pain had caused her heart to constrict. Bless him. And bless Libby, who had carried that sorrow—and another—for so long.

She heard a rustle in the back and, turning around, spotted Lila, who had paused to accustom her eyes to the dim light. Weezer signaled to her. Lila had taken a vacation from the casino to come to Whitefish to care for Kylie after the Chisholms left. Weezer was grateful Lila had made this second trip to be here for Trent and Libby today.

The minister entered from the side and lighted the candles on the altar, then quietly withdrew. From the organ loft came the soft, poignant strains of Brahms's "Lullaby." Lila clawed in her handbag for a tissue, then gripped Weezer's hand.

A door opened at the back of the church and the Chisholms entered, followed by Trent, walking between Kylie and Libby, who clutched a book under one arm. Halfway down the aisle, Libby reached for his hand, and he smiled down at her with such tenderness that Weezer, who rarely cried, blinked rapidly. When the group reached the first pew, they moved in and sat down.

The only other person in the congregation was Libby's friend Lois, who slid into the row across from Weezer and Lila.

When they all were settled, Reverend Jeter, a liturgical stole around his neck, entered from the sacristy. For a brief time he stood silent, his head bowed. When he looked up, he focused on Trent and Libby.

"We come together today to remember and honor the hope with which you received the news, Libby, that you were to bear new life into the world, and to grieve with you the untimely loss of those lives. We cannot know the full answer to the question 'Why?' But we can be certain that God understands your sorrow and shares your tears, just as he promises comfort and healing."

Weezer could see Libby's throat working. Trent sat with his head bowed.

"God, grant to us now the knowledge that these unborn children are also encircled by your arms of love. Libby and Trent have come here today to commend…" He hesitated.

"Scooter," Trent said in a strangled voice. Libby slipped her arm around Trent and pulled him close.

The minister smiled encouragingly, then continued. "…to commend Scooter to your never-failing love and care along with…"

Libby glanced at the minister, the tears now evident on her lashes, and shook her head sadly.

"…her unnamed baby who died stillborn. Into your loving care and compassion we commend these tiny beings, knowing you have been rocking and tending them all along."

Weezer had never been so proud of Trent. He'd confessed to her his past insensitivity. Looking at him now, she had no concerns for the future.

"Libby?" The minister beckoned her forward. "Trent?"

The couple rose and stood before him. "Libby, in your hands you hold the record of those first few months of your pregnancy. What have you chosen to do with it?"

Libby looked at Trent, who moved closer and encircled her waist, then back at Reverend Jeter. "I entrust it to you as a symbol of my continued healing and of my desire to embrace my future."

Weezer was just able to make out the words on the cover of the book Libby handed the minister. *My Baby Book.*

"Trent, what else do you and Libby bring today as an offering?"

Trent reached into his pocket and pulled out a check. "In memory of these unborn children, we want to present the church with funds to redecorate the nursery."

The minister took the check, then holding it aloft, faced the altar. "Gracious God, we offer you this gift to the nurture and enrichment of small children. May their lives be blessed by this expression of love."

When Libby returned to the pew, she put her arm around Kylie and kissed her on the forehead. Georgia was dabbing at her eyes with a handkerchief and Gus kept clearing his throat.

"To the friends and family gathered here, we ask for your support of Libby, Trent and Kylie. As they face the mysteries of life and death, strengthen the bonds of this family, we pray."

Lost in her memories of the little boy dive-bombing off curbs on his bicycle, hurdling fences with the abandon of a mighty elk and laughing gleefully after his first ski jump, Weezer didn't hear much of what followed. No. Instead, she sent up her own prayer: "Let them bring forth new life."

EPILOGUE

May

"DADDY, no! You can't come in here." Kylie, dressed in a bouffant pink taffeta dress, leaned against the door of the church robing room.

"Please?" Trent teased his daughter from outside in the hallway.

Georgia and Libby exchanged amused smiles.

"It's against the law," Kylie said with exasperation. "You can't see the bride before the wedding."

"Could you give her a message then?"

Kylie stood back, hands on her hips. "Okay."

"Tell her I love her and can't wait."

Libby winked at Kylie. "Tell him ditto."

Kylie put her mouth to the door. "Ditto! Now, go away."

As she studied herself in the mirror, Libby acknowledged that no matter how long a woman had to wait, seeing herself as a bride was like looking at a strangely beautiful new person. The satin gown, understated yet elegant, flowed from a long-sleeved lace bodice. She hardly recognized herself.

"You look lovely, dear," Georgia said, approaching with a fingertip veil. Holding it up, she asked, "Would you let me?"

"I'd be honored." She bent her head so the shorter woman could affix the combs. When she'd finished, Libby studied her reflection again. Their first wedding all those years ago had been a spur-of-the-moment trip to Las Vegas, a few mumbled words by a production-line minister, followed by a hasty dismissal. In the mirror now, staring back, was a genuine bride, lucky enough to be marrying Trent Baker for the second time.

"How much longer?" Kylie bounced on her toes, eagerness lighting her blue eyes.

"Soon," Georgia said, slipping her arm around her granddaughter. Then they both stood silent, admiring Libby.

"You look like a Barbie bride," Kylie breathed in awe.

Smiling, Libby turned to face them. "Thank you both so much for everything. For accepting me. Loving me."

"It's easy," Kylie said.

"Ditto," Georgia said with a just-between-us-girls smile.

"Thank you, too, for understanding why I needed to choose this day for my wedding."

"Mother's Day," Kylie said proudly.

"All my life until now, Mother's Day has been painful for me. Lonely."

"I can imagine," Georgia murmured.

And Libby knew she could. After all, she had lost a daughter. "I so much wanted reasons to celebrate this occasion, and after today, Kylie and I will both have mothers, and you, dear Georgia, will have me as a daughter." She couldn't hold back her grin. "All that and a wedding anniversary, too."

Georgia held out her arms. "I hope I don't muss you, but I want to hug you and tell you how much I love you."

Libby stepped forward. "You're more important than any dress." Happy tears threatened, but she blinked them back. "And I love you."

"Me, too," Kylie said, stepping into the group hug.

And then it was time. Libby couldn't resist peeking into the church, which was full, four whole pews occupied by her second-graders and their parents. She put her hand over her mouth in delight when, next to Mary, she spotted Doug, and beside him, sitting quite close, the new kindergarten teacher. Then Georgia took her seat, and Kylie, serving as Libby's honor attendant, waited breathlessly for the organ to strike up the wedding march. One minute before the ceremony was to begin, Libby glanced outside, astonished to see a limousine pull up to the curb. The driver hopped out and hastened to the back, opened the door, then stood aside. Libby gasped. The senator.

He ran up the steps, pausing in the narthex to remove his hat and coat. Then he moved toward Libby, his cheeks red with exertion. "I didn't miss it, then."

She smiled, still surprised to see him. "No, you didn't."

He glanced toward the nave, then back at her. "I don't suppose you'd let me walk you down the aisle."

Thankfully, she understood it wasn't a serious question. She laid a hand on his lapel. "You know better than that. You raised an independent woman. No one can give me away but me."

"Somehow I knew that," he said. "Before I go in, though, I want to say you're the most beautiful bride I've ever seen, and I've seen a good number." Then he leaned over, kissed her briefly on the cheek and whispered, "I hope you'll be very happy."

"Thank you. I'm pleased you made the effort

to come." Glancing into his moist eyes, an unfamiliar sensation swept through her, and she realized that further healing was possible. "On second thought, I'd be honored if you would walk me down the aisle."

The organ swelled, and he offered her his arm. Although she was vaguely aware of the smiles and approving nods of the guests, her eyes never strayed from the handsome man standing beside Chad. The man she'd waited for her whole life. The man who had given her a daughter and now promised her babies.

And looking into his eyes, so full of love for her, she couldn't wait to begin trying.

But for now, he and Kylie were family enough.

Trent reached out his hand as she neared the front of the church, drawing her to him. She greeted him with a radiant smile. He was absolutely the right man.

* * * * *

Love Inspired®

HEARTWARMING INSPIRATIONAL ROMANCE

Contemporary,
inspirational romances
with Christian characters
facing the challenges
of life and love
in today's world.

**AVAILABLE IN REGULAR
AND LARGER-PRINT FORMATS.**

For exciting stories that reflect traditional values,
visit:
www.ReaderService.com

LIDIR11

Love Inspired SUSPENSE

RIVETING INSPIRATIONAL ROMANCE

Watch for our series of edge-
of-your-seat suspense novels.
These contemporary tales
of intrigue and romance
feature Christian characters
facing challenges to their faith...
and their lives!

**AVAILABLE IN REGULAR
& LARGER-PRINT FORMATS**

For exciting stories that reflect traditional values,
visit:
www.ReaderService.com

LISUSDIR11

INSPIRATIONAL HISTORICAL ROMANCE

Engaging stories of romance,
adventure and faith,
these novels are set in
various historical periods
from biblical times
to World War II.

NOW AVAILABLE!

For exciting stories that reflect traditional values,
visit:
www.ReaderService.com

LIHDIR11

Harlequin®

HARLEQUIN HEARTWARMING

HEARTWARMING AUTHOR
Judy Christenberry
TAKES YOU ON A JOURNEY OF LOVE.

Katie hasn't regretted her choice of refusing Gabe's
proposal; although, over the past ten years, life has
been a little lonely. Now Gabe is back in town and
he wants to embrace the home his grandmother left
to him. There is just one stipulation in order for him
to take over the house of his dreams–he must marry
Katie! The idea of baring his soul to Katie a second
time sure doesn't sit well with Gabe. But without her,
he'll never find the peace he's looking for.

Find out if Gabe and Katie are meant to be in:
The Wedding Promise

Coming soon!
Available wherever books are sold!

www.eHarlequin.com

HW36428

Harlequin®

HARLEQUIN HEARTWARMING

A HEARTFELT STORY FROM
FAN-FAVORITE AUTHOR

Jillian Hart

Cadence Chapman has been cautious in
safeguarding her heart ever since her love,
special forces soldier Ben McKaslin, left town.
Now Ben is back and in one defining moment,
an emergency has him leaping instinctively
to the rescue—and locking eyes with the
captivating woman he left behind.

Could this be fate giving them a second chance
at love?

What Matters Most

Coming soon!
Available wherever books are sold!

www.eHarlequin.com

HW36431